Also by

MW01703018

MORE - Ava Michaels used to think she was special. As a child, she fantasized about having magical powers . . . making things happen. She felt different from others her age, and just knew she was meant for something important. But, like most kids, Ava grew up and eventually accepted the fact that her childish dreams were just that, and maybe a normal life wasn't so bad after all.

Now a young college student, Ava begins to wonder if there were more to her childhood fantasies than she thought. She's haunted by terrifying nightmares of a frightening man chasing her, determined to catch her, to take her—a huge hulk of a man with one blue eye and one green. Even during daylight hours, there are moments her hair stands on end with an uneasy prickle of awareness . . . and she just can't shake the feeling that she's being watched.

Unable to decide if she's imagining things or just plain crazy, Ava finds an unlikely ally in Caleb Foster, a brilliant and mysterious man who comes to her rescue as a Physics tutor, but in reality has another mission in mind. What he shows Ava challenges her view of the world, shaking it to its very core.

The thing is, Caleb's not quite what he seems. In fact, he's not entirely human, and he's not the only one.

Together, the duo faces a threat from an ancient race bound to protect humans, but only after protecting their own secrets—secrets they fear Ava may expose. Now they're after her, bent on her capture or maybe even her extinction.

Fighting to survive, Ava has to depend on Caleb to lead her through the strange new world opening up before her. A world of magic and mystery, where she learns she's not
actually normal . . . she's not even just special.

She's a little bit more.

Thanks for reading! TM Franklin

The Guardians

Book 2 in the MORE Trilogy

By
T.M. Franklin

TWCS
Publishing House

First published by The Writer's Coffee Shop, 2013

The Writer's Coffee Shop
(Australia) PO Box 447 Cherrybrook NSW 2126
(USA) PO Box 2116 Waxahachie TX 75168

Paperback ISBN- 978-1-61213-171-9

E-book ISBN- 978-1-61213-172-6

A CIP catalogue record for this book is available from the US Congress Library.

Cover image by: © Depositphotos.com / Francesco Cura
Cover Artist: T.M. Franklin

www.thewriterscoffeeshop.com/tmfranklin

Glossary of Terms

First Race/The Race – Ancient people who've lived alongside humans throughout history. They are more advanced technologically than humans, have superior physical and mental abilities, and devote themselves to helping humanity grow and evolve. They are considerably fewer in number than humans, so maintain secrecy above all else in order to protect themselves.

Guardian – Race member who has broken away from the Council. Guardians disagree with the Council's stand on Half-Breeds and devote themselves to helping Half-Breeds escape the Council, learn to control their abilities, and live peacefully either in a Colony or back in the human world.

Guardian Colony/Colony – Group of Guardians living together in hiding from the Council. A Colony is a safe haven for Half-Breeds.

Half-Breed – A person of mixed human and Race heritage. The Council sees them as a threat to Race secrecy because they are often unable to control their Race abilities.

Heterochromia/HC – A difference in color in two structures that are usually alike in color. In the *MORE* trilogy, HC refers to the Race trait of having two different colored eyes.

The Law/Race Law – The highest governing force of the Race. The primary tenet of the Law is to aid in the development of humanity, but to never endanger the Race or compromise its secrecy.

Mimic – person capable of imitating a Race imprint after only brief contact with the subject.

New Elysia – Race city in the Rocky Mountains, approximately fifty miles from Kalispell, Montana. Seat of the Race's Ruling Council.

Protector of the Race/Protector – Race member entrusted with enforcing the Law, primarily through hunting down Rogues and Half-Breeds under orders from the Council.

Pyrokinesis – The ability to set objects or people on fire or to supernaturally project fire from one's own being through the concentration of psychic power.

Race Imprint – A kind of electric shadow left behind by a Race member. Also known as a Race Signature.

Rejuvenation cube/R-cube – A small, grey, gelatinous cube that helps restore Race power when it's been depleted by use. An R-cube is a supplement made up of, among other things, vitamins, protein, and electrolytes. It tastes like plastic.

Rogue – Race member who rebelled against the Council and lives for pleasure. Rogues don't care about keeping the Race a secret, and in fact often flaunt their abilities and use them to gain power. The Council sees them as the greatest threat to the Race.

Shifter – Race member with the ability to teleport.

The Ruling Council/The Council – The five-member ruling body of the First Race. The Council is charged with maintaining Race Law, protecting the Race, and resolving conflicts within the community.

Telekinesis – The ability to move objects with psychic power.

Tracker – Race member with an enhanced ability to follow even a minimal trail.

Veil – Camouflage that hides a Race member's true appearance, making them appear ordinary so they can fit in among humans.

Chapter 1

A loud crack overhead was the only warning. Ava's head snapped up, and she caught a glimpse of black and blue before a thick branch fell toward her. She threw out a hand—more reflex than out of any real need—and the branch shifted its trajectory, landing several feet away on the spongy forest floor.

"You'll have to do better than that," she said quietly, well aware he could hear her.

She continued down the path, every sense on alert. The call of a crow in the distance obscured the faint crunch and splinter of debris underfoot.

Is that—

A rustle of movement to her left had her ducking behind a tree trunk, peeking around the edge into the thick forest. She caught the faint whooshing sound behind her and spun just in time to stop the large rock hurtling toward her. She smiled, bouncing the rock up and down a bit in the air, testing the limits of her telekinetic ability.

Show off, she heard whispered through the trees.

With a smirk, she sent the rock shooting back through the forest in the direction of the voice, laughing at the surprised yelp in response.

"Come on!" she shouted. "You going to hide in the trees all day or fight like a man?"

Ava stood with her feet braced apart and head thrown back, listening intently. For a long moment, only the quiet sounds of the forest met her ears. She closed her eyes, focusing on her enhanced hearing, listening deeper . . . farther.

There.

The faint in-and-out of breathing grew louder as she focused on it, and she opened her eyes, turning in the direction of the sound. Pushing her eyesight beyond normal human levels, she spotted him hiding behind a tree —a peek of denim, a glimpse of pale blue cotton.

She ducked behind her own tree, heart pounding as she considered her next move. There was no way she could catch him. She wasn't fast enough. She could try to throw something, though.

She glanced around frantically for something—pinecones were useless, the scattered sticks too small. A boulder several feet away was too big—she wasn't sure she could even lift it, let alone force it between the trees. She'd need to try something else.

Ava took a deep breath and closed her eyes, focusing her mind as Caleb had taught her. She pictured the tree where she saw him hiding and tried to will her body to shift to that very spot.

Visualize your body . . . your very cells dissolving, dissipating into the air. See them coming together where you want them to be.

Easier said than done.

You'll feel yourself growing lighter, almost floating, and before you even realize what's happening, it's like you're there . . . but you're not.

Ava frowned. Caleb didn't always make much sense.

She forced herself to breathe slowly and evenly, blocking out the sounds around her and focusing on her own heartbeat. She pictured herself floating, coming apart in the air. A tingle worked its way across her skin, now easily recognizable as her Race power coming to life. Her pulse quickened. Maybe she could do this.

Strong arms imprisoned her—one across her neck, another at her waist—not tight enough to cut off the air supply, but she was definitely immobile.

Ava cursed under her breath.

"So what now?" a low voice growled in her ear. "You going to try and push me? Throw some rocks at my back?" His arm tightened slightly, making her gasp. "I've got you right where I want you."

"You cheated."

He laughed, loosening his hold to step back. "I did not!"

Ava turned and leaned back against the tree, glaring at the sight of his bright blue eyes sparkling with mirth. She crossed her arms over her chest. "You did, too."

Caleb grinned and reached out to tweak her earlobe. "And how exactly did I cheat?"

"Well, I'm sure there's a rule against . . ." Ava scrambled for an answer, then smiled smugly. "Distracting me. It's very dangerous to distract me when I'm trying to shift. I could end up inside a tree or something."

He laughed. "That wasn't going to happen."

"You don't know that."

"Yes, I do." He stepped toward her, toying with the strings on her hoodie. "You weren't going to shift, Ava. I would have felt it."

She deflated, knowing he was right. "Why can't I do it?"

"Not everyone can."

Ava exhaled heavily. "It would just be so cool, you know?"

He smiled and leaned in to kiss her lightly.

Ava felt the familiar tingle of his power meeting hers.

"You can do lots of other cool stuff," he reminded her.

She could. Since her, for lack of a better word, *breakthrough* at the Rogue lair, Ava's telekinesis had proven to be a powerful gift, and one she was getting better about controlling. The same could be said for her enhanced senses, another Race trait that was becoming second nature to her. She no longer had to concentrate quite so hard to access her superior vision and hearing. If anything, it had become more instinctual. She had tuned in to conversations across campus, for example, before she'd even realized what she was doing. She felt kind of bad about that, to be honest. Just because she was a superhuman being didn't mean she had a right to be rude.

But shifting continued to elude her. Caleb made it look so easy, disappearing and reappearing without breaking a sweat. Long distances were more challenging, but Ava was still a little jealous of his innate gift. It would be so handy on those mornings she overslept and was late for class.

Caleb was quick to remind her that not everyone was the same, and although Race members all shared certain traits, things like shifting and telekinesis were hit and miss. She knew she should be happy with what she *could* do, especially since she seemed to be more powerful than many others already. The face-off with the Council had proven that.

It wasn't that she wanted more, really. She simply wanted to be prepared —prepared if the Council came after her again or if the Rogues staged another attack. She knew, deep inside, that it wasn't over, and Caleb agreed, even though he'd never said as much out loud. He'd been true to his promise to train with her, pushing her limits and working to develop her gifts. He could also become easily distracted, however—as he seemed to be at that moment.

Caleb propped a hand on the tree behind her, nuzzling along her neck and placing a soft kiss behind her ear.

"We're supposed to be training," Ava said, a little breathless and maybe a bit distracted, as well.

"Too much training isn't good for you."

She laughed. "Oh, and where did you hear that?"

He trailed kisses down her neck, sucking lightly at her collarbone where it peeked out from under her shirt. "Common knowledge," he said into the hollow at her throat. "All work and no play . . . blah, blah, blah." Caleb waved an idle hand as he scraped his teeth lightly against her skin.

Ava gasped. "You make a valid point," she said, her voice trembling, revealing his effect on her.

He lifted his head with a victorious smirk. "I knew you'd see it my way."

"Cocky."

His response was muffled because Caleb chose that moment to kiss her properly.

It had been months since the first time Caleb kissed her, but Ava still had yet to get used to the electrifying sensation. It wasn't only the physical act, the press of lips to lips, which was *spectacular*—all hot and wet and demanding and . . . *hot*—but kissing Caleb also sparked a mingling of their power. She recognized it now, the electric tingle of Caleb's Race gift sizzling along her skin, penetrating into her very center, and slowly—*deliciously*—wrapping itself around her power, the two weaving together in a sensual dance that left her dizzy once he pulled away. It was why she always fought it when he tried to stop.

She felt a little pathetic about it, as though she had absolutely no control over her own body. She didn't, at least when it came to Caleb. Still, it was more than lust—more than simple physical attraction. Ava was relatively sure she was in love with Caleb, although she had yet to say the words out loud. Maybe it made her a coward, but she was an old-fashioned girl and wanted him to say it first. Or maybe old-fashioned had nothing to do with it. Maybe she just didn't want to make a fool of herself.

It was possible.

She couldn't complain, though. They'd only grown closer since they had returned from the Race city of New Elysia three months earlier, even with Ava's newly tapped power still wild and erratic and both of them unsure what the Council's next move would be. He'd succeeded in his goal as her tutor to help her pass physics, and even though she no longer had need of him in that capacity, he was just as patient when it came to helping her with her Race skills. Even if most training sessions eventually devolved into make-out sessions.

Not that Ava fought it too much. Kissing Caleb was incredible. The way he touched her, and that thing he did with his—

A vibration in her pocket brought Ava out of her thoughts.

Caleb pulled back slightly but kept his body pressed up against hers as she took her phone out of her pocket.

"My mother." Her head fell back against the tree as she groaned, thumb hovering over the *Ignore* button.

Caleb laughed. "You know if you don't answer, she'll just call back."

Ava shrugged, punching the button and stuffing the phone back in her pocket. "Maybe not. Maybe she'll leave a message." She wrapped her arms around Caleb's neck, tugging him closer and twisting her fingers in the dark hair at his nape.

He smiled against her lips, his warm breath sending a shiver down her spine.

The phone rang again and Ava grumbled, tugging Caleb forward stubbornly when he tried to pull away.

"You might as well answer it," Caleb said, untangling himself to reach into his inside coat pocket and pull out his glasses.

He didn't need them, but they helped him fit in at school and made him less noticeable. Also, Ava liked them, to be perfectly honest. They were cute.

He took her free hand in his. "We should be heading back anyway. It'll be dark soon."

Ava frowned, but answered the phone and allowed Caleb to lead her down the path to the edge of the woods. "Hi, Mom."

"Sweetie, I wanted to check and see what you've decided about spring break," her mother said, a little distracted, as if she was doing something else at the same time. It wasn't unusual. Sarah Michaels was nothing if not a multitasker. "You know we'd love to see you. And Caleb, of course."

Her voice had softened on Caleb's name, and Ava couldn't help rolling her eyes.

Caleb smirked, obviously hearing it as well.

Her parents adored Caleb and had since they first met him over Christmas break. She hadn't actually *intended* for them to meet, but Caleb had insisted on accompanying her home to Oregon for her own protection. With wide, innocent eyes, he'd promised he would keep his distance if she wasn't ready for him to meet her parents yet. Of course, Ava couldn't very well tell him the idea terrified her, so she'd shown up on her parents' front porch with Caleb by her side. The smile on his face had been more than a little smug, if she hadn't been mistaken.

In the end, it had been a blessing having him along. In addition to the obvious benefit of having him sleeping down the hall in the guest room and unlimited access to him during the day, he'd helped her investigate some of the questions that had come up after she'd learned of her Race blood. She'd always known she was adopted—abandoned nineteen years earlier at a local church when she was only a few days old—but being back home had given her the opportunity to try and find out more about what had happened.

One afternoon, they'd visited the priest who had found her. He'd long since retired and moved to Coos Bay, but with Caleb's shifting ability, they'd made the distance in an afternoon, and with his power to push—a mild compulsion gift that helped him get what he wanted—they'd talked their way into the retirement home and sat with Father Gallagher for about an hour.

Unfortunately, he hadn't been able to tell them much. He said that night he'd been at the hospital, counseling Ava's parents, who'd just lost their own baby. He'd returned to the rectory, and a noise had drawn him to the front of the church, where he found Ava bundled in a blanket inside a cardboard box—no note, no identification of any kind.

The box, of course, was long gone, but the blanket had been stored in Ava's attic along with other baby clothes. She'd dug it out, trying her best to reassure her mother that she was simply curious about her past, nothing more.

The adoption itself hadn't been exactly official. No paperwork had been filed with the state. Not even the police had been notified about Ava's abandonment. The priest had simply tapped into his connections at the hospital, and the infant who had died became a Jane Doe, and Ava had become her parents' daughter.

Ava realized, as the truth had come out, that someone Race had had a hand in keeping the adoption under wraps, not to mention influencing her adoptive parents to leave behind their own lost biological child. Ava had never questioned how they could essentially replace one baby with another, like in some bad soap opera. Her mother had always called Ava a gift from God and left it at that. As she had spoken with the priest, however, Ava realized that someone had most likely helped her mom and dad with the transition, perhaps even blurred the memory of the loss so they could more easily accept their new daughter. The thought made Ava shudder.

In the end, Sarah had been supportive in the way that only a mother could be—after all, now that Ava was an adult, there was little chance the authorities would step in and take her away—and Ava had felt another wave of guilt about concealing her Race identity from her mother. It was something she constantly battled—wishing she could tell her parents everything, but needing to protect them from the truth for their own good.

Unfortunately, the investigation had proven fruitless anyway. The only tie Ava had been able to find to her past was that blanket—soft, white flannel with white stitching around the edge and a stylized H with curved sides embroidered in one corner. She and Caleb had tried to track down the image, thinking perhaps the H referred to a nearby hospital or even a women's shelter, but they could find no connection to anything within several hundred miles.

Another dead end.

She'd taken the blanket with her back to Allenmore College, though. It was the only connection to her other life, the life before she became Ava Michaels. She kept it tucked away in the bottom of a drawer, somehow comforted by its presence—proof that all the incredible things she'd been through over the past few months were real and not the figment of an overactive imagination.

"Ava, are you listening to me?"

She took a deep breath, shaking off the memories to focus on the phone call. "Yes, Mom." Caleb squeezed her hand, and Ava smiled sheepishly in response. "I don't know about spring break. I'll have to see." Caleb snickered, and she shot him a nasty look.

They had been planning a trip of their own, just the two of them, but she'd yet to work up the courage to tell her mother that. Caleb had teased her about it to no end, saying she was brave enough to face the Council and a room full of Protectors, but her mother made her want to run and hide. It wasn't really that she was *afraid* of her mother, though. It was just that Sarah Michaels had considered Ava and Caleb all but engaged since he'd come home with her at Christmas. Telling her they were going on vacation together would kick-start the wedding plans for sure.

They neared the edge of the forest and Caleb released her hand, popping a couple of R-cubes in his mouth to prepare for the shift.

She wasn't sure exactly where they were—somewhere in western Wyoming, on a bluff overlooking the Mississippi River valley. They generally had to shift a half dozen times or so to find an isolated spot to train, and Caleb preferred the protection that a forest provided. That meant either the woodlands and ravines of Wyoming or the Badlands of South Dakota, both equidistant from Allenmore College in northwestern Missouri. Shifting took a lot out of Caleb, especially long distances, but he seemed to be getting more comfortable with pushing himself to even fifty miles at a time. A couple of cubes before and after, fifteen minutes of rest, and he was ready to go again. Apparently, she wasn't the only one getting stronger with practice.

He turned to her, hands tucked in his pockets and brow raised in question.

"Look, Mom, I've got to go," she said. "I've got a big test tomorrow, and I'm almost to the library, and they really don't like you to talk on the phone in there because it . . . you know, disrupts everyone—" She glared at Caleb's amused chuckle. She never had been any good at lying.

"All right, honey," her mother replied. "Let me know about spring break, okay? We thought it might be fun to have Uncle Bobby and everyone over to meet Caleb."

Ava fought back a groan. That was something she would never subject Caleb to. Uncle Bobby had a habit of pulling out his teeth so he could click *The William Tell Overture* on his gums. "Okay, Mom. I'll let you know. Love you." Her mom returned the sentiment, and Ava hung up.

Caleb snorted.

"Shut up," she muttered.

"You need to tell her sometime."

"I know. I will." She moved toward him, wrapping her arms around his waist.

"When?" he asked.

"Soon."

Caleb held her close, pressing a kiss to the top of her head. "Just think. You and me, alone . . . traveling the country, seeing the sights."

"You sure you can handle all that shifting?"

"I'll be fine," he said. "I can't wait to show you the Grand Canyon, Niagara Falls . . ."

"Times Square."

"The Met."

"Disney World."

Caleb laughed. "Of course, we can't miss Disney World. I'll even get you one of those Mickey Mouse hats with your name embroidered on it."

Ava sighed. "It's going to be perfect."

"Yes, except for one thing."

She peeked up at him. "What?"

"Your mother filing a missing person's report when we don't show up at her house." Ava made to shove him away, but he only held her tighter, chuckling slightly. "I'm kidding," he said. "I know you'll tell her when you can."

"I will."

"I know." He bent to kiss her once more. "Ready?"

"Ready."

Ava closed her eyes and pressed her face into Caleb's chest, knowing better than to try and watch as they shifted. She'd done it once—only once—and ended up on her knees throwing up all over Caleb's shoes once they'd landed. It was an experience she had no desire to repeat. So instead, she held on tight and inhaled deeply, Caleb's warm and spicy scent instantly calming her as the ground fell away and the wind whipped around them in a swirling vortex.

Tiernan Ross leaned against a tree and cracked his knuckles then his neck before sighing heavily. The sun had just disappeared over the horizon and the spring evening was warm, a slight breeze rustling through the trees, but Tiernan couldn't enjoy his surroundings. He sighed again, impatiently tapping his fingers on his thighs.

He hated waiting.

He especially hated the ridiculous assignment he and Katherine were currently shackled with, courtesy of the blasted Council, thank you very much. Monitoring Caleb Foster's little girlfriend wasn't only mindless duty, it was unnecessary, as far as Tiernan was concerned.

And boring. He couldn't forget boring.

Ava Michaels obviously wasn't going to talk. In the months since she returned to Allenmore, she'd said nothing to anybody about the Race nor given any indication she was tempted in the least to do so. But that wasn't all the Council was concerned about. Her power definitely made them more than a little nervous, and Tiernan couldn't blame them. He'd experienced it firsthand himself, and it stung—not to mention annoyed the hell out of him—when he remembered the helplessness of being strung up like a Christmas goose in front of the Council and all of his fellow Protectors.

Yeah. He still held a bit of a grudge about that. Even though he had to admire the girl's guts. To stand up to the Council like she did? To say no to Madeleine Foster and the other suits? Tiernan smiled a little at the memory. It was something he might have done himself—if he'd had the power to back it up. He'd never admit it to Caleb or Ava, of course. He could barely admit it to himself.

"Anything?"

His sister's voice drew Tiernan out of his thoughts, and he turned to see her approaching from across the campus. She smiled when she reached him, smoothing back her straight, black hair when the wind blew it across her face. His would match if he didn't keep it closely shaved, but that was where the resemblance between the siblings ended. Where Tiernan was immense and intimidating, with his mismatched blue and green eyes and a fierce scar running down the right side of his face, Katherine was tall and willowy, with unmarred porcelain skin, one blue eye, and one lavender. She wore the contacts many Race preferred to hide the heterochromia. Katherine being Katherine, she chose lavender instead of blue. She'd always tended toward more exotic tastes.

Tiernan shrugged. "Not yet. They should be back soon, though."

Caleb was nothing if not predictable. When he left on these training sessions with Ava, he always shifted from the isolated spot behind the library, and reappeared shortly after dusk. He sometimes wondered if Caleb did it on purpose, to show Tiernan he had nothing to hide.

As if on cue, Caleb appeared in the shadows, holding Ava close and stumbling a little as they encountered solid ground. Ava pulled his arm over her shoulders and supported his weight as she handed him something he popped into his mouth—R-cubes, Tiernan assumed. After a few minutes, they walked slowly away toward Ava's dorm.

"You want to follow them this time?" he asked Katherine.

She laughed slightly. "Nope. It's your turn, little brother. I'm off until tomorrow night." Without another word, she turned to walk away, waving over her shoulder in response to Tiernan's soft curse.

Sometimes family was a real pain in the neck.

He started after Caleb and Ava, staying back far enough that Caleb wouldn't detect him. It was more out of protocol and habit, though. It wasn't as if Caleb didn't already know he was being followed.

He did, of course. Which was one more reason this assignment was absolutely ludicrous.

Tiernan's cell phone vibrated as he took up his usual spot across from Ava's dorm. He frowned at the screen, wondering why Andreas Petrov, of all people, would be calling him. It was rare that an actual Council member contacted him, and when it did happen, it was usually Rafe.

He answered the phone, trying to keep the hesitation out of his voice. "Ross."

"There's been a change of plans," Petrov said in his smoothly accented voice.

"A change?" Tiernan could only hope he was being pulled off babysitting duty and put to work at something useful. Even hunting down Half-Breeds was more interesting.

"The Council has decided to assign another Protector to keep tabs on Miss Michaels."

Tiernan smiled in satisfaction. "Do you want me to come in? Or are you sending me out right away?"

"Slow down. Slow down, Ross," Petrov said, chuckling lightly. "Who knew you were such an eager beaver?"

Tiernan bit back an annoyed retort and took a steadying breath. He tried to relax his clenched jaw but ended up speaking more through his teeth than around them. "Just trying to do my job, sir."

"Yes, well, be that as it may, I will be e-mailing you the brief on your new assignment. It's highly classified, Ross. That means your eyes only on this. Not a word, even to your sister."

"Of course, sir."

"Katherine will remain on the team watching Miss Michaels. You're to tell her nothing."

"I understand." It wasn't the first time he and Katherine had been ordered to keep secrets from each other. "If I may, sir. Where will I be going?"

"Nowhere, at least for now."

"Sorry, sir?"

"It's not that complicated, Ross, try and keep up," Petrov snapped. "Your assignment is there at Allenmore. Review the brief, and we'll be in touch."

The call disconnected, and Tiernan's phone pinged with the arrival of a new e-mail. He thumbed at the screen, waiting for the decryption protocols, and opened the file sent by the Council. He flipped through the pages, eyes widening with confusion and downright shock when he read the information within.

What in the . . .

His eyes snapped up as Caleb stepped out of Ava's dorm, flashing a mocking salute in Tiernan's direction before he headed off toward his apartment. Tiernan hesitated, his gaze flicking up to Ava's window briefly before he turned to walk away.

She wasn't his mission anymore.

What he couldn't wrap his mind around, however, was why the Council had apparently decided that Caleb Foster was.

Chapter 2

Caleb was getting annoyed. Or perhaps *frustrated* was the more appropriate word. It wasn't only that the Council was watching Ava, it was the fact that they'd sent *Tiernan Ross* to do the watching—the Race's best tracker—as if Ava was a flight risk.

Where was she going to go? It had been months, and she'd given the Council no reason for concern. Still, his contacts told him she was on the radar, still considered a threat, both because of her strong gifts and the fact that she was raised as human. It was unheard of—a member of the Race hidden in the human world for so long with no idea who or what she was. And for the Council, the unknown was always perceived as a threat.

He spotted Tiernan as he left Ava's dorm, although he knew the Protector wasn't trying to hide. Tiernan had no love for Ava, but Caleb knew he thought his current assignment was beneath him. To Caleb's surprise, instead of staying at the dorm, Tiernan approached him, matching his pace.

"Evening," Caleb said with a questioning lift of his brow. "Something I can help you with?"

Tiernan shrugged. "Just out enjoying the fresh air."

Caleb smirked. "Yeah. I always took you for a nature lover. I assume Katherine's taking over?" He waved a hand back toward Ava's dorm.

"I don't know what you're talking about."

"Sure, you don't," he said with a tired sigh. "So to what do I owe the honor?"

Tiernan was silent for a long moment. "The Council isn't letting up on her."

It was a statement, not a question, so Caleb didn't bother responding.

Tiernan glanced at him sidelong. "It's been months. Why do you think they're so worried?"

Caleb took a deep breath. This was . . . odd. "You know why. She has a lot of power."

"Yeah." Tiernan rolled his shoulders as if remembering how she'd used that power against him. "But that's not all. You think it's the Rogues?"

Caleb came to a stop, turning to face him. "Why do you care all of a sudden?"

"Just curious." He looked away with another shrug. "*If* I'd been watching a girl for months, and *if* she'd given no indication of betraying the Race, I might wonder why the Council wasn't calling off the dogs."

"*If*." Caleb eyed him carefully before turning to continue toward his apartment. "I have no idea what the Council's thinking, Tiernan. If you have any insight, I'd love to hear it."

Tiernan walked alongside him and appeared to be deep in thought. He kicked a rock and tucked his hands in his pockets. "You have any interesting assignments lately?"

Caleb started a bit at the change of subject. "You know I can't discuss that."

"So you *have*."

"I didn't say that."

"Come on. I've been bored out of my mind. Entertain me."

Caleb's eyes narrowed. It wasn't like Tiernan to be so talkative or to express interest in someone else. "What's up with you?"

Tiernan stiffened and stopped abruptly, looking up at Caleb's apartment building. "Nothing. Just making conversation." He shuffled on his feet before jerking a thumb over his shoulder. "I should go." He started to leave but glanced back. "Why do you walk?"

"What?"

"From Ava's to here. Why do you walk instead of shifting?"

Caleb shrugged. "I like to walk."

Tiernan nodded once before he turned to slip away, melting into the shadows. Caleb went into his apartment building as the Protector took up a post outside, far enough away that Caleb couldn't sense him unless he was trying, but close enough to he could monitor his movements.

Early the next morning, Caleb was jolted out of a deep sleep by the vibrating of his cell phone on the nightstand. He glanced, bleary-eyed, at his alarm clock, groaning when he saw it wasn't quite six o'clock. He didn't have class for three hours. Caleb was not amused.

He fumbled for the phone, sighing heavily when he recognized the number on the screen, and answered the call with a barely intelligible, "Foster."

"Good morning, sunshine," a cheerful voice responded.

"Bel." Caleb sat up against the headboard, rubbing at his eyes. "Do you know what time it is?"

"Oh, don't give me that. If I recall correctly, the last time you called me, it was the middle of the night, and you dragged me out of a rather comfortable bed."

Maribel Castro had been the first person Caleb had turned to when he'd gone on the run with Ava the previous fall. Although a trusted associate of the Council, Bel was also involved with a splinter group called the Guardians—former Protectors who took issue with the way the Council handled Half-Breeds. The result of a forbidden union between a human and a member of the Race, Half-Breeds were considered unstable—unable to handle whatever Race gifts they might inherit—and a potential threat to Race secrecy. The Council sent out Protectors to track down such people for containment and, in some cases, extermination. So when Caleb had been sent to detain Ava—then deemed a potential Half-Breed—he'd turned to Bel and the Guardians to protect her. The plan had been simple—get to a safe house and then on to the Guardian Colony in Ontario.

Ava, however, rarely stuck to plans.

"Caleb? You awake?" Bel's prodding jerked Caleb out of a near-doze.

"Yeah, yeah. I'm here," he mumbled. "What's up?"

"We need your help. Nothing fancy. Just transport for a Half-Breed up to the Colony."

Caleb yawned but slid out of bed and grabbed a duffle bag from his closet. "When? Where?"

"You're to rendezvous with Balaam in Milwaukee tonight, six o'clock your time for the handoff." Bel paused, and Caleb could hear the shuffling of papers over the phone. "Balaam will lead any Protectors south while you shift the Half-Breed, Evan, north."

Caleb nodded even though Bel couldn't see him.

He was familiar with Balaam's ability to mimic any Race member or Half-Breed. Because of their individual mental capabilities, each gave off a unique electrical signature. Balaam was able to imitate that.

Caleb frowned. Correction. Not *every* Race member gave off the signature. Ava didn't, and Caleb wasn't sure why. She'd been fitted with a psychic block as a baby, which blocked her Race abilities; it was possible that parts of the block were still in place and that was why she didn't give off a Race imprint. It was just one more mystery among a host of them where Ava was concerned.

He yawned, his jaw cracking as he threw some clothes into the duffle bag. "Six o'clock. Evan. Milwaukee. Got it."

"Don't be late."

Caleb tossed the phone onto the bed and finished packing. He needed to meet Ava for coffee and tell her he was leaving for a few days. Caleb didn't like it, but it actually helped that he knew Tiernan would be watching her.

Even if he was sent to protect the Council *from* her, he knew that if push came to shove and any Rogues showed up, Tiernan would protect *her* from *them*.

Not that she really needs it.

He smiled. Ava had become a formidable opponent, her powers growing every day. In truth, he couldn't blame the Council for being nervous.

If he didn't know she was on his side, he might be, too.

Ava smiled when she saw Caleb waiting for her outside the campus coffee shop, balancing two cups as he adjusted his backpack. He gave her the vanilla latte with a quick kiss to her cheek, and she took his hand as they set off across campus toward her English literature class. It always filled Ava with a little bit of glee that she got to start her day with Chaucer and Bronte instead of Pascal and Bernoulli. Sure, physics had brought her Caleb, but she couldn't say she missed the class.

Without warning, Caleb yanked her into the shadows between two buildings and pulled her against him, wrapping his arms tightly around her.

She barely had enough time to clench her eyes shut when, with a dizzying whirl, the ground dropped out from beneath her. When she opened her eyes, she stumbled, blinking uncertainly until she realized he'd shifted them to the top of the bell tower. The campus was spread out before them in a grid-like pattern of green and brown, the town of Witteville sparkling in the morning sunshine just beyond.

When Caleb released her, she smacked his arm, and his coffee sloshed out of the hole in the plastic lid. "You need to warn me before you do that!"

Caleb grinned. "Then it wouldn't be a surprise."

She shook her head but couldn't keep from smiling herself. Taking a sip of her coffee, she crossed to the low brick wall circling the huge bell at the top of the tower and dropped her backpack at her feet. "You do realize if we ever get caught up here, we're going to be in a lot of trouble."

He shrugged, lowering his own bag to the ground. "I like to live dangerously."

"Mm-hmm." She faced him and leaned on the wall, setting her cup down next to her. "I do have class, you know?" Not that she was that worried about it. Spending time with Caleb was always more fun than bonding with Chaucer.

"I know. I needed to talk to you alone for a minute."

Ava didn't like the sound of that. "What's wrong?"

"Nothing's wrong. I just have to leave town for a few days."

Ava fought down a rush of concern. "For the Council?"

"Guardians."

Ava nodded, turning back around to look out over the campus. She knew

Caleb had been secretly working with the Guardians on occasion, unbeknownst to the Council. The Guardians operated in the shadows, and if the Council knew he was helping them, he'd not only lose his position as a Protector, he could be tried as a traitor to the Race. She couldn't blame him for wanting to get involved, though. She knew firsthand how frightening it was to be hunted by the Council and the appalling way Half-Breeds were treated. Still, it *was* dangerous. And she couldn't help being worried.

"I could go with you." She kept her back to him, not wanting him to see exactly how much it meant to ask, how much she really hated to be apart from him.

"You know that won't work," he said quietly. "I can't shift you and him."

She nodded. "Well, be careful, okay?"

He drew closer and set his coffee cup next to hers before reaching out to rub her shoulders lightly. He pulled Ava back against his chest, his arms crossed over hers and their fingers tangling. "I'll be fine. And you know Tiernan and Katherine are around if you need them."

She smiled wryly. "You really think Tiernan would help *me*?"

Caleb laughed. "Well, maybe Katherine. I think she likes you."

"I doubt that."

"Here," he said, untangling one of his arms to fumble in his coat pocket. "I have something for you." He reached around and held his open hand in front of her, a small, polished wooden box lying in his palm.

She glanced up at him over her shoulder. "What is it?"

He shrugged, a hint of pink creeping up his cheeks. "Open it and find out."

Ava took the box as Caleb loosened his hold on her, his arms falling slowly to his sides. Absently running her fingers over the smooth wood, she turned around to face him. "It's not my birthday."

"I know when your birthday is." He smirked, and Ava laughed lightly. Caleb knew pretty much everything about her, actually. Having been assigned to her, knowing every detail about her had been part of his job, at least until their relationship had developed into something more.

"So what's the occasion?" Ava couldn't resist prodding a bit, since Caleb was so adorably embarrassed.

His face flushed a little more as he shook his head in exasperation. "No occasion. Just . . . something to remember me by while I'm gone."

A rush of warmth raced through Ava at that—the idea that Caleb *wanted* her to think about him, *wanted* her to miss him—and she looked down at the box, her own face heating rapidly. She lifted the lid of the box, and her heartbeat sped a little then seemed to stop altogether when she saw its contents. A hammered pewter pendant hung on a black leather cord, and she brought it closer to examine the design: two linked circles, and where they overlapped, a woven knot, obviously Celtic in design. Two gleaming stones were set in the larger circles, one blue and one green. Ava smiled, realizing the stones were the color of Caleb's eyes—his true eyes, when he wasn't wearing his contacts.

"It was my mother's," he said quietly. "The only thing my father gave her that she kept."

Ava blinked back tears, rubbing her thumb over the green stone. "It's beautiful," she said. "But I can't accept this. It's too important to you." She held it out, but he wrapped her fingers around the pendant, holding her hand tightly.

"*You're* important to me."

"But . . . your mother . . ."

"She wants you to have it, too," he said, swallowing thickly. "I think it's her way of letting you know that even though she has to fulfill her duties to the Council *officially*, she's glad you're in my life, *personally*." He leaned in to kiss Ava, their clasped hands pressed against his chest.

Ava melted against him, the feel of his power familiar yet not diminished in its intensity. When he reluctantly pulled away many minutes later, they were both breathing heavily.

"Here, look," he said, his voice raspy as he opened her hand. "The two circles are a symbol of both our worlds, the two stones representing humanity and the First Race. My father added the knot in the middle for my mother—a symbol of unity." He traced the twisted metal with a fingertip. "Actually, it became a symbol for the Guardians later on, so she could no longer wear it, for obvious reasons. But she always kept it close. Even after he left. And now . . . now, I want you to have it."

Ava examined his features, seeing nothing but sincerity there, and looped the necklace over her head before kissing him again. "Thank you," she said softly. "I love it."

"You're welcome."

They stood there for a moment, wrapped in each other's arms, before Ava looked up at him again. "You never talk about your father."

He shrugged. "There's not much to tell. He wasn't around."

She fingered the necklace. "But if your mother kept this, she must have missed him, at least a little."

Caleb pulled away, sighing heavily. "That's a long story," he said, checking his watch. "And one we probably can't get into right now. Not if you're going to make it to class on time."

Ava wanted to protest, but Caleb had taken on that stiff look that always accompanied any mention of his father. He only moved back a fraction, but in that moment, it felt as though he was miles away. His jaw twitched with tension, his eyes hard, and she recognized the look of him getting lost in thoughts of the man who'd abandoned him and his mother. Ava could push it. She'd tried to before, but the closest Caleb had ever come to opening up about his feelings on the topic was to say that he didn't know much about his father and didn't feel the need to.

She left it alone and simply reached up to touch his cheek, waiting.

She didn't have to wait long. He looked down with a soft smile and pulled her close, getting ready to shift. "I'll tell you everything once I get back," he said, the promise clear in his eyes.

He seemed almost nervous at the prospect, but she didn't mention it, instead asking, "Which will be?"

"Soon," he said with a laugh. "Few days. A week at most."

"Okay. I can do a week." She tucked her face against his chest and closed her eyes. "But any longer and I'm coming after you."

Caleb laughed.

Little did he know, she wasn't kidding.

That evening, Caleb waited at the rendezvous point, a nondescript coffee shop on a street corner in Milwaukee. He checked his watch again, impatient to get this assignment over and done with. He'd pushed himself, shifting rapidly and wolfing down R-cubes so he could get where he was going and back home again.

Of course, he hadn't taken into account having to wait for the Half-Breed. All he could think about was getting back to Witteville and to Ava. He didn't like leaving her alone, both for personal and professional reasons. Despite his reassurances to her that she would be looked out for, he felt a lot more comfortable when he was the one doing the looking.

He felt a telltale prickle up the back of his neck, indicating a Race presence nearby, and turned to watch the door to the coffee shop, sipping a cappuccino as he waited for Balaam and the Half-Br—*Evan,* he corrected —to appear.

After a few minutes, the two men walked in, Balaam raising a hand in greeting as soon as they were through the door. They joined Caleb at his table and took a seat as Evan looked around nervously.

Caleb smiled and held out a hand. "You must be Evan. I'm Caleb, your ride north."

Evan looked at him in confusion, and Caleb was forced to reevaluate his initial impression. He wasn't a man, but a boy—a teenager, at most—all spiky blond hair and wide, innocent eyes, with a sprinkling of freckles across his nose.

Caleb glanced at Balaam, raising an eyebrow in question.

Balaam, however, turned to the boy, resting a comforting hand on his shoulder. Despite the man's large and rather intimidating frame, thick black dreadlocks, and curling tattoos around his muscular, dark-skinned arms, he had a way of soothing frightened Half-Breeds. "Caleb is going to make sure you get to the Colony safely," he said, his voice a low rumble. "I'll lead anyone following us away." His dark eyes were intent, reassuring.

Evan nodded and turned to Caleb smiling hesitantly. "It's nice to meet you. Thanks . . . for helping me."

"That's my job," Caleb said lightly, offering his hand again.

This time, Evan shook it.

"You two should get going," Balaam said, getting to his feet. "I think we have Protectors about half an hour away. Luckily, no shifters, as far as I can tell, so I should be able to keep them busy long enough for you to get away." He reached out to touch Evan again, closing his eyes and breathing deeply for a moment.

Caleb knew it was how the man focused in on Evan's unique signature so he could mimic it, and he waited patiently until Balaam stepped back with a nod.

"Good luck," he said before stepping out the door without another word.

Caleb got to his feet and tossed his empty cup into the trash. "Come on," he said to Evan. "We need to find someplace less . . . busy."

They left the coffee shop, and Caleb led him down the street and into a dim alley he'd scouted when he first arrived in Milwaukee. "Did Balaam tell you how this works?" he asked.

Evan swallowed, his Adam's apple bobbing as his gaze darted toward the slimy walls and down to the littered ground. He finally focused on Caleb and seemed to square his shoulders. "He said you could . . . teleport us?"

He'd said it more as a question than a statement, and Caleb grinned. It wasn't the first time he'd had such a reaction. "Yeah. We're going to have to get close, I'm afraid." He waved the boy over and turned him around. Men generally tended to be more comfortable if they weren't face-to-face. "Cross your hands over your chest," he said, folding his arms over Evan's firmly. "This will be quick, only a few seconds, but take a deep breath and close your eyes. It can be a little disorienting."

Evan nodded.

Caleb could feel his heart racing under his arm. "It's okay," he said. "Try and relax and it will be over before—" Caleb stiffened at the familiar tingle of a Race presence nearby. He cursed under his breath.

"What is it?" Evan asked.

"Someone's coming," he whispered, his hold on Evan tightening in urgency. "Brace yourself; we've got to go now."

They shifted, reappearing in an empty field. Evan staggered as Caleb's knees buckled and he leaned into him.

"Sorry," Caleb said, his voice cracking as he reached into his pocket for some R-cubes. "That was a long one. I need a minute."

"Are you okay?"

Caleb chewed and swallowed with a nod. "Yeah. You?"

Evan nodded, still looking a bit stunned. He turned around in a circle. "Where are we?"

"About fifty miles north of—damn." Caleb shot to his feet. "They're here."

"Who?" Evan paled. "How?"

"I don't know. Balaam was wrong. They must have a shifter . . . and a tracker of some kind." He reached for Evan. "I won't be able to get us far, but we need to shake them. I'm going to try several short shifts instead of a long one." He popped another cube. "Ready?"

Evan closed his eyes, his hands trembling under Caleb's. "Ready."

Caleb took a deep breath and shifted, beginning to wonder if this was one mission he would fail.

They made it to the Guardian Colony, Caleb dead on his feet and leaning heavily on Evan as they approached the gate. He remembered little of the next twelve hours, spending them sleeping, for the most part, and waking only to consume some cubes and water, and a little soup on occasion, before exhaustion took him again.

When he finally woke, Bel was there by his bed, waiting to ask him about what had happened. Unfortunately, Caleb didn't have any answers. He hadn't seen who'd pursued them as far as the Canadian border before they had apparently lost him, or *them*, and although they'd waited anxiously for Protectors to close in, there had been no attack.

Someone, somehow, had tracked him, and Caleb couldn't fight the fear that he and Evan hadn't *escaped* that person, but that he or she had let them get away.

"But why?" Bel had asked when he expressed the thought out loud. "It doesn't make any sense. If it was Protectors, why wouldn't they have taken you, or even followed you here?"

Caleb didn't know, and at that point, he found he didn't care. All he wanted to do was recover and head back to Allenmore, perhaps utilizing more conventional travel options for the trip home. He wasn't anxious to shift again.

Three days later, he left the Colony, happy to see Evan fitting in well with some of the others his own age. He'd learned the boy had been orphaned by a car accident, leaving him miraculously uninjured. The fact had led the Protectors to close in on him, but at least this time, the Guardians had won. The boy was free. Caleb had succeeded in his mission.

He hugged Bel, nodding to Gideon in farewell, but still not comfortable with a more demonstrative gesture where the Guardian leader was concerned.

Perhaps in time.

Rebuilding that relationship, or rather, *building* it, would definitely take a lot of time. He turned quickly and shifted away from the Colony without looking back. He planned to take a train from Winnipeg, then possibly a bus once he got across the border. He preferred not to fly if at all possible, since shifting wasn't the best option when he was miles above the ground.

Caleb stopped to rest in a thick forest about thirty miles from Winnipeg, sitting on a fallen log as he chewed on some R-cubes and a protein bar. He took comfort in the quiet around him, the faint rustling of leaves or chirp of a bird overhead. He smiled as his mind wandered, as it often did, to Ava and her reaction to his gift of the necklace. He knew he had to tell her more about his parents. It was essential that she know what she was getting into before their relationship progressed any further.

And he definitely wanted it to progress. He'd known that for a while.

But Ava was still learning what it meant to be Race, and there were things she needed to know about him—about *herself*—and sooner rather than later. He just hoped it wouldn't scare her away because, although it terrified him, he didn't know what he'd do without her.

A branch snapped, and Caleb jumped to his feet, eyes scanning the surrounding trees. He swallowed the rest of his R-cube and held his breath, listening for other signs of movement. A rustling drew his attention, and he almost laughed out loud when a squirrel darted across the ground in front of him and bounded up a nearby tree.

"Not cool," he muttered.

It stopped on a branch, scrutinizing Caleb with a tilt of the head before darting higher up the tree.

Then he felt it; that telltale tingle up his spine that he'd come to recognize as he'd raced to the Colony with Evan. He knew, somehow, whoever had been chasing them had found him again. Whoever it was wasn't after Evan at all, but after him.

Caleb warred with himself, half wanting to run and half wanting to confront whoever was tracking him. The problem was he was relatively certain it was more than one person, and he had to assume they had a nefarious purpose. Why else would they stay in the shadows? Perhaps the Council suspected he was working with the Guardians. Or, even worse, maybe the Rogues had tracked him down in an attempt to get to Ava.

He stiffened as they came closer.

Not two . . . three, possibly more.

There was no way he could take on that many, so Caleb used the seconds he had to reach out with his Race gifts, trying to gather as much information as possible about the approaching group. He would relay it to Bel—or to Gideon—and together they could try to determine who was out to get him.

He closed his eyes, focusing until the last possible moment, and popped another cube into his mouth before starting a series of shifts toward home.

It was going to be a long trip.

Chapter 3

Caleb was gone for five days, sixteen hours and twenty-seven minutes, not that Ava was counting. He appeared on her doorstep late Thursday evening, his face drawn and haggard, but smiling as he pulled her close for a sweet kiss.

"Hey you two, get a room!" Ava's roommate, Lucy, called as she passed by on her way to the bathroom.

"I have one," Ava said with a flippant toss of her hair as she pulled Caleb inside.

"Yeah, but you *share* it," Lucy said, poking her head back around the corner and holding up a finger as if she was making a brilliant observation. "And some of us spend our Friday nights alone and lonely and don't need to be reminded of what we're missing."

Ava laughed.

Lucy may have lacked on the long-term-relationship front, but she hardly spent all her weekend nights home alone. Tall and slender with sleek blond hair and gorgeous blue eyes, Lucy Matthews never wanted for male companionship. She just hated to commit, saying there were a lot of fish in the sea, and it was her job to throw back the tiny ones.

Ava wasn't sure what that meant, exactly, but it seemed to be Lucy's motto. And who was Ava to dispute her best friend's motto?

Caleb stopped a few steps in the room, lacing his fingers with hers. "Come on," he said, kissing her again. "Let's go for a walk."

"A walk?"

He grinned. "Well, maybe not a *walk* so much."

Ava tried to look skeptical, but it was difficult when she would follow Caleb anywhere. She let him pull her back out of the room, ignoring Lucy's catcalls of "Don't do anything I wouldn't do!" as they raced down the stairs and out the back door of the dorm into the fenced area housing the dumpster.

"Romantic," Ava said with a wry smile.

Caleb snorted, glancing around carefully to ensure they weren't being observed before pulling her close.

"You sure you're up for this?" Ava asked as he popped an R-cube into his mouth. "You seem kind of tired."

He swallowed, smiling as he brushed a finger over her cheek. "We won't go far. Ready?"

Ava nodded and tucked her head against his chest, smiling at the feel of his heartbeat under her cheek. She hadn't truly realized how much she'd missed him until he was back, warm and strong, and wrapped around her, his scent familiar and comforting as she nuzzled against him.

The ground dropped away beneath her feet and her grip around his waist tightened in reflex, wind whipping her hair about her face as she clenched her eyes shut against the whirling dizziness that accompanied shifting. She focused on her breathing, in and out, counting to herself until the wind died down and they landed on firm ground. Ava took a deep breath and opened her eyes to find they'd shifted to the grasslands on the banks of the Missouri River. It was one of Caleb's favorite places to visit, especially at night, when the campers and fishermen went home, and they could lie in the high grass and stare up at the stars.

He pulled her down beside him on the ground, and she lay back on her elbow, Caleb's head pillowed on her stomach and the moon casting the planes of his face in shadow. With training and school and Caleb's assignments, it was rare to have these quiet times, times to simply enjoy being together, touching each other. Ava brushed her fingers through his thick dark hair, twisting it a little, and he sighed contentedly, his eyes drifting closed behind his glasses.

He looked a little thin, his tall, lean frame spread out in the grass—a disguise, of course, the Veil that kept the world from seeing his true form. Ava had seen it—the perfection of him, all golden skin and corded muscle—although she didn't look through Caleb's Veil often, and never without asking. It was rude, she'd learned. And she actually liked Caleb's Veiled body. It was beautiful in its own way and familiar to her while the other was otherworldly and a little bit intimidating.

"You sure you're okay?" she asked after a while.

"It's been a tough few days," he replied. "Lot of shifting."

"Did everything go all right?"

Caleb hesitated—only briefly, but it was enough for Ava's instincts to kick in. "What happened?"

He sighed again and opened his eyes enough to glance at her sideways. "Sometimes it would be easier if I could lie to you."

She tugged his hair lightly. "Yeah, but then I'd have to hurt you."

"You'd have to catch me first."

"You think you could shift before I could bind you?" she asked with teasing grin. "Didn't you see Tiernan hanging upside down in the Council chamber?"

Caleb shook his head and closed his eyes again with an amused half smile. "Show off." He turned onto his side, throwing an arm across her stomach.

"Tell me," she said quietly, laying her hand on his arm.

Caleb was silent for a long moment. "Someone followed us. Well, followed *me*."

"Followed you?" A lump formed in Ava's throat. "Who? Why?"

"I don't know. I didn't stick around to find out."

"I don't understand."

Caleb sat up, turning to face her as she did the same. "Someone was able to track my shifts. I lost them when we got to the Canadian border, or at least I thought I did . . ." His eyes took on a faraway look, and he furrowed his brow as if trying to solve a complicated puzzle.

"Caleb?"

"Sorry." He shook his head, blinking rapidly a few times. "Anyway, they picked me up again when I left the Colony."

"How do you know it was the same person?"

"I know. And not person . . . *people.*"

Ava scooted closer to him, wrapping her arms around his bent knee. "How do you know you lost them this time?"

When Caleb looked up, he couldn't hide the worry in his eyes. "I don't. Not for sure. All I know is I don't feel them now." He tilted his head. "Do you?"

Ava closed her eyes, reaching out with her Race senses. For whatever reason, her gift seemed more intense than his—more intense than most, according to Caleb—and she was often able to sense Race presence from much greater distances. She breathed slowly and deeply, focusing as Audrey had taught her at the Guardian safe house all those months ago, searching for the faint tingle to alert her one of her own kind was nearby.

"No," she said with a heavy exhale as she opened her eyes. "I only feel you. Maybe you should go to the Council. Tell them what happ—"

"I'm not going to the Council."

"But it could have been Rogues."

"It wasn't Rogues," Caleb snapped. "I don't know who it was, and I'm not telling anyone until I know more."

"But—"

"Ava, let it go!" Caleb moved away from her, his back stiff. After a moment, he glanced back, and the frustration on his face softened when he saw her shocked expression. "I'm sorry. I don't mean to yell. I'm just tired. It's been a long few days and I really want to relax for a bit, you know?"

Ava was still a bit stunned by his reaction. Caleb was always patient with her, sometimes agonizingly so, and it was unlike him to snap at her like that.

He reached out and took her hand, rubbing his thumb over it lightly. "I'm sorry."

She nodded, licking her lips nervously. "It's okay."

"It was difficult," he said after a moment, "being away from you."

Ava moved closer until they were sitting side by side, shoulders touching. "It was hard for me, too."

"You felt it, then?"

Caleb watched her carefully, as if the question was some kind of test, as though her reply was important. She thought very carefully about exactly *how* she felt.

"I . . . missed you," she said slowly. "But it was more than that. It was like . . ." She looked up and searched the sky as if amidst the stars she could find the right words. "It was like something was wrong. Something missing. I don't know. That probably doesn't even make any sense." She blushed and drew her knees up, wrapping her arms around them, and rested her chin on top.

"It makes sense," Caleb said quietly.

She looked up, but he was gazing out over the horizon, lost in thought.

He took a deep breath. "When we—Race—are . . . involved with someone, we form a bond, not just on a physical and emotional level. You've felt it, right? When we're close?" He looked at her, a small smile on his face.

Ava thought of all the times she'd indulged in that feeling of their gifts mingling, their power twisting back and forth between them, and nodded slowly.

He swallowed, taking her hand, and she felt it once again. "It only gets stronger over time," he said, lifting his free hand to trace the curves of their joined fingers with the tip of his own, sending sparks of awareness over her skin everywhere he touched. "And even stronger the more . . . *intimate* . . . the connection."

He let the words sink in for a moment, and Ava shifted nervously as what he was saying hit home.

"It can be overwhelming," he said, his gaze on their interlocked fingers as he rubbed his thumb gently over hers. "The bond can be . . . addictive. It's why we have to be so careful." He looked into her eyes. "It's why we have to take things slow."

Ava tried to absorb his words, his intense gaze. "Are you saying we could become addicted to each other? Like a drug?"

"The bond is very powerful. We're taught from a young age to respect it." He cleared his throat, rubbed at the back of his neck, and he focused on their joined hands once again. "But this life is all new to you, so you need to know what's in store if we stay together. The intensity of our connection will grow to be more than you can imagine."

"I don't mind," Ava said quickly.

Caleb looked up in surprise, a bark of laughter escaping before he could stop it. Ava blushed, of course. He reached out to graze the color with his knuckle. "I don't either," he said quietly, his hand dropping to cup her cheek. "But we *should*. The bond is not something to be taken lightly."

They sat in silence for a moment, then Caleb smiled and his gaze dropped as he reached out to touch her necklace. "You're wearing it."

"Of course. I never take it off."

He slid his hand around it, rubbing the stones with his thumb. "It's said to have power, you know."

"Power?"

"The necklace." He fingered the blue stone. "Azurite stimulates mental activity." Then the green one. "Fluorite grounds excess energy and is supposed to promote clarity and peace. Together they're supposed to help focus your abilities. I thought it might help you in your training."

"Really?" Ava said with a skeptical tilt of her head. "You really believe all that stuff—crystals and magic stones?"

Caleb shrugged. "It's all electrical impulses. Everything." He released the necklace and waved his hand in a broad sweep. "The world around us, the air, the ground, you and me. It's how we're able to do what we do, by manipulating cells and molecules and electricity and magnetism. The stones are a part of that. It's not out of the realm of possibility that they could help."

"Huh." Ava tried but failed to hide her doubt. "If you say so."

"You're a telekinetic with a boyfriend who can teleport, and you're having trouble with this?" Caleb laughed, getting to his feet and holding out a hand to Ava. "Come on, let's give it a try.

Ava narrowed her eyes, barely able to make out Caleb's tall frame as a cloud passed over the moon. After five days, sixteen hours, and twenty-seven minutes without him, training was the last thing on her mind. Still, she was intrigued and gripped his hand as he pulled her to her feet.

"You think it will help me shift?" she asked.

Caleb laughed, pulling her in for a quick kiss. "Couldn't hurt. But let's try something else first."

She glanced around the dark clearing. "No rocks to throw."

"I was thinking we might try something more physical."

Ava raised an eyebrow, intrigued, and ran a finger over his stomach. "Oh, really?"

He snorted. "Not *that* kind of physical. I swear, you have a one-track mind." He kissed her again to soften his words, but gave her a stern look. "Work first. Play later."

"Spoilsport." She frowned then clapped her hands and rubbed them together, ready to try whatever Caleb suggested. "All right, then, what do you want me to do?"

"I still can't figure out why your strength and speed are so lacking," he replied.

"Thanks."

"Oh, now, don't take it so personally. You know what I mean," he said, shoving her shoulder lightly. "For some reason, those gifts are still blocked for you. I've been thinking it's the same with your electrical imprint and the Veil, for that matter."

No matter how hard Ava tried, she was unable to lift the camouflage that presented her as an ordinary human—average height, slender, pale skin that freckled in the summer, and long, light brown hair. The only visible evidence of her Race heritage was her mismatched brown and hazel-gold eyes, but those were easily hidden, thanks to her colored contacts. While Ava could see through the Veil of others, and others were able to lift their Veil with enough focus, she couldn't. No matter what she did, she looked human. Normal.

"So you think the block's still there?"

"Well, at least some of it. It's the only thing that makes any sense," Caleb said, searching the area and settling on a grove of cottonwood trees. He started leading Ava toward them. When they reached the trees, he scrutinized them carefully, testing them with a hand before settling on one with a trunk about a foot in diameter. He waved her forward.

"Try to push it." Ava closed her eyes, and he touched her shoulder to get her attention "*Without* telekinesis."

She stared at him for a moment, and he extended an arm toward the tree with a slight bow. Tentatively, she approached the tree and placed both palms on it.

"Try to clear your mind . . . focus," he said quietly. "Think about how it felt when the block came down back at the Rogue lair. Picture it in your mind, crumbling brick by brick."

Ava took a deep breath, Caleb's voice fading to a low rumble in the background as she focused on her own power. She called it forward, feeling the familiar tingle winding through her, radiating from deep within. She searched for the block keeping it at bay, tried to picture it flowing through her bloodstream and into her muscles. A warm vibration heated her chest, and Ava gasped, one hand flying up to touch the pendant around her neck. She could feel it vibrating under her fingers, and it seemed to intensify her power somehow.

"Now push it," Caleb said.

Ava tensed and took three quick breaths before leaning into the tree, every muscle tightening as she shoved with all her strength.

Nothing happened.

"Again." Caleb's voice was tight, and she felt him touch her arm, boosting her power with his own.

She focused on that feeling, envisioned the block falling down—breaking apart—and pushed again.

And again.

Finally, she opened her eyes, glaring up at the stubborn tree, her fingers digging into the bark.

"Nothing's happening," she grumbled, leaning against the tree in defeat. "I can't do it."

"Come on. Try again," Caleb said, a hint of irritation in his tone.

Ava turned to glare at him. "I can't do it."

"Of course you can't if you don't even try." He stepped away, turning to another tree and pushing it with all his might. The tree shuddered with a low groan before bending under Caleb's power, falling to the ground with a crash as the roots popped up from the ground, and spraying dirt in all directions. He brushed off his hands, turning to her with a challenging look. "See? You just have to *try*."

"I *did* try." Ava was more than a little annoyed at his superior attitude. "What is wrong with you?"

Caleb threw his head back, rubbing his hands over his face before he stalked a few steps away from her.

Ava watched him warily. "Caleb?"

He looked back over his shoulder, but didn't meet her eyes.

"What is it?" she asked, her irritation vanishing as concern twisted in her stomach. "What's wrong?"

He shook his head slightly, as if to clear it, and turned to walk back to her. He reached out to touch her cheek gently. "I'm sorry. I . . . I'm just tired. I didn't mean to take it out on you."

Ava took a step closer, sliding her hands under his coat and gripping his shirt as her anger evaporated. "Maybe we should head back? So you can get some rest?" She hoped he'd argue the point, but Caleb only nodded sadly.

"Yeah . . . yeah." He pulled her close and pressed a kiss to the top of her head. "I'll take you home."

Ava clung to him as he shifted them back to campus, held his hand as he walked her back to her dorm, and tried to ignore the uneasy feeling that something was very, very wrong.

Late that night, the ringing of a phone roused the occupant of a lavish home in New Elysia, the Race city hidden on a mountain about fifty miles from Kalispell, Montana. With a groan, the man disentangled himself from the naked limbs of his bedmate, who rolled over, taking the sheets with her as he fumbled for the phone.

"Yes?"

"He's back at Allenmore," a familiar voice reported.

"Any problems?"

"None. Everything went according to plan."

"Good, that's good." The man swung his legs over the side of the bed, leaned forward onto his knees as he yawned, and scrubbed a hand over his face. "What about the girl?"

"No change."

The man stood and padded quietly out of the bedroom and down the hall, crossing the darkened living room to pour himself a drink at the bar. "We will have to help that situation along, it appears. What of the Protectors?"

"No indication they were aware of our presence," the voice said, a hint of smug satisfaction in his tone.

"Don't underestimate the Ross siblings." The man took a gulp of his whiskey and winced as it burned on the way down. "Tell your men to watch themselves."

"They always do, sir." He cleared his throat. "So what's next?"

The man sighed, years of planning weighing down his shoulders. They'd come so far, their goal finally within reach, but the timing of all of this was crucial. Any mistakes could be devastating.

"We proceed according to the timetable," he said. "I want daily updates on Foster. No one makes a move until all the pieces are in place, understood?"

"What about Elias?"

Elias. A critical piece of the puzzle.

"Protectors are closing in on him as we speak. He should be in Council custody within the week." He finished his whiskey and sucked on an ice cube before letting it drop back into the glass. "I don't have to tell you what's riding on all of this."

"No, sir."

"Don't let me down." He hung up without another word and crossed to the window, looking out at the darkness.

His home sat on a slight rise overlooking New Elysia, and his gaze flitted over the sleeping city, drawn to a light here and there. He wondered if the people below realized that their lives were about to change. That their whole *world* was about to change.

No. No, they have no idea.

But one day very soon they would, and they would no doubt thank him for it. He closed the curtain, smiling at the thought, and turned to head back to the bedroom, leaving his empty whiskey glass on the hall table.

He still had a few hours to sleep. The sleep of the righteous.

And then, with the morning sun, he'd get back to work.

Ava sat up in bed, unsure of what had awakened her, but unable to shake an uneasy feeling in the pit of her stomach. She'd had an odd dream but couldn't recall the details of it, only fleeting glimpses of familiar faces—Caleb, Madeleine, Tiernan—and a sensation of running and panic.

She shuddered, drawing the blankets up over her shoulders as she hugged her knees. She hadn't had such dreams in months—not since the psychic block crumbled at the Rogue lair—and had assumed that the dreams were a result of her Race instincts trying to get her attention. Once she'd connected with them more fully, the dreams had disappeared, but for some reason those instincts seemed to be on high alert recently.

Ava glanced at Lucy's bed, hoping she hadn't disturbed her, but her roommate lay huddled under the blankets, breathing evenly. Ava slipped out of bed and made her way to the window to peer through the blinds. It only took a moment for her to spot Katherine standing in the shadow of some trees.

Although different Protectors appeared throughout the day, including Tiernan, on occasion, Katherine generally preferred the night shift. It amplified her gift—an unusually strong Veil that could render her nearly invisible to humans, as well as most Race when she wanted—but Ava was always able to see her clearly, something that both irritated and impressed Katherine.

The Protector looked up, obviously feeling Ava's presence, and waved a hand in greeting. Ava rolled her eyes but waved back before letting the blinds close. She turned to go back to bed and stopped abruptly, that uneasy feeling suddenly growing stronger. She closed her eyes and focused her thoughts, reaching out with her Race gift. She could feel Katherine clearly, but there was also something more.

Someone . . . more.

Ava slipped back to the window, parting the blinds enough to peer through. Katherine looked up again and tilted her head in question, obviously wondering what her charge was doing. Ava ignored her, heart pounding as she searched the shadows for whatever—*whoever*—had triggered her instincts. Her power sparked as she narrowed her eyes, looking deeper, farther—into each dim doorway and along each shadowed corner.

Just like that, the feeling evaporated, and the only Race presence she felt was Katherine's.

Ava blinked in surprise, reaching out again in a fleeting attempt to recapture the sensation, but it eluded her like water trickling through her fingers. She looked down at Katherine, but the Protector was thumbing through her phone, seemingly unperturbed. Obviously, if there was someone out there, it was someone who didn't overly worry Katherine.

Ava frowned.

She had been on edge lately, nervous, and she couldn't figure out why. Her encounter with Caleb earlier had left her uneasy, verging on paranoid. He'd seemed *off* somehow, like something was bothering him, but when she had questioned him about it, he'd simply said he was tired and she was reading too much into his foul temper. Combined with the return of her strange dreams and whatever had just happened, Ava felt off-kilter.

She sighed and got back into bed, pulling the covers over her head. Perhaps she *was* being paranoid. Sure, the Rogues were out there, and the Council still wasn't convinced she wasn't a threat, but she had Caleb watching her back—and Protectors as well. Not to mention that if she'd proven anything lately, it was that she could take care of herself.

She wasn't writing off her instincts yet, though. Caleb had told her time and time again to trust them, that they had the potential to save her life. But until she could figure out what they were trying to *tell* her, Ava decided she'd keep her concerns to herself. There was no point in panicking until there was something to actually panic about.

One last time, Ava closed her eyes and searched for that unknown presence, just to be sure.

Nothing.

Well, if there was someone out there, Ava would be on the lookout for him. Until then, she had to get some sleep. She had an English quiz in the morning and a full shift at the diner after. On top of all of that, spring break drew closer with every passing hour and she still hadn't told her mother she wasn't coming home.

Tomorrow. Definitely tomorrow. Everything can wait until then.

Chapter 4

Other than a few texts on Friday, Caleb didn't hear from Ava again until Saturday evening, when he showed up to walk her home after a shift at the diner. She was tired, so he didn't linger, simply kissing her softly before she turned to walk into her dorm. She flashed him a quick smile as the door shut behind her, and he sighed when he lost sight of her, ignoring Katherine, who stood off in a cluster of trees, playing with her phone. He wasn't sure he was handling the situation with Ava well at all.

He'd tried to warn her about the bond, but it was difficult to explain if you'd never witnessed it in person, never seen both sides, as he had. Not many had because once bonded, it was rare for the two partners to be separated, except by death. Which, of course, dissolved the bond and, in a strange twist of fate, made the separation a bit more tolerable.

But to be torn from your bonded mate while still alive? Well, Caleb was one of the few with intimate knowledge of the pain that could cause. Did cause. Still caused, actually.

He had no doubt that Ava was the one for him, but he was determined that she understand what she was getting into, and that would take some time and unfortunately, a little chat with his mother. He knew it would be uncomfortable for Ava, to say the least, but Madeleine Foster could probably explain things better than anyone. Still, it was not something he was looking forward to bringing up with his mother. She would no doubt have her own opinions about Caleb's relationship and his plans for the future.

That was what happened when your mother was the leader of the Council and your girlfriend was number one on the Council's watch list. So, yeah. It was complicated.

He heard Ava enter her dorm room and call out a hello to Lucy, and he turned to walk away, shuffling a bit on the gravel path. Before he could think better of it, he angled toward Katherine, who kept her eyes on her phone until he cleared his throat to get her attention.

"Oh," she said with a wide-eyed blink. "Hello, Caleb. Fancy meeting you here."

"Katherine," he replied with a nod. "You seem to be pulling Ava duty quite a lot lately."

She shrugged, not denying it. "Tiernan's on another assignment."

"Really?"

"Very hush-hush. He won't even tell me what it's about."

"Interesting." Caleb leaned against a tree and crossed his arms over his chest. "So the Council's found something more important that Ava. Strange that I haven't heard a whisper." Not that his mother discussed Council business with him, but Caleb had contacts in a lot of places, and he usually knew when something was up.

Katherine raised a perfect brow. "Don't look at me. I'm as in the dark as you are."

"I'm getting a little tired of being in the dark," Caleb snapped. "The Council needs to remember that it acts for the Race, not the other way around."

"Big talk, Protector," Katherine said with smirk. "Better be careful, or you'll be labeled a radical. Or worse yet, a revolutionary."

"Well, maybe it's time someone stirred the pot a little." Caleb straightened and kicked a rock. It pinged off a series of trees and disappeared around the corner of a building.

"That doesn't sound like you." Katherine pocketed her phone and peered at Caleb curiously. "I mean, I've heard rumors of you and the Guardians . . ."

"Like that's a big secret."

"But bad-mouthing Mommy and the Council?" Katherine snickered at Caleb's dark look. She'd always loved getting under his skin. "I'm just saying it's refreshing to hear you thinking for yourself, that's all. Maybe the girl's been a good influence on you."

"Ava doesn't have anything to do with it." He leaned in, his eyes glittering in the darkness. "Hasn't it ever irked you, Katherine? We're the most powerful beings on this planet, and we're relegated to . . . to chauffeur duties and babysitting. Doesn't it seem like our time could be better spent elsewhere?"

Katherine stared at him, eyes wide with surprise at the underlying vehemence in his voice.

"We're supposed to be Protectors. From whom? It seems a bit ridiculous, is all. Half-Breeds are some horrible threat? Or maybe the humans? I'm not sure I see it."

"Caleb, what are you talking about?" Katherine whispered as she glanced over her shoulder, suddenly nervous. "You can't say things like that."

Caleb opened his mouth to respond, but after a moment, shook his head, letting out a self-deprecating laugh. "Sorry. Ignore me," he said. "I'm just tired. Need a few cubes and a good night's sleep, I think."

Katherine let out a quiet breath, all teasing gone. "That's probably a good idea."

He forced a smile. "Yeah . . . yeah. Forget I said anything. I don't know what's gotten into me lately."

"Don't worry about it," Katherine replied. "You know I won't mention it again."

Caleb turned to leave, but stopped when she touched his arm.

"Be careful, Caleb. You of all people should know you don't want to end up in the Council's crosshairs."

He nodded, but his jaw was tense, and he didn't meet her eyes. "It's fine. I'm fine. I'll see you later, Katherine." She released him, and he walked away through the trees, a little embarrassed at his outburst.

It was true that he'd been feeling jerked around by the Council lately, but that was really nothing new. The Council had always operated on a need-to-know basis when it came to the Protectors, and he'd never had a problem with it before. Caleb had always taken his responsibilities as a Protector seriously, and even when working with the Guardians, only did so because he thought he was doing the right thing—for his people, as well as the humans and Half-Breeds. For a moment when talking with Katherine, however, he'd felt an unfamiliar irritation . . . a *frustration* with his role in Race society, and he wasn't sure why.

He pulled a couple of R-cubes from his pocket and chewed them thoughtfully. He really wasn't in the mood for walking. A quick shift home and some sleep, and everything would make more sense in the morning.

Ava flipped through her notes, but she could feel Lucy watching her—again—and didn't need her Race senses to know something was on her mind. She looked up, only to have Lucy drop her eyes immediately to the book Ava knew she wasn't really reading.

"What?" she asked.

Lucy blinked innocently. "Hmm?"

If she hadn't known her so well, Ava might have bought it. "Don't 'hmm' me," Ava said, slapping her textbook shut and shoving her notes aside. "You've got something on your mind. Out with it."

Lucy bit her lip, eyeing her roommate nervously. "It's just . . . I'm not sure if I should say anything."

"About?"

Lucy pushed her books aside and crossed the room to sit cross-legged next to Ava. After a moment, she reached out to squeeze Ava's hand, a sad and almost pitying look on her face.

"Okay, now you're freaking me out," Ava said, forcing a laugh.

"Sorry." Lucy winced, but she didn't pull away. Instead, she took a deep breath. "Okay, it's about Caleb."

Of all the things Ava had imagined, that wasn't one of them. "What about Caleb?"

"How . . . serious are you guys?"

Ava wasn't even certain how to answer that question. Sure, she knew how she felt about Caleb, and she was pretty sure she knew how he felt about her. But it was complicated. They seemed stalled in a way, especially after their recent conversation about the bond. Ava avoided thinking about it because part of her didn't know what it meant, and part of her was worried about what it *could* mean.

"We're pretty serious, I guess."

"You guess?" Lucy squeezed her hand again.

Ava felt the urge to tell her everything. She couldn't, of course. That would put Lucy's life in danger, not to mention her own and probably Caleb's as well. But she could talk to her about *some* of it. The *normal* stuff. The *boy-girl* stuff. Maybe if she left out all the supernatural, life-threatening parts. After all, Lucy was her best friend. And she did have more experience with guys than Ava did. A lot more.

"I love him," she said quietly, the words foreign on her tongue, though she'd thought them plenty of times.

"Yeah, that part's pretty obvious." She scooted next to Ava and put her free arm around her shoulders. "And?"

"And . . . it's good. It's really good." Ava said, not meeting her eyes.

"But?"

Ava glanced at her sidelong. "You sound like a Schoolhouse Rock song." At Lucy's blank look, she sang tunelessly, "*Conjunction Junction, what's your function?* I swear, Luce, your childhood was sorely lacking."

Lucy smiled but didn't let her off the hook. "But?"

"But," Ava said and sighed. "I'm just not sure where it's going. He's holding back."

"How do you mean?"

Ava gave her a significant look, and Lucy gasped, her eyes widening as her mouth formed an astonished O.

"You mean you haven't?"

Ava shook her head, her face hot.

"But you've been together for months!"

Ava shrugged. "We're taking it slow."

"Well, that's . . . fine." Lucy patted her hand. "I mean, there's nothing wrong with taking your time."

"There's not, right?"

"Of course not." Lucy fidgeted a bit then exhaled heavily. Her words flowed out in a rush. "It's just, I saw him—Caleb, I mean. Although who else would I be talking about, right?" She laughed nervously.

"And?" Ava wasn't sure where this was going, but she had a feeling it wasn't good.

"And he wasn't alone." The words came out in a final rush. "*Hewaswithawoman.*"

"What?"

"I mean, it doesn't mean anything, right?" Lucy sounded as if she were set on high speed. She didn't even pause for breath as the words rushed out of her mouth in a torrent. "They were only talking. And I don't want to make it seem like a big deal, but I saw them, and I kind of waved, but he looked a little upset that I did—"

"Luce—"

"And she was *gorgeous*! I mean, no offense, you know I think you're beautiful. You *are* beautiful, but she was gorgeous, and it just hit me as odd —"

"Lucy—"

"And I hated not saying anything to you, because we tell each other everything, right?"

"Lucy, slow down." Ava shifted to face her on the bed, one leg tucked under her. "What woman?"

She shrugged. "I don't know who she was. She's tall and, like I said, gorgeous. Pale, but in a pretty way, not sickly, long straight black hair . . ."

Ava's stomach flipped.

Katherine.

"And they seemed to be having this intense conversation. I mean, not like fighting, but . . . involved."

Ava knew she had to tread carefully. "It's okay, Luce. I know her."

"You do?"

Ava nodded, forcing a smile. "Yeah. She and Caleb work together."

"She's a physics tutor?" Lucy looked skeptical.

Ava laughed. "No. He has another job."

Doing what?

Ava feared she was painting herself into a corner. "Back home on school breaks, you know?"

"So what's she doing here?"

What is *she doing here?*

"Oh, you know, she's pretty new at it, and Caleb kind of works as a consultant when he's away. They're old friends, so he's helping her out." It sounded weak and full of holes, even to her. She held her breath, remembering the old adage that the simpler a lie, the better. If in doubt, shut up. She reached for her book, like the conversation was over.

"Are you . . ." Lucy ducked her head, trying to meet her eyes. "Are you sure that's it? I mean, it didn't look like a work conversation."

Ava forced herself to meet Lucy's gaze. "I'm sure. It's nothing, Luce, really."

"Okay," she said slowly. " 'Cause you know I've totally got your back, right? If that witch was making the moves on your man . . ." She clenched her fists like a boxer. "I would take. Her. Out."

Ava laughed. "I appreciate the thought," she said. "But it's really not necessary. Caleb and me, we're good."

"Well, the offer stands." Lucy stood up and went back to her own bed, flopping down and still managing to be graceful about it. "You'd do the same for me, right?"

Ava grinned. "In a heartbeat."

In a confinement facility in New Elysia, Elias Borré considered his surroundings with an indifferent air. It was nice, as prisons went; more like a small condo than a cell. The one-bedroom unit was comfortably furnished; the only thing lacking was anything that could be used as a weapon—like knives in the kitchen or mirrors in the bathroom.

He sat on the rather stiff sofa, watching the door, as he had for the past hour or so, too distracted to concentrate on reading any of the drivel lining the nearby bookshelf. He'd appeared briefly in front of the Council before being assigned his "quarters" and was scheduled for further questioning the following morning.

The Council had procedures, after all, and even Rogues were allowed time to rest. It was all so very civilized. He eyed the cameras they didn't even bother to hide, wondering who was watching, and resisted the urge to make a crude gesture.

Borré felt the presence of another a few seconds before a quiet knock sounded at the door. It was irritating, since he was locked in—the knock only reinforced the illusion of privacy. It's not as if he could stop anyone from coming in anyway. He didn't bother getting up but remained on the couch as the door opened and the person he'd been expecting entered.

Borré glanced significantly at the cameras.

"Don't worry," his visitor said, taking a seat in a chair across from him. "They've been dealt with."

He didn't elaborate, and Borré didn't pursue the point, instead relaxing back into the sofa cushions. "Have you heard from Sloan?" he asked.

"Foster's back with the Michaels girl. Sloan and his men are keeping tabs on both of them."

"His men?" Borré raised a brow. Sloan Bartok usually worked alone. He never needed anyone else.

His companion smiled, but it didn't reach his eyes. "Simply ensuring all bases are covered. He knows how important this is." He rubbed at his lower lip. "He asked about you."

Borré nodded. "Yes, well, it's difficult for him. We work so closely, and with this . . . development." He waved a hand to indicate his surroundings. "He's not used to it." There was more to it, of course, but Borré did not feel compelled to reveal it.

"I don't completely understand it, myself," the visitor said. "Why allow yourself to be captured by the Protectors? I know it has to do with Foster —"

"Foster's but a tool. A piece of the puzzle."

"Don't you think I deserve to see the whole picture?"

"You deserve," Borré said with a pointed look, "the reward you will earn when this is all over."

The man's jaw tightened, but he nodded in acceptance. "What of the girl?"

Borré smiled. "Sloan knows what to do. The girl will come to us in time." He stood, crossed to the window overlooking the city, and tapped on it with a knuckle—plastic, not glass.

Typical.

"Why not *take* her?"

Borré frowned in irritation. "Because *getting* her is not the point, old friend. No, she will join us of her own free will."

"And if she doesn't?"

Borré smiled icily. "She will. They all do, eventually."

Ava knew it was a dream, but it didn't matter to her heart. It raced as she walked down the street through a dark neighborhood, a brisk wind cutting through her coat and whipping her hair around her face. She could see lights in one house centered in a cul-de-sac at the end of the street. She made her way toward it, stepping around a discarded basketball and a wayward Rollerblade.

A chill ran down her spine as she looked up at the modest two-story home, and she spun around, certain she wasn't alone. She scanned the area but could hear nothing above the wind until a squeaky rattle drew her attention to a loose street sign, hanging crookedly from a single bolt.

152nd Court SE

Slowly, she turned again to face the house only to see a dark figure standing in the shadows near the front porch. Her senses tingled. He was Race.

"Hello?" she called, but the figure either didn't hear her or chose to ignore her.

The front door opened, and a man emerged, carrying a plastic garbage bag. He whistled lightly and headed for a pair of cans already sitting on the sidewalk. He turned to glance back at the house, and the dim light from the front door was enough for Ava to identify who he was: Officer Nick Simmons from the campus police department. The one who helped her when she was attacked by Tiernan all those months ago. Back when all her nightmares had centered around the Protector.

Ava's breath quickened as the dark figure followed Officer Simmons, slipping silently through the yard. The illumination from the house didn't seem to reach him, and he remained hidden in the shadows. Ava was unable to make out any details. He was a shrouded specter, the only glint of light from a blade clutched in his right hand.

She shouted out a warning to Officer Simmons, but he didn't respond, continuing instead to the curb to deposit the trash into a can and smash it down with a slight grunt. He turned to go back to the house and came face-to-face with the mysterious pursuer. Officer Simmons opened his mouth to speak, but all that came out was a gasp, his body clutching around what Ava knew was the knife.

"No!" she screamed, trying to run toward him—to help in some way—but her feet wouldn't move. It was as though she was slogging through knee-deep mud, the ground sucking her in with every fruitless step.

Officer Simmons fell to the ground, blood spreading out in a sickening bloom across his shirt.

The attacker whirled around and was gone.

Officer Simmons gurgled, blood spurting from his mouth, and with his last breath, his head fell to the side, and his dead eyes latched on to her accusingly.

"I'm sorry," she gasped. And then she awoke, sweating and fighting for breath, with tears streaming down her face.

"Ava? You okay?" Lucy's raspy voice drifted over from across the room.

Ava willed her heart to slow, forcing a note of calm into her voice. "Yeah. I'm fine. Go back to sleep," she whispered. Ava sat unmoving for several minutes, even as she gripped the sheets to ground herself, listening to Lucy shift under her covers until she was breathing steadily again.

Quietly, Ava slipped out of bed, grabbed her shoes and a coat, and headed out of the room. She couldn't explain to Lucy where she was going or why, but she didn't dare waste any time getting there. Pulling her hair into a haphazard ponytail, she raced down the stairs and out the back door, knowing Katherine would be waiting there. Instead of trying to avoid her, Ava ran right up to her.

Katherine raised a brow in surprise. "Good evening," she said, taking in Ava's disheveled state with a long, slow look. "Out for a little stroll, are we?"

"I need your help." Ava knew she was wild-eyed and more than a little frantic. She hoped it would help her case. "There's someone in danger. We have to protect him." She reached out to tug at Katherine's sleeve. "Do you have a car? No, of course you don't. Why would you need a car?"

"Slow down," Katherine said calmly. "Tell me what's going on."

"There's no time. He could be there right now." Ava scrubbed at her face. "Look, I'm going. Your job is to watch me. So you can either help or I guess follow me and hope I don't get murdered."

The corner of Katherine's mouth lifted the tiniest bit. "Come on," she said finally. "I'll find us a car."

They raced toward the edge of campus.

Well, Ava raced. For Katherine, it was more of a slow jog. Ava spared a minute to be aggravated yet again that she still wasn't as fast as the rest of the Race.

Katherine scanned the cars parked along the side of the road, then moved toward a red Mustang convertible with the top down.

"We're lucky it's been an early spring," she said as she hopped over the side into the driver's seat. Even snow showers were not uncommon in early March in Missouri, but unseasonably warm temperatures had some people breaking out the short sleeves and, fortunately for them, putting the tops down. Katherine reached under the steering column to pull out a handful of wires.

"You sure you know what you're doing?" Ava asked, opting to open the door instead of climbing over.

Katherine shot her a glare. "I was doing this before you were born." The engine roared to life, and she let out a little squeal. "Sixty-six, Candy Apple Red Mustang convertible . . . a very good year."

She wiggled her eyebrows, and Ava realized it was the first time she'd actually seen Katherine excited about anything. But now was not the time. "Head east," she said as Katherine put the car in gear. "Toward Belmont Park."

Katherine sped through town, and in a few minutes, they wound past the park to the neighborhood Ava now recognized from her dream. She watched the street signs, letting out a distressed sound when she spotted the crooked one identifying 152nd Court Southeast.

"Turn here," she said quietly. "To the cul-de-sac at the end of the street. And be careful."

To her surprise, Katherine didn't have an indignant response to that. Instead, she slowed down a little and turned off the headlights, her superior sight more than enough to avoid any obstacles.

The wind picked up as she pulled to a stop, and Ava scrambled out of the car, searching the area in front of the house with first her eyes, then reaching out with her Race senses.

"What is it?" Katherine asked, coming up to stand beside her. "What's happening?"

"I'm not sure," Ava replied slowly. She walked toward the house, avoiding the basketball and the Rollerblade, just like in her dream. A light flicked on upstairs two houses down and Ava caught a glimpse of someone peering out the blinds before it went out again a few minutes later.

Her eyes darted back and forth from the front door to the shadow of the trees where she'd seen the mysterious figure in her dream. But he wasn't there. Perhaps she was early. Maybe she'd gotten there in enough time to warn Officer Simmons.

Or maybe she was too late. Her eyes flashed to the garbage cans at the sidewalk, but there was no body lying next to them.

Thank God.

That didn't necessarily mean anything, though. Her dreams were not always literal and could have been a reaction to a *potential* threat, not necessarily a specific one.

She made her way to the front door and knocked—first tentatively, and then with a bit more force—glancing over her shoulder to where Katherine stood in the shadows, ready to intervene if it was necessary. In a few minutes, the door opened, and Ava exhaled in relief when she saw Officer Simmons standing before her, rumpled and sleepy, half-mast eyes blinking in confusion.

"Ava? Do you know what time it is? What are you doing here?"

Oh, now that's a good question.

"I was, uh . . ." She scrambled for an answer and settled on the first one to pop into her mind. "I couldn't sleep and was just . . . walking and I thought I . . . uh . . . I saw something suspicious."

"Really?" He squared his shoulders, instantly in police mode. "Where?"

"I'm not sure," she said. "I thought I saw someone in the shadows." When he started to step out onto the porch, she moved to block his way. "They're gone now, I think. I just thought you'd want to know. I mean, I didn't know it was you, Officer Simmons, obviously, since I didn't know where you lived. But I thought whoever lived here would want to know." She heard a quiet snort behind her and decided she owed Katherine a kick in the shins. "So, yeah. You might want to keep an eye out. You know. Just in case," Ava said. "Be careful."

"Okay," Officer Simmons said slowly. "Thanks for the warning."

She nodded once and turned to leave, then had a thought. "By the way, have you taken your garbage out tonight?" His mouth dropped open a little, and Ava was pretty sure he thought she was a nut. Not that she blamed him.

"Yeah," he said. "I took it out a few hours ago. Are you sure you're all right, Ava?"

"Me?" Ava floundered a bit. "Yeah. I'm fine. Really. Sorry to bother you." She backed down the porch stairs, waving weakly. "You have a good night."

She turned to hurry down the street, checking to make sure he'd gone back inside before getting into the car. Katherine was already there, of course, waiting in the driver's seat and wearing a wry smirk.

"Care to tell me what that was all about?" she asked as she started the engine.

Ava sighed. "When I figure it out, I'll let you know."

She stared out the window as they made it through the quiet town back to campus. She'd been so certain that her dream was more than a dream. Obviously, either she'd misunderstood it or it was just her subconscious messing with her. Ava should have felt reassured, but she didn't. Instead, an unsettled tension weighed on her shoulders, and just like with Caleb, her intuition continued to prod at her, insisting that something wasn't right. The problem was she had no idea what to do about it.

Sloan Bartok stood on a rooftop a safe distance away, watching as the red Mustang finally turned around and left the neighborhood. His pale red hair curled around his head, blowing wildly in the wind, and he shoved it distractedly out of his face, annoyed.

He'd never been one to question orders, mainly because he knew he wouldn't be given any answers, but the night's assignment had proven an exercise in frustration. First, he'd been sent to intercept the cop, only to be diverted to Allenmore to the girl's dorm then back again to the cop's suburban neighborhood, but simply to watch from afar. It seemed a ridiculous waste of time, not to mention a waste of his particular skill set.

He pulled out his cell phone and dialed a familiar number, breathing deeply to maintain his composure.

"Yes?" a voice answered.

"The girl was here, just as you said."

The line was silent. Only Sloan's slow breaths measured the long seconds until the voice replied quietly, "And?"

"She's gone now. She spoke with the cop and then took off with Katherine Ross."

"Katherine? Really?" the voice said. "That's a bit surprising. I was unaware the two had become friendly."

Sloan didn't say anything. He'd learned that often it was simply best to wait for instructions.

"You know what to do. It should look like a crime of passion. Cover your tracks carefully. We don't want any inconvenient questions."

"Yes, sir."

"A witness or two might be helpful, though. I assume you can handle that?"

Sloan almost rolled his eyes, a bit insulted by the question. "Already taken care of, sir."

"Excellent. Thank you, Mr. Bartok. Your efficiency will be rewarded."

"Thank you, sir."

"Inform me when the job is done," he said. "Oh, and Mr. Bartok?"

"Yes?"

"Don't forget the wife."

The phone went dead, and Sloan slid it into his pocket as he rolled his shoulders to loosen his muscles. He checked his weapon, then thought better of it and holstered the Glock. He reached down and slid the hunting knife he kept under his pant leg out of its sheath. Even in the darkness, the blade flashed as it caught a glimmer of light from the moon, and Sloan smiled in satisfaction. He didn't often use weapons—given his gift, he didn't need to—but this particular assignment called for unorthodox methods.

He leapt from the rooftop and walked casually down the sidewalk toward the cop's house, the knife gripped loosely in his fingers. He whistled and flipped it in the air, catching it first by the blade, then the handle. If things went according to plan, he'd be done before dawn. Maybe grab some breakfast before he went home. He could go for some pancakes.

Sloan stopped at the curb, looking up at the front porch for a moment as he flipped the knife again. Gripping the handle firmly, he went to work.

Chapter 5

Ava stared at the clock on the classroom wall, the tick-tick-tick keeping pace with the thudding of her heart. Her English professor rambled on about allegories in *The Faerie Queene*, but she couldn't even track the conversation.

Caleb was gone. He'd disappeared without a word two days earlier, and she had no idea where he was. She'd finally broken down and asked Katherine, but she seemed genuinely surprised. She had tried to reassure Ava that sometimes Protectors were called out for emergency assignments at a moment's notice.

"I'm sure he'll contact you when he can," she'd said, but her eyes had betrayed her own concern. Which had been enough to really worry Ava. She was relatively certain that Katherine had never been one who was easily concerned. At her continued prodding, Katherine had tried to contact Tiernan to see if he knew anything, but so far she'd been unable to reach him.

Ava sighed as the minute hand moved ever so slowly, finally settling on the eleven as the professor announced a quiz the following afternoon. She couldn't even summon the energy to groan with the rest of the class but got up and left the room, her backpack bumping heavily against her hip.

She had no idea what to do. She knew Caleb was a big boy—more than able to protect himself—but her instincts continued to scream at her that something was wrong. Ava felt weak, powerless, left to flounder about helplessly, and she didn't like the feeling one little bit.

She started toward the dorm then whirled around, deciding to go by Caleb's apartment once more, just in case. She checked her phone, but didn't call him again, having texted and left numerous voice mails already.

She swore if he was okay, she was going to kick his—

Well, first she was going to hug him. And kiss him.

Since he'd been gone, she'd truly begun to understand what Caleb was talking about when he'd warned her of the so-called addiction. She felt tense and unsettled without him nearby, her power reaching out as if searching for him, needing his presence to fill a hole she hadn't realized was forming. If Caleb was right and that feeling only intensified the closer that they got? Well, it was a little scary, to be honest.

So, yeah. First, she was going to touch him and relieve this ache inside her. But then she was definitely going to let him have it.

Ava hitched her backpack up higher on her shoulder and gasped as a familiar sensation tingled along her skin. The hair stood up on her forearms and the back of her neck, and she spun around, her heart racing wildly.

"Hi," Caleb said, scratching at his neck nervously. "You're losing your touch. I can't believe you didn't sense me sooner."

Ava gaped at him. "Well, I've kind of had a lot on my mind. My boyfriend disappeared without a word two days ago. I've been a little worried." She fought the urge to grab him and nuzzle into his neck, despite the fact that she could feel her gift reaching toward him—and his reaching back.

"Yeah. I'm sorry about that," he said, brushing a finger down her arm. Her skin tingled where he'd touched her, even through her clothes. "Last-minute assignment and I was constantly on the move or I would have called."

Ava nodded, feeling tears prick her eyes. She knew she should be strong about this. Caleb was only doing his job—trying to help people—and she knew she should be supportive. She was just feeling so . . . not.

"Hey," he said softly, finally moving to take her in his arms. "I'm fine. Really. I'm sorry you were worried. If there was a way to get word to you, I would have. You know that."

Ava took a deep breath, settling against his chest as their gifts mingled and swelled to fill the hole inside her. "I know," she said. "Where were you, anyway?"

"West coast." He pushed her hair back over her shoulder and tipped his head to brush his lips over her ear.

"For the Council?"

He snorted. "No."

"The Guardians, then?"

"What's with the third degree?" he snapped. At her shocked expression, he blinked and shook his head slowly. "Wow. I'm sorry. I don't know where that came from," he said. "It's just been a long couple of days. I missed you."

"I missed you, too." Ava tried to relax, to enjoy Caleb's warmth, his touch, but a twinge of uneasiness nagged at her. "Are you okay?" she asked.

The strangest thing happened. Caleb smiled, assured her he was fine, apologized again, and leaned in to kiss her. And in that moment, Ava *knew* he was lying. It was as if he'd put on a mask—one that most people might not be able to see through, but one she could tell was a façade. A Veil atop his Veil.

"Come on," he said, taking her hand and pulling her along. "Let's go to my place and order some pizza or something. I'm starving."

Ava warred with herself, wondering if she should challenge him further. He was keeping something from her, but she could also tell that he was tired. She knew fulfilling his duties as a Protector while helping out the Guardians put a lot of pressure on him, so it was possible that was it. Maybe he was trying to put on a brave face so she wouldn't worry. It would be so like Caleb to try not to be a burden, out of a misguided notion of chivalry.

She opted for a gentler approach, squeezing his hand. "You know you can talk to me about things, right?" she asked quietly. "I mean, if something's bothering you, I'd want to help."

He lifted her hand to his lips and kissed it gently. "I know," he said. "And really, I'm fine. I just want to curl up on the couch with you, eat some greasy food, and maybe watch a horrible reality TV show and veg out, okay?"

Ava watched him carefully, still unconvinced, but she smiled and nodded anyway. "Okay, that sounds good."

He grinned and they walked the rest of the way in silence, Ava's instincts protesting the whole way.

It was late when a sound roused Ava from where she'd been drowsing, leaning against Caleb on his living room sofa. Actually, she realized it wasn't a sound, but a *feeling*, a tingling of her awareness. Caleb stiffened, shifting under her cheek, and she sat up and rubbed the sleep from her eyes.

"What is it?" he asked.

She held up a finger, reaching out with her Race senses.

There's someone . . . just on the edge. No, coming closer.

"Can't you feel it?" Ava stood abruptly and walked to the window, peering through the curtains. "Someone's coming."

"Are you sure? I don't—" Caleb froze. "I feel him now."

"Who do you think it is?"

A knock sounded at the door, and Caleb got up from the sofa, rubbing a hand over his face. "I think we're about to find out."

Ava moved to his side, and instinctively, Caleb positioned himself in front of her before opening the door. Tiernan stood on the other side, his face grim and stance intimidating.

"Tiernan?" Caleb stepped back to allow him to enter. Instead of coming inside, however, he moved forward, effectively blocking the doorway with his hulking frame. "Is something wrong?" Caleb asked.

"You're wanted before the Council."

"What? Why?" Ava asked, her instincts on high alert. "I haven't done anything!"

"Not you," Tiernan said gruffly. "Him."

"I don't understand," she babbled, her gift rising in an impulse to protect. Something was wrong. Very wrong. "It's the middle of the night. Can't this wait until tomorrow?"

"I'm afraid not." Tiernan crossed his beefy arms over his chest. "Come on, Caleb. Let's go."

Caleb took a step backward. "What is this all about?"

"You know they don't give me that information. I'm just following—"

"They don't tell you everything. But you know *something*." Caleb's jaw twitched as he stared Tiernan down. "Give me something, here, so I don't go into this blind."

Ava could feel the tension radiating off both of them in waves. "Caleb, what's going on?" she asked.

"Where have you been, Caleb?" Tiernan asked. "Why have you been hiding from the Council? Why did you run from me?"

"I wasn't aware I had to answer to you!"

"You knew I was there. You deliberately tried to lose me."

Caleb snorted. "I succeeded."

"What?" Ava pushed between them. "Why were you following him?"

Tiernan ignored her. "Does the name Elias Borré mean anything to you?" he asked Caleb.

Caleb shrugged. "No. Should it?"

He'd taken another step back into the room, and Ava watched as Tiernan matched his movements. She reached down for her gift, felt it twist through her, waiting . . .

"He's a Rogue who was, up until yesterday, in Council custody," Tiernan said through gritted teeth. "You saying you don't know anything about that?"

"What are you insinuating?" Caleb asked, taking another step backward.

Ava took a deep breath, her power sparking along her nerve endings. She wasn't sure what was going on, but she didn't like it. Not one bit.

Tiernan stepped forward, casting a wary glance in Ava's direction before focusing on Caleb again. "The Council thinks you helped him escape."

Ava let out a choked sound. "That's ridiculous!"

"They saw you on the security cams. Your imprint was left in his cell."

"This has to be a mistake!" Ava put herself between Tiernan and Caleb, heart pounding as her gift flared, aching to protect him. "You know this is wrong, Tiernan. Caleb's no traitor."

"They've got evidence that says he is." He stepped around Ava and zeroed in on Caleb, muscles rippling as he stretched his arms in a way that he probably intended to be nonthreatening, but really wasn't. "Don't make this harder than it needs to be."

Ava could feel it a split second before it happened. Before Caleb lunged for his bag, yanked it against his chest, and started to shift. Before Tiernan wrapped his hands around Caleb's throat, bringing him back before he could completely vanish. Before her gift shot out of her and slammed Tiernan into the far wall, toppling furniture along the way and cracking the plaster. She held him there, incapacitated against the wall, and turned frightened eyes to Caleb.

But if she hoped for answers—for promises—she got none, only a whispered, "I'm sorry," before Caleb shifted away into the night.

"Caleb?" Ava stared at the spot where he'd been standing, unable to believe what had just happened. He couldn't have left her there alone with Tiernan, with no explanation.

"You have to let me go after him." Tiernan choked, barely able to get the words out.

Ava realized her gift had tightened its hold on him so she loosened it a little—but only a little.

He took a deep breath, but he still couldn't move beyond that. "He's running from the Council. If I don't bring him back, they're going to send others after him. They're going to send *everyone* after him."

"He didn't do it," she said, although her voice lacked the conviction she'd felt only a few minutes earlier. "He couldn't have. He wouldn't."

"I tracked him to New Elysia myself," Tiernan said. "I let my guard down, thinking he was there on Council business, but—" Tiernan's muscles tensed, and Ava knew he was fighting against her binding. "They have him on camera taking Borré out of the city. He hurt a lot of people, Ava."

"No. That can't be right." Her mind raced, and she felt tears prick at her eyes. "You can't be right."

"Ava, listen to me," Tiernan snapped. "The Council has suspected Caleb for a while now. They pretty much knew about the Guardians. But with his background, they gave him some leeway on that. He's hardly the first—" He bumped his head back against the wall, his frustration clear. "But then they assigned me to watch him, and I knew it was more than the Guardian thing. They don't tell us much. We're just hired muscle, after all.

"But I did some digging around, and something's definitely being going on with Caleb, Ava. He's been spotted with suspected Rogues, and then this thing with Borré—"

"No." Ava shook her head and tightened her hold on Tiernan, choking off his words. "You're wrong. Caleb wouldn't work with the Rogues. Never."

But . . .

He'd been different the past few weeks. Disappearing for days at a time. Vague about where he'd been. Defensive when she questioned him.

He'd lied to her. She'd known it, but didn't want to admit it.

She'd known something was wrong, something was off. But *this*? This couldn't be.

Tiernan struggled, his breath wheezing in and out slowly, skin red with exertion, veins bulging.

She loosened her hold and he took a deep breath.

"Could you please stop doing that?" he growled.

"Sorry," she replied, distracted.

"You've got to let me go," he said, still gasping. "Caleb's in trouble, Ava. If he's working with Rogues he's in serious trouble."

Stunned, she blinked up at him through unshed tears. "What?"

"I promise I won't hurt him. I'll make sure he's safe."

"You'll take him to the Council."

"He'll get a fair hearing." His blue and green gaze was unwavering, his scar jagged and white against his flushed skin. "If the Council learns he's on the run, they'll send assassins. It'll be shoot first, ask questions later. And shifter or not, they have ways of tracking him down."

The thought sent a chill down her spine. She knew all too well the resources the Council had at its fingertips. She also knew that regardless of what Tiernan promised, a fair hearing before the Council was no guarantee of justice. If they had the evidence he said, Caleb's fate was all but sealed. Even his mother couldn't save him if they believed he was in league with the Rogues.

No, she couldn't let that happen. But she couldn't let the Council send assassins after him either. There was only one solution.

"I'll let you down," she said, walking slowly toward Tiernan. "I'll let you go after him. But you've got to do something for me."

He glared at her, and she knew he was imagining wrapping those meaty hands around her throat. Again.

"What?"

"Take me with you."

"What?" Despite his precarious position, he laughed. "You're out of your mind."

"I want answers, and I want to hear them from Caleb," Ava said, lifting her chin stubbornly. "So, that's the deal. You want to go after Caleb, you've got to take me with you."

"You'll slow me down."

It stung, but it was true. Ava didn't let it show.

"You'll have to figure that part out."

If Tiernan had laser vision, Ava figured she'd have been barbecued. His eyes narrowed. "How do you know I won't agree and dump you at the first opportunity?"

Ava smiled wickedly. "I'm a lot better at this now," she said. "How do you know I can't grab you from a mile away and hang you from the nearest tree?" She couldn't. Not by a long shot. But she knew her training sessions with Caleb had been unobserved, so Tiernan had no way of knowing that.

She held his gaze, hoping he wouldn't call her bluff.

He didn't. His frown intensified, if that were possible, and he growled out a resigned, "Agreed."

"Really?"

His lip curled in a snarl. "Don't make me say it again."

Ava let out a relieved breath, but she took a few steps back before she released him. He rubbed at his arms, shaking them a bit to get the blood flowing, and she eyed him warily.

He raised a mocking eyebrow. "Now you're nervous? Like you couldn't slam me back up there in a second?"

She laughed weakly but reached for her backpack to check for the basics she always carried with her. Recent experience had taught her to be prepared. "So, you ready?" she asked, depositing her textbooks on Caleb's table before zipping her backpack closed. She had a feeling she wouldn't be studying in the near future and didn't want to be weighed down.

Tiernan didn't respond. He just headed for the door.

Ava shrugged into her heavy coat as she trailed after him, quickening her steps. "How do you know where he's going?" she asked as they hurried down the stairs.

Tiernan crouched at the bottom, staring at the sidewalk and then the grass along the edge. "I'm a tracker," he said. "That's what I do." He tilted his head back and closed his eyes as he inhaled deeply. After a moment, he opened his eyes and headed toward the parking lot.

"Where are we going?" Ava asked, jogging at his heels.

"East," he replied, not slowing his steps. "But we can't run . . . obviously." He cast a disdainful look her way. "So we're going to need a ride." He came to a stop at the street, eyeing the parked cars appraisingly.

"Don't tell me, let me guess." Ava pretended she wasn't trying to catch her breath. "We're going to steal a car."

He raised a brow. "Borrow."

She sighed. "You and your sister have a lot in common, you know that?"

He ignored the comment, striding toward a black sports car.

Within minutes they were on their way, Ava clutching the door handle as Tiernan sped toward the edge of town.

"I hope you know what you're getting yourself into," he said as he shifted gears, tires squealing a little as he rounded a corner.

"You're not the only one," she replied under her breath. She pulled her feet up onto the seat and wrapped her arms around her knees. They'd find Caleb, and she'd figure out how to help him. Until then, she was just along for the ride.

The girl was a pain in the neck.

She kept asking Tiernan where they were going. How he knew which direction to turn. Why he kept sticking his head out the window. He didn't have time to explain. Not that he could, really, even if he wanted to. His tracking ability was something as natural to him as recognizing the smell of apple pie, or the taste of peppermint. It was part of him. He just knew. He could sense Caleb, as long as they weren't too far behind him.

The problem was they were falling farther behind him every hour. It was her fault, of course. She couldn't match his running speed, so they had to use a car, which meant sticking to the roads while Caleb could go cross-country. And Caleb knew he was being tracked. He kept doubling back, shifting one direction then running another to throw them off. Tiernan was left to trail after him like an awkward puppy, stumbling over his own feet. He didn't really see an alternative, though.

He glanced at Ava sitting innocently in the passenger seat.

Innocent. Right.

The girl slammed him up against that wall as if he was nothing more than an annoying fly. It was humiliating. Irritating. But he had to hand it to her, she had guts. She stood right up to him and glared unblinkingly into his mismatched eyes. Not many—human or Race—would dare such a thing. Still, it was unnerving to have someone like that sitting next to him. He felt at a disadvantage, which was decidedly where Tiernan preferred *not* to be.

He came to a crossroads and stopped to scan the horizon. The homes were farther apart—not quite farms, but with generous lawns out front and well-tended gardens in the back—and he could spot a town in the distance off to the right.

"What is it?" Ava asked.

"Give me a minute." He rolled down the window and turned to scent the air, listening . . . searching with all of his senses.

Ava's stomach growled, and he turned on her with a frown.

"What?" she asked. "I can't help it."

"Well, try," he snapped. "I can't hear with you making all that noise."

"It's a biological function! In case you haven't noticed, we've been at this for hours. Not that I'm complaining, but I can hardly be blamed for my empty stomach's reactions."

He glared at her, and she set her jaw stubbornly. Her stomach growled again and her cheeks flushed, but she didn't look away.

With an irritated grumble, Tiernan reached over the seat to where he'd tossed his bag in the back, and fumbled inside it. He threw a slightly smashed protein bar into her lap and snagged one for himself, ripping the plastic with his teeth and eating half in one bite.

"Thanks," she said quietly, pulling off a piece of her own bar. "You might have mentioned you had these before."

"I was a little busy," he replied through a mouthful of granola and chocolate. Ava grimaced slightly, but said nothing. He turned back to the window and tried to seek out Caleb again.

"It's no use," he said after a few moments, wadding up the wrapper and tossing it into the backseat. "I'm getting a faint sense of a trail, but I can't tell which direction, other than a vague—that way." He waved his hand toward the town. "You getting anything?"

Ava shook her head. "I've been trying, but he's beyond my reach, I think."

With a sigh, Tiernan stepped on the gas and turned right. "We'll need to ditch this car. Find a place to hole up until I can get some backup," he said.

Ava stiffened. "You can't call for backup. They'll know he ran."

Tiernan shot her a sideways glance. "I have a contact in the Council. He's the one who put me on Caleb in the first place, and he's made it pretty clear that he wants to talk to him—not kill him." He spotted a grove of trees off to the side of the road and pulled behind them. "I think he'll give me the resources I need to find him, without alerting the rest of the Council." He grabbed his bag and got out of the car, slamming the door behind him.

"You think?" Ava followed him anxiously. "That isn't very reassuring."

"Look." He stopped and turned to face her, trying not to smile in satisfaction when she faltered back a step as he loomed over her. "I know you're worried about Caleb, but this is all I've got right now. Unless you have a better idea?" When she said nothing, he nodded. "Okay, then. Let's go."

Ava grumbled something under her breath, but he ignored it and headed toward town, trying to be as inconspicuous as possible. It was difficult without the Veil, but that was something Tiernan had sworn off long ago, along with the ridiculous contact lenses that the majority of his people favored. They wanted to fit in with humans. He had no such desire.

Still, when they approached a motel set back off the highway outside of town, he figured it wouldn't hurt to be a little less intimidating. He was a bit out of practice, but managed to pull the Veil over him a bit—just enough to smooth his scar and make him seem a little smaller, a little more forgettable. In that moment, he envied Katherine's gift of near-invisibility but figured this was better than nothing.

"Whoa," Ava murmured.

"Shut up."

"You look kind of like Michael Cera."

"I said, shut up." He peered at her sidelong. "Is that the guy from *Zombieland*?"

"No, that's Jesse Eisenberg," she said, tilting her head. "Although, now that you mention it, you kind of look a little like him, too." Her eyes widened. "Wait a second. You saw *Zombieland*?" She seemed stunned that he would ever watch a movie.

"I do have a day off once in a while, you know." He strode toward the motel office without looking back.

"But *Zombieland*? It's not very, well . . . *you*, is it?"

He stopped in his tracks. "Not *me*? Who doesn't like zombies?"

"Oh." Ava blinked at him. "Of course you'd root for the zombies. Makes perfect sense now."

"It's not their fault they're zombies."

"And trying to eat Jesse Eisenberg's brain."

Tiernan couldn't believe he was having this conversation. "We don't have time to discuss film choices," he said, starting toward the hotel again. "You coming?"

She trailed after him, and they managed to secure a motel room with minimal fuss.

Once they were inside, Tiernan pulled out his phone to call Andreas.

"Andreas? Really?" she whispered as he waited for the call to connect. "I figured it would be Naomi." The woman had shown favor to Ava when she'd appeared before the Council, so it was no surprise Ava would suspect it was her.

Before he could respond, Andreas answered the phone with a curt, "Yes?"

"I have a bit of a situation."

"What kind of situation?" He heard a door close in the background and assumed Andreas had moved to a more private setting. "Foster?"

"He's on the run."

Andreas cursed under his breath, and Tiernan ignored the fact that Ava was practically bouncing on the bed, wondering what was going on.

"Can you track him?" Andreas asked.

Tiernan flicked his gaze up to Ava. "That's proven a bit of a challenge. He knows I'm on his trail, so he's been shifting steadily since he disappeared. He must have a stash of R-cubes. I can't keep up by traditional means. I need someone who can track shifts."

He heard Andreas inhale deeply on the other end of the phone. "This is disappointing, Ross. Caleb Foster has detailed knowledge about the Council and the Protectors. If he's turned his back on us . . ."

He was silent for a long moment, and Tiernan waited, ignoring Ava's anxious expression.

"Still, I think it best that we keep this between ourselves for now," Andreas said.

"I thought you might feel that way." Tiernan nodded at Ava in a reassuring manner. "How would you like to proceed?"

"Well, fortunately, I've recently come across a young man with the specific talents necessary to address your . . . predicament."

"A sensor?" Tiernan waited as he heard some papers being shuffled.

Andreas didn't answer his question but after a moment, asked one of his own. "What is your current location?"

"Motel in a town called Matlock, near the Nebraska border."

"Stay put," Andreas ordered. "Stay out of sight. I'll be in touch." The call disconnected, and Tiernan drew a deep breath.

"Well?" Ava was apparently irritated she had to ask.

"He's getting someone to help us." He stood and stretched, then crossed to the windows and peered out at the empty parking lot.

"So what do we do in the meantime?"

"We wait." Ava's stomach rumbled, and he shot her a wry grin. "And maybe order a pizza."

Chapter 6

Waiting was not Ava's favorite thing to do. She paced. She flipped through channels on the television. She checked her cell phone for missed calls or texts from Caleb—there were none, by the way—and she pretty much drove Tiernan insane. Not that you could really tell. The man gave new meaning to the word stoic, simply sitting by the window and peering through a gap in the curtains. He did his best to ignore her, but every time she got up, she saw a muscle twitch in his jaw and knew he was annoyed.

"Pizza's here," he said a moment before a knock sounded at the door.

Tiernan stayed in the shadows, letting Ava handle the interaction with the pizza delivery guy. They settled in around the cardboard box, and Ava downed two slices before taking a long drink of her Coke.

"So, this sensor," she said and wiped her mouth. "What exactly can he do?"

Tiernan shrugged. "Track shifters."

"How far?"

He shrugged again.

"Well, you're just a fount of information, aren't you?" she snapped, taking up another piece of pizza and pointing it at him. "If we're going to work together, you'll need to be more forthcoming with information."

"We're not working together."

"What do you call it, then?"

He curled his lip. "Barely perceptible tolerance borne out of distrust and blackmail?"

She snorted. "So sensitive." Ava took another bite of pizza before asking, "So is this sensor coming here?"

"I don't know."

"Well, how else is he—"

"I said, I don't know!" Tiernan glowered at her. "We're just supposed to wait."

"Wow, is that how you operate?" she asked. "No questions? Just following orders?"

"It's my duty. You wouldn't understand." His tone was the slightest bit mocking, and Ava, of course, took offense.

"I understand *duty*," she said. "I just don't understand how you can do your job if you're kept in the dark all the time."

"They tell me what I need to know." Tiernan looked out through the window again, effectively shutting down the conversation.

Ava rolled her eyes and flipped the channel on the television, settling on the local news as she finished her pizza. She stared at the screen but let her mind wander, wondering about where Caleb was and what he was doing. She surreptitiously checked her phone again, and footage of a familiar house flashing on the television caught her eye. She reached for the remote to turn up the volume.

". . . body was found early this morning by his wife, Beth Simmons. She told police she hadn't seen her husband since Saturday evening, when the two had an argument . . ."

"Oh no," Ava whispered. "No. It can't be."

"What?" Tiernan turned his attention to the television as Officer Simmons' photograph filled the screen.

". . . witnesses testify that a young woman visited the victim's home late Saturday night and was possibly the last to see him alive . . ."

"No. Oh no, no, no . . ." Ava chanted, her eyes wide and frightened as her own picture appeared.

"Police are calling this woman, Ava Michaels, a person of interest in the case. They stop short of calling her a suspect, but our sources say there is strong evidence linking Michaels to the murder of Officer Simmons. Mrs. Simmons herself says Michaels is the reason she left home on Saturday."

A crying woman appeared on the screen, apparently Mrs. Simmons. *"I'd suspected he was having an affair for some time. And when I found out it was with a student at the college, I confronted him about it. He admitted to being involved with that woman, and I was so angry."* She wiped at her eyes with a tissue. *"He was going to break it off. He promised me. But I never thought . . ."*

The woman dissolved into sobs, and Tiernan reached over to take the remote and click the television off.

Silence hung in the air, punctuated by Ava's ragged breaths. "I can't believe it," she murmured.

"So." Tiernan cleared his throat. "You knew him?"

"He . . . he helped me," she said, still in a daze. "When you . . . when you came after me. He helped protect me."

"And you . . ." Tiernan rubbed a hand over his shaved head. "You . . . and he . . . uh . . ."

"No!" Ava shot to her feet. "No, of course not! I don't know what's going on, but I didn't have an affair with him. And I definitely didn't *kill*—" She choked on a sob and sat down heavily on the bed. "Oh God, he's dead. They think I killed him. What in the world is happening?"

Tiernan stared at her for a long moment. "It looks like someone's trying to set you up."

Ava swiped at her eyes. "But who? Why? I don't understand any of this."

He stood and paced across the room and back again. "Well, if none of this is true—"

"It's not!" Her hands clenched into fists. "None of it."

Tiernan nodded. "If that's the case, whoever it is would need to manipulate the witnesses—"

"Someone saw me," Ava said, half to herself as she remembered the neighbor peeking through the blinds. "I was there Saturday night, but it was dark. I didn't think . . ." She rubbed at her temples and tried to think back.

"You were there?"

"I saw him," Ava said quietly. "I talked to him." She looked up at Tiernan, eyes bright with tears. "I had a dream. I thought someone was going to hurt him."

Tiernan's jaw tightened. "Looks like you were right."

She laughed humorlessly. "Yeah . . . yeah. Good to know." She stood, tangling her hands in her hair. "What am I going to do? I have to go back. Turn myself in, right? Try and clear my name?"

"I really don't think that's the best option."

"But if I don't, they'll think I'm guilty." She threw her hands in the air in frustration.

"I've got news for you. They already think you're guilty." At her irritated glare, he huffed and rolled his eyes. "Look, you shouldn't do anything until we figure out what we're dealing with here. Whoever's behind this isn't putting all his hope in one witness who happened to see you at that house. Someone pushed his wife, maybe even pushed Simmons, too."

"Pushed? You think it's Race?"

"Well, something made her think her husband was having an affair that never happened."

Even in her panic, Ava felt a trace of relief that Tiernan seemed to believe her without question. "Who?" she asked, her mind whirling with possibilities. "The Council? Or maybe Rogues?"

"No way to know for sure. At least, not yet."

"But why?" She looked up at Tiernan but he had no answers. Her gaze fell to her twisting fingers. "It's got to be the Council."

Tiernan frowned. "Think about it. The Council has no reason to do this. Why would they frame you for murder?"

"To get me to go to them for protection? Keep me locked up nice and tight in New Elysia?"

"Not really their style. To harm an innocent human violates Race Law."

"You think that would stop the Council?"

Tiernan fixed her with a steady look. "The Council isn't perfect, but it is dedicated to upholding the Law."

Ava slumped back down onto the bed, her eyes fixed unseeing at the blank television screen. "So it has to be a Rogue."

"That would be my guess," Tiernan said. "And if that's the case, this is only the beginning." He pulled a chair over and sat down to face her. "What do they want with you?"

Ava sighed. The Council had asked her the same question endless times —she'd asked it herself—but she'd yet to come up with an answer. "I don't know. Arthur, the Rogue who took me, he ranted about me having some higher purpose, being one of them. It didn't make any sense. None of this makes any sense."

Tiernan considered that for a long moment. "It's possible some of the Rogues are joining forces. Maybe they hope you can help them."

"Help them what?"

"Do what they do best. Cause trouble." He sat back, crossing his arms over his chest. "At any rate, there's nothing you can do right now. Not until we figure all of this out."

She raised a brow. " 'We'?"

He shrugged. "The Rogues are a threat to the Race. Protecting the Race is my job. So . . . you just became my job."

"Lucky me."

"Look on the bright side," he said, standing and crossing the room again to peer out the window. "You wanted to find Caleb. Now you know I won't let you out of my sight until we do."

"I repeat," Ava said wryly. "Lucky me."

Despite her anxiety, exhaustion won out, and Ava ended up curled up on the bed half-dozing as they waited for instructions from Andreas. The sun had just set when the call finally came, and Tiernan snapped his phone up off the table to answer it before Ava even realized it was ringing.

The call was brief, peppered by a couple of "Yes, sirs" from Tiernan, and Ava was wide awake when he finally hung up.

"Well?" she said as he stood up, shrugged on his jacket, and grabbed his bag.

"We go west."

"West? That's it?" She crammed her feet into her shoes and swept up her backpack, following him out the door, only to slam into his back. He shoved her back into the room unceremoniously and whipped the door shut, leaving barely a crack to peek out.

"What is it?" Ava whispered, trying to see under his arm and failing. She moved to the window to peer through a gap in the curtain.

"Don't let him see you," Tiernan snapped.

"Who?" Ava still couldn't see anything—only the back of a car parked at the motel office.

A black and white car.

"Oh no." She yanked the curtains closed, panic rising in her chest. "Is that the police?"

"It could be nothing." Tiernan kept his voice low, still looking out the crack in the door. "Or . . ."

"Or?"

He glanced at her. "Or, it could be that the motel manager also watches the news."

"Crap." Ava ran her hands through her hair, tugging lightly before pulling it into a ponytail. "What are we going to do?"

Tiernan shut the door quickly, trying not to slam it. "He's coming this way." Tiernan headed for the bathroom, frowning when he spotted the tiny window over the toilet. Striding back into the room, he tossed his bag on the bed and squared his shoulders. "I'll try not to hurt him too badly," he said, meeting Ava's frightened eyes.

"No!" She hurried back to the window, thinking quickly. "I think there's another way." She willed her heart to slow, reaching for her Race gift through the layers of panic and fear and freaking out. "Give me a second."

"We don't have a second."

Ava ignored him, her gift swelling through her, responding to her call as she focused on the bumper of that black and white car. "Come on . . ." she murmured. She envisioned the brake releasing . . . the gearshift sliding down to neutral . . .

"Ava?"

They could hear the footsteps approaching now . . . low voices . . .

The police car began to roll backward, and Ava's lips curled into a victorious smile. The car turned, coming to a quick stop then started rolling forward. "That's right, a little faster . . ." she whispered, pushing it with her gift.

A startled cry outside told her the diversion had worked, and she saw the police officer and motel manager running toward the car, chasing it as it rolled into the street.

"Now." Ava hitched her backpack higher onto her shoulder. "Let's get out of here." She kept her focus on the car, increasing the speed as they ducked out of the motel room and headed in the opposite direction, keeping to the shadows.

"Nice job," Tiernan said grumpily, as though it hurt him to say it.

Deciding that was the best she was going to get, she asked, "Where are we going?"

"I'm to check in every hour for directions," he said, scanning the parking lot then setting off toward the center of town.

Ava trailed after him, hitching her backpack onto both shoulders and giving the police car one last push as it turned a corner heading away from town, the police officer running full speed behind it. "Shouldn't we get out of town? That cop isn't going to be kept busy for long."

"We need a ride," Tiernan said tersely. "It's the only place to get one."

"What about the sensor? I thought he was coming with us."

"Apparently, he doesn't need to."

He strode quickly, but Ava knew he was holding back so she could keep up. Barely.

"He must be quite powerful. Andreas said he could track Caleb from where he is," he said.

"Wow. That's pretty impressive." She jogged alongside him, her pack bumping against her back. "Can a lot of sensors do that?"

Tiernan was silent for a long moment. "He's the first one I've heard of."

He seemed a bit uncomfortable about that, and Ava wondered if it was because he was leery of the sensor's power or because Tiernan had been unaware of his existence. She tended to lean toward the latter. Tiernan didn't seem to be the kind of guy who liked to be caught off guard.

They came to the town's main street, the storefronts on either side closing down for the night except for a restaurant and what looked like a biker bar. A slow grin eased onto Tiernan's face when he spotted the bar.

He didn't look at her, just threw a "Stay here," over his shoulder before starting across the street.

"What are you going to do?"

"I'll be right back," he said. He slipped into the shadows as he neared the bar and disappeared inside.

"Oh, crap." Ava glanced nervously up and down the street as she figured out his intent.

Tiernan lounged against the brick wall near the entrance, eyes wandering purposefully as people passed by. After a few moments, he walked into the bar, following a group of scruffy men in leather jackets.

Ava wrung her hands and stopped abruptly when she realized she was doing it, annoyed at the cliché. She started to cross the street then thought better of it, returning to a bookstore window and pretending to examine its contents. Her gaze darted to the bar entrance every few seconds while she kept an eye open for the police. Tiernan eventually emerged, glancing up and down the street before approaching a group of motorcycles. He hovered over them for a moment before he straddled one, the lights flipping on a moment before the engine roared to life. He pulled a wide turn in the road and stopped at the curb next to her.

"Get on," he said, scooting forward a little on the seat.

"You can't be serious," she said, eyeing the bike with dread. "Those things are dangerous."

He glanced over his shoulder. "Not as dangerous as the drunk guy I stole the keys from once he notices it's missing."

Ava's eyes narrowed. "Yeah, like you're really scared."

To her surprise, Tiernan laughed.

"It looks kind of old," she said, not getting any closer to the bike. It was big and shiny . . . with metal studs all along the seat. Definitely not her.

Tiernan practically caressed the bike as he ran his hand over the emerald-green gas tank. "Seventy-two Harley Softail. It's a classic." He reached back to pluck a black half-helmet emblazoned with a skull and crossbones off the backrest and held it out to her expectantly.

She frowned but took it, her stomach fluttering nervously as she buckled it on. "Don't you have one?" she asked.

Tiernan revved the engine. "Quit stalling. Get on."

Resigned, Ava did as she was told, wrapping her arms around Tiernan's thick waist and clenching her eyes tightly shut as they sped out of town under the darkening sky.

They continued west, stopping every hour or so to stretch their legs and call Andreas, through South Dakota and across the Wyoming border, angling slightly north toward Montana. Then, after a late-night call, they were ordered to turn abruptly south at Sheridan.

"Sensor says Caleb's trying to lose us," Tiernan said, cracking his neck as he shoved his phone into his pocket and climbed back onto the bike.

Ava's heart sank at his words. "Maybe he's doing what I'm doing. Trying to find a way to clear his name."

"Maybe." Tiernan didn't seem convinced, but to his credit, he didn't challenge her. Instead, he jerked his head toward the back of the bike. "You coming?"

Ava yawned widely as she got on behind him.

"I hate to do it, but we're going to have to ditch this bike," he said. "We need to keep going, and you're going to fall asleep and fall off."

"No, I won—" Ava's yawn gave her away.

Tiernan smirked and started the bike.

They traded the motorcycle for a Jeep at a park and ride at the edge of another nondescript town, then zigzagged their way southwest through Wyoming, stopping midmorning for a few hours of sleep at an isolated rest stop, and again that evening to fill up with gas and grab some food at a mini-mart in Riverton.

Tiernan's phone rang as they wolfed down stale doughnuts and coffee. Ava was still exhausted, but she fought her drooping eyelids, swallowing the last of her coffee and retrieving another from the store while Tiernan spoke to whoever was on the other end. He was in the Jeep, its engine idling, when she returned.

"Caleb's stopped," he said, peeling out of the parking lot. "The sensor says he hasn't moved in the last hour. He must think he's lost us."

Ava was suddenly alert, her stomach churning wildly. "Where is he?"

Tiernan checked the rearview mirror and stepped on the gas. "Utah.

Andreas said the sensor's closing in on a more precise location, but for now, we're heading to Salt Lake City."

Ava leaned against the passenger side window, snoring lightly, as they finally crossed the border into Utah.

The sky lightened, the second sunrise since Tiernan had gotten any decent sleep himself, and he yawned, shaking his head and blinking to try and stay alert. He picked up his phone, pressing the speed dial for Andreas as Ava sighed in her sleep next to him.

He had to admit the girl had impressed him a bit. Other than the need for conventional transportation, she'd been less of a burden than he'd expected. She did ask a lot of questions, which was annoying, and never failed to state her opinion, no matter how wrong or irritating, but overall, she was . . . *not horrible.*

He smirked at the thought, his expression growing grim as Andreas answered the phone.

"We're a little over an hour out of Salt Lake City."

" 'We'?" Andreas repeated, and Tiernan winced. He'd been so careful to avoid mentioning Ava until then. Obviously the lack of sleep was making him sloppy.

"Yes, sir," he said, clearing his throat. "Ava Michaels is with me. She was . . . rather insistent about it." He wondered if he should relay his suspicions about Officer Simmons' death and the Rogues, but to his surprise, Andreas laughed.

"I've known Miss Michaels was with you all along, Ross," he said. "This sensor is surprisingly talented. He's not only been tracking Caleb, but you as well. He recognized right away that you weren't alone."

"I'm sorry, sir. I should have mentioned it."

"Yes, you should have," Andreas said, his voice chilling. "You should also remember that keeping things from me—from the Council—is a futile effort and also one that could prove quite dangerous. For you."

"Yes, sir." He quietly relayed the information about the murder and Ava's suspected involvement. "She claims innocence," Tiernan said, glancing at Ava, who was still sleeping peacefully.

"Yes, well. She would, wouldn't she?"

"She's not a killer, sir." Tiernan was a little surprised at how strongly he believed it. "Someone is setting her up."

"Well, that is neither here nor there at the moment," Andreas replied. "We'll deal with the problems of Miss Michaels at a later time. Your priority is Caleb Foster. I've assured the rest of the Council you have matters well in hand. Do not prove me wrong, Ross."

Tiernan bit back a retort. "Yes, sir."

"There is some interference keeping the sensor from zeroing in on Foster's precise location, but he is confident he will break through it soon," Andreas said, the topic of Ava forgotten, at least for the moment. "I suggest the two of you find a place to lay low for a little while. Maybe get some sleep. You'll need to be on your game to confront Foster. And Ross . . ."

"Yes?"

"Miss Michaels. Will she be a problem when it comes to Foster? I don't need to remind you what your responsibility is in this situation, do I?"

"No, sir."

"You're to bring him to me. Will she try and stop you?"

"She's not convinced he's helping Rogues," he said, watching his words in case Ava was listening. "She wants to talk to him. Her biggest concern is his safety."

"Then you'll convince her he'll be safe here," Andreas said shortly.

Tiernan glanced at Ava just as her eyes opened, fixing him with a quiet look.

"Yes, sir," he said, unable to see any other option.

They pulled off the highway onto an isolated gravel road that wound through a thick canopy of trees. A couple of miles into the forest, Tiernan finally pulled off the road, crashing through some brush before parking the Jeep out of sight.

"Nice spot." Ava shot him a wry look.

He ignored her, leaned his seat back, and closed his eyes, crossing his arms over his chest. "There's nothing we can do until I get word from Andreas, so you might as well get some sleep."

"I've *been* sleeping."

He opened one eye and frowned at her. "I haven't. So be quiet."

She was. For about thirty seconds. "What's going to happen?" she asked quietly, as if speaking in lower tones made it all good. "You know, when we find him?"

Tiernan sighed. "I need to take him to the Council."

"But . . . you'll let me talk to him first, right?"

He sat up and rubbed at his eyes before answering. "If it's possible. Yes."

"What do you mean?"

"He might try to run again. I'll have to stop him if I can." He turned to her. "He'll be safer with the Council than he would be on the run."

She nodded.

"Will you try to stop me?"

Ava considered that for a long moment. "I don't know," she finally whispered.

Tiernan shook his head and closed his eyes. Within a few minutes, he was breathing deeply, asleep.

She turned to look out the passenger window at the trees and brush beyond, letting her mind wander. She jumped when her phone vibrated in her pocket. With a quick glance at Tiernan, she fumbled for it, her breath catching at the text from Caleb.

It's not what you think. I'm sorry.

She stared at the phone in shock and worry and reached for the car door handle.

Tiernan stirred. "Where are you going?"

"Little girls' room. I'll be back in a second," she said, willing her voice not to wobble and praying she could get out of the car before her phone vibrated again and Tiernan noticed.

Luckily, he just shifted in the seat, tucked his chin into his chest, and went back to sleep.

Ava got out of the car and walked into the cover of some trees. She wanted to call Caleb, craved hearing his voice, but she couldn't risk Tiernan overhearing. And she didn't dare walk far enough away to ensure that wouldn't happen.

It would probably take an hour anyway. Stupid super hearing.

She texted Caleb back instead, erasing and retyping several times thanks to her trembling fingers.

Are you all right? Where are you? What's happening?

She paced back and forth in the little clearing between two trees, waiting anxiously.

I'll explain soon. Everything will be all right. Just trust me.

It took all of Ava's self-control not to scream in exasperation. She did let her gift loose a little—enough to throw a couple of pinecones zinging off through the forest.

How? The Council thinks you're working with Rogues! They'll send assassins if you don't come in.

She'd almost given up getting any response at all until her phone buzzed once more.

Don't trust the Council.

And that was it. She texted him three more times, but got no response, and finally gave in and dialed his number. It went directly to voice mail. Again.

Ava reached up and touched her necklace through her shirt, fighting tears. She wanted to trust Caleb, wanted to believe him that he could explain the whole mess, but she couldn't fight the feeling that she was missing something. Something big. She closed her eyes and felt for her gift, the necklace warming under her fingers. She didn't let her power loose, just let it trickle through her body, centering and calming her. After a while, she took a deep breath, letting her gift settle within her again.

She turned to walk back to the car and got in quietly. Tiernan didn't stir, so she closed her eyes and tried to get some sleep.

Chapter 7

"You got anything?" Tiernan asked as they pulled to a stop somewhere in the mountains east of Salt Lake City. They'd finally gotten a call, the sensor directing them to the isolated area, but they'd had to abandon the Jeep, taking to the rough terrain on foot.

"Not yet," Ava replied, tightening the straps on her backpack as she set off after him. "Maybe when we get a little closer."

"You can feel him, right?" Tiernan asked, not meeting her eyes. "I mean, you and Caleb . . . you . . . uh . . ."

Ava flushed, realizing what he meant. "Yes. I feel him," she said, clearing her throat. "Just not at the moment."

Tiernan nodded and climbed up a rocky slope, Ava scrambling up behind him. "The sensor said due south from where we left the car," he said, lifting a hand to shade his eyes as he looked up at the sun. "Should be close in about an hour. Let me know as soon as you feel him . . . or anyone."

"You think there are others?"

"Well, someone may be shielding him," Tiernan replied as he started walking again. "Andreas said that's why the sensor was having so much trouble."

"And you think it's a Rogue."

Tiernan didn't answer.

They trudged along for several minutes, and Ava appreciated that he didn't complain once about her slowing him down. For a huge, scary monster, Tiernan really wasn't such a bad guy.

The silence was getting to her, though, her mind on a constant repeat—the look on Caleb's face as Tiernan confronted him, Caleb disappearing without even looking her way, his texts . . . her feeling for a while now that something had been off with him. She knew Caleb. She knew she could trust him. But all of the evidence against him was . . . unsettling. Frightening. And she had absolutely no idea what would happen when they finally caught up to him. Sure, Tiernan had promised she could talk to him. The problem was the Council had evidence against him. Of course, from current personal experience, she knew that evidence didn't always prove the truth. And if Caleb was found to be a traitor, even his mother couldn't save him, regardless of her position with the Council.

She half slid down a slope, coming to a stumbling stop next to Tiernan, who was taking a long drink out of a water bottle. "Could a Rogue be setting Caleb up as well?" she asked.

He handed her the bottle, frowning as he considered her words. "I suppose it's possible. I wouldn't have thought so before, but now . . ."

She sipped from the bottle, swirling the cool water around in her mouth before swallowing. "The question is why? Why would a Rogue want the Council to think Caleb was helping him?"

"Maybe to protect whoever *really* released Elias Borré?"

"Who is this guy, Borré, anyway?"

Tiernan shrugged, taking the bottle from her and putting it back into his bag. "I don't know anything about him other than the fact he's a Rogue. And he's apparently pretty powerful."

"So how would Caleb even get to him?"

"Maybe he had help."

"What if . . ." Ava started up another hill with Tiernan walking beside her. "What if it's the same guy? The one who killed Nick Simmons. And the one who set up Caleb?"

"I don't think so." Tiernan scratched at the scruff on his chin. "Borré escaped early Saturday morning. Simmons was killed late Saturday night." He glanced sidelong at Ava. "I suppose a shifter might be able to do both —"

"No," she said stubbornly. "Don't even try to point the finger at Caleb."

He raised a brow. "What I was *going* to say is it's far more likely that it would be two different people."

"Two Rogues. Working together?"

"It used to be unheard of," he said with a humorless smile. "Until your recent experience, that is."

Ava swallowed thickly, remembering her time as a prisoner in the Rogue lair. Until then, Rogues were thought of as disorganized, selfish—each operating on his own, with greed and lust for power his only motivation. The fact that a group of Rogues conspired to capture her was worrisome to the Council.

Well, to be honest, it didn't make Ava feel all that great either.

"Of course, all of this is pure speculation," Tiernan said. "And ignores the fact that Caleb never denied helping Borré escape. And he ran, which only makes him look even more guilty."

Ava opened her mouth to defend Caleb again, but was interrupted by the ringing of her phone.

Tiernan glared at her. “Are you out of your mind? Why do you still have your phone?”

Ava glanced at the display. “I don’t recognize the number, but it’s a Witteville prefix. It might be Lucy.”

“Your roommate?” Tiernan’s face was red with fury. “You’re wanted by the cops, in case you don’t remember. And they may not be Race, but they can trace a cell phone. It might even be them calling.”

Ava felt like such an idiot. She knew that. She’d just been so worried about contacting Caleb, she hadn’t thought it through.

“If it’s Lucy, I need to talk to her,” Ava told him. “She’s got to be wondering what’s going on. I disappeared without a word and now with the police looking for me . . .” She watched Tiernan carefully, and he finally gave a begrudging nod.

“Make it quick,” he said. “And then, destroy that thing.” He took a few steps away, presumably to give her at least the illusion of privacy, and turned his attention to the ground at his feet.

“Hello?”

“Ava? What in the world is going on?”

Ava let out a relieved breath at the sound of her friend’s voice.

“I’ve been trying to reach you for hours. Didn’t you get my voice mails?”

“I’ve been kind of in and out of service,” she said lamely. “Where are you calling from? I didn’t recognize the number.”

“Pay phone,” she said with an almost irritated huff. “I’m not an idiot.”

“I know that—”

Lucy continued talking as if she hadn’t heard. “The police came to our room, Av. They said you killed that campus police officer. They went through all your stuff. Asked all these questions. They called your parents.”

“Oh, no way. They talked to my parents?”

“Yeah, and they are freaked out. Haven’t you called them?” Lucy took a breath. “Ava, what is happening? Are you all right?”

Am I?

Ava wasn’t exactly sure how to answer that question. “I didn’t kill anyone,” she said.

Lucy snorted. “I know that. That’s what I told the cops. There was no way you were sleeping with that guy. I told them you had a perfectly hot boyfriend, and Av, not to speak ill of the dead, but that cop was *old.*”

Lucy believed her. So whoever had tampered with the witnesses hadn’t gotten to her. Ava supposed she had Katherine to thank for that. She suspected the Protector was still keeping watch outside her dorm, even if she wasn’t there.

Katherine.

Ava couldn’t believe she hadn’t thought of her before. Katherine had been with her. Katherine had *always* been with her.

"But why do they think you did it?" Lucy asked, interrupting her train of thought.

Ava let out a heavy sigh. "I don't know, Luce. Someone else killed him and made it look like I did. I don't know who and I don't know why, but I'm trying to figure it out."

"Are you crazy? Ava, you need to get back here and talk to the police. You can't handle this on your own!"

"I'm not alone," she said, casting a glance at Tiernan.

"Is Caleb with you? The police were looking for him, too."

"No, not Caleb. I have a . . . friend in law enforcement. He's helping me get to the bottom of this, and he's keeping me safe, Luce. You don't have to worry."

"I don't know, Av—"

"The cops think I'm guilty, Luce. And there's too much evidence against me right now. You know they'll lock me up if I come back, and I'll never be able to figure out what's happening."

Tiernan crossed his arms over his chest and tapped at his watch.

"Look, Luce, I have to go. Just . . . trust me, okay?"

"You know I do." She could hear tears in her friend's voice, and it broke her heart.

"I'm going to fix this, but I can't come home right now. It's not safe."

"What are you going to do?"

"I'm not sure." Ava swallowed thickly, trying not to cry herself. "But if you talk to my parents, let them know I'll call them when I can. I'll have to destroy this phone, or the police will find me."

"God, Av . . . be careful. Please?"

"I will. You too, okay?" She considered her next words, but only for a second. "And you know that woman you saw with Caleb? The pretty one with black hair?" Tiernan raised a brow, but she ignored him.

"Yeah," Luce said.

"If anything weird happens, you'll probably see her around—"

"But—"

"Don't ask," Ava said sharply. "Please listen, okay? If you ever feel scared or think someone's around, you can trust her. Her name's Katherine. She'll . . . protect you."

"I don't understand any of this."

"I know you don't," Ava said softly. "Just don't forget, okay? It's important."

Lucy was quiet for a long minute. "Okay. Katherine. Got it."

"I'll be home soon." And with that, Ava hung up.

Tiernan shot her an exasperated look. "Katherine? Are you crazy?"

"Maybe." Ava waved off his question with a distracted hand. "But that's beside the point. *Katherine,* Tiernan." She reached out without thinking and grabbed his beefy arms tightly. "She was with me when I went to see Nick Simmons!"

Tiernan did not seem as impressed with Ava's epiphany as she'd hoped.

She huffed in frustration. "Don't you get it? She or you or one of the others has been monitoring my every movement. She can clear my name!"

"It's not that simple—"

"Why not? She can go the police and tell them—"

"Tell them what, exactly, Ava?" Tiernan pulled away and scrubbed a hand over his head. "That there's no way you could have killed that police officer, despite the witness who put you at the scene? That she knows this because she's assigned to follow your every movement to ensure you don't expose the existence of a Race of super beings?"

"Well, no. Not that. Obviously." Ava faltered a bit, but pressed on. "She could say she's a friend who was with me at the time of the murder. It doesn't matter; we can figure it out—"

"The Council will never allow it."

Ava couldn't understand why Tiernan was being so difficult. "But—"

"But nothing!" he snapped. When Ava blinked at him, stunned, he drew a deep breath. "Try to understand, Ava, there is nothing—*nothing and no one* —more important to the Council than protecting the secrecy of the Race. They will never agree to allow one of their Protectors to expose herself to human authorities, let alone get involved in something as high-profile as the murder of a police officer. And Katherine will never go against the orders of the Council."

"But we could at least try . . ." Ava's voice trembled as Tiernan turned his back on her.

"That's only part of the problem," he said, surveying the landscape. "Even if we could get you cleared of this, we still don't know who's behind it. Which means they know more about you than you know about them." He glanced at her over his shoulder as if waiting for her to finish the thought.

"So if we don't figure out who it is—*why* they're doing all of this—they could do something else," she said quietly. "Go after me in some other way."

"Or those you care about."

Ava's throat closed up as it hit her once again that Officer Simmons had died in some kind of twisted ploy to get at Ava.

Who would be next?

"Do you think they'd hurt my parents?" she asked after walking a while in silence.

"I think, right now, they think they've got you right where they want you," he replied. "As long as that's true, there's no reason for them to hurt anyone else."

"So we have to be careful." Ava pushed aside a branch to duck under it. "Stay a step ahead of them."

"Well, we have to *get* a step ahead of them first." Tiernan shot her a wry look, and Ava couldn't keep back a small smile.

"In the meantime, you think you could ask Katherine to keep an eye on Lucy for me?" she asked. "I'm still a bit freaked to think they're in Witteville. Whoever they are."

Tiernan watched her for a long moment before taking out his phone and sending a quick text message. Without waiting for an answer, he tucked it back into his pocket.

"That's it?"

He shrugged. "She won't ask questions. I told her it was import—" He stopped abruptly, tilted his head back, and closed his eyes, inhaling deeply.

"What is it?" Ava asked.

He took another breath and opened his eyes, his gaze darting around the trees and settling on a spot near the base of a large rock. He approached it and knelt to run his palm over the soil.

"It's him," he said. "Or it was, not too long ago." He stood up and scented the air again. "I have the trail." He spared a moment to grab her cell phone and smash it under his heel before striding away.

Ava felt a rush of panic as she hurried after him, up another hill and finally following a narrow path through the trees. A few clouds obscured the sun overhead, and Ava shivered and stiffened as her gift flared to life.

"I feel someone," she said, reaching for Tiernan's arm. "Not Caleb, but someone else."

"Where? I don't sense anyone."

She pointed forward, along the trail. "We're not that close. Not yet."

Tiernan nodded, and they continued forward, both tense and on high alert. After a while, he glanced back at her. "How many?"

Ava swallowed. "At least four," she said. "Maybe five or six. But I don't sense Caleb."

"He could be shielded." Tiernan said, as if she needed the reminder. He scanned the area around them and pointed to a high outcropping of rocks. "That might give us a better vantage point. We can't get too close without tipping them off, but maybe we can get a better idea of what we're dealing with up there."

They circled around and up the rocks, Ava guiding them along the way. The Rogues were still on the edges of her intuition, so she knew they probably couldn't feel her yet, but they climbed in silence anyway, unwilling to take any chances. When they reached the top of the outcropping, they slid to the edge, flat on their stomachs, and searched the area below.

Ava closed her eyes for a moment and pointed off to the left. "That way."

Tiernan squinted, and she knew he was trying to focus through the trees. "Ah," he said after a moment. "That explains it."

"What?" Ava peered through the trees, focusing her own vision. "I don't see anything."

"It's there, hidden behind some brush," he whispered. "Between those two big trees."

Ava stared for a long moment, then a breeze blew at the branches, and she spotted a dark opening. “Is that a cave?” she asked.

“They’re underground,” Tiernan replied. “That would explain why the sensor had so much trouble and why even you couldn’t feel them until we were almost right on top of them.”

Ava bristled slightly, but there was no accusation behind his words.

“Fortunately, they’re in the same boat,” he said. “Let’s hope they don’t sense us.” He glanced at her. “You sure Caleb isn’t in there?”

Ava frowned. “I don’t feel him. But if he’s shielded underground, maybe there’s too much interference.” She wasn’t sure if she should hope he was inside or not.

Tiernan slid back from the edge of the cliff and leaned against a rock. “We need to lure them outside,” he said. “Get them away from the cave so we can search it and see if we can find him. Even if he’s gone, there could be intel that would be valuable to the Council.” He eyed her carefully. “We’re going to need a distraction.”

Ava felt a slow smile tug at her lips and let it develop into a full-blown grin. “Well, that is something I can definitely provide.”

Tiernan left Ava on the rock outcropping and climbed back down to the edge of a clearing. He could make out the entrance to the cave from where he was but was far enough away that the occupants wouldn’t notice him unless they were looking.

He sincerely hoped they weren’t looking.

He slid his bag off his shoulder, removed his pistol, and tucked it into his waistband before hiding the bag under some leaves. He checked the knives sheathed at his ankles and waited for Ava to make her move. He’d told her to count to a hundred, but he had no idea how fast she counted.

Is she a ‘one-thousand-one, one-thousand-two’ counter . . . or maybe an ‘and-one, and-two’ counter?

A large rock flew across the clearing and smashed into the brush covering the cave opening.

Apparently, she’s a straight ‘one-two-three’ counter.

Tiernan breathed steadily, every muscle tensed as he waited to see what would happen. After a few moments, another rock flew into the cave, and then a larger one smashed into a tree to the side of it. He heard a shout from inside the cave and stiffened, fists clenched and eyes focused on that sliver of cave opening.

A man emerged—not one Tiernan recognized, but definitely Race—and Tiernan ducked behind a tree out of reflex, and peered around the edge. The man walked hesitantly, firmly gripping a rifle as he scanned the surrounding trees.

A crash sounded in the distance, and the man whirled about, aiming into the forest.

Tiernan smirked. Ava was good at distractions.

"There's someone out there!" the man shouted back into the cave. "Come on, and bring Christopher!"

Another man and a blond woman emerged from the cave, both holding weapons, followed by a slight, dark-haired man Tiernan recognized from the fight at the Rogue lair when they'd rescued Ava.

The pyrokinetic.

He winced. That wasn't good.

Ava continued to throw rocks and branches through the forest, luring the little group away from the cave.

Tiernan slipped closer. He could feel one more person inside. He glanced up at Ava, hoping she felt the same thing. It felt strange to rely on someone else after so many years working on his own. The only person he truly trusted in the world was Katherine, and even with her, he preferred to call the shots. Not that she didn't push it. Frequently.

Ava nodded and held up one finger in agreement, then went back to distracting the others as Tiernan moved silently toward the cave.

The crash of rocks and branches in the distance covered his movements, and he reached for the knife at his ankle when he got to the entrance, his back pressed against the cold rock as he took a quick, assessing glance inside. With a sharp breath, he descended into the darkness, waiting a moment for his eyes to adjust before he proceeded, his fingers trailing along the chilled walls of the cave.

It was larger than Tiernan had expected, tall enough for him to stand upright, and extended down and back to where it disappeared around a sharp corner. He proceeded through the tunnel around several twists and turns until he came to a large, well-lit cavern that apparently served as some kind of command center. A bank of computers was set up against one wall, the rest of the room filled with stacked crates and boxes. He started toward the computers to take a closer look, but as he rounded a large crate, he noticed another smaller tunnel branching off from the cavern. He could tell that whoever was still in the cave was somewhere in that direction.

Just as he was about to head down the tunnel, he felt another presence approaching quickly from the opposite direction. He turned and ducked behind the crate, only to see Ava appear from the main tunnel, headed straight for him.

Perfect.

"What are you doing here? You're supposed to be the distraction."

She waved a hand. "They're chasing rocks all over the place out there. We have time." When he continued to glare at her, she cocked a brow. "Not enough to sit here and argue about it, but—"

"All right." He relented, albeit reluctantly. "Let's go, but stay behind me."

"My hero," she said, batting her eyelashes.

Tiernan ignored her and set off through the tunnel. It wasn't long before they came to a dead end, a stone wall facing them, and two openings on either side blocked by makeshift metal doors.

"This one," Ava whispered, touching to the door to the right.

Tiernan nodded and pressed his ear to the door, listening for a moment before giving it a tentative shove. It stood firm, somehow wedged into the thick rock.

"Stand back," he told Ava as he drew his pistol. He took a deep breath and kicked the door.

With a crash and a shower of dirt and rocks, it collapsed forward onto the dirt floor, revealing a small room carved into the rock. A young woman sat curled up on a cot in the corner, watching him with wide and frightened eyes. Tiernan held the gun pointed at her as he advanced into the room, but the girl didn't move. She sat, paralyzed, not even blinking, until Ava reached out and touched his arm. He'd been so intent on the girl that he hadn't even realized Ava had followed him into the room.

"I think you can put that away." Ava started to step around Tiernan, but he threw out an arm to stop her.

"She's just a girl," Ava said.

"Looks can be deceiving." He'd seen it too many times. Deadly purpose wrapped up in innocent packaging. For all he knew, this girl could burst their internal organs with a thought.

"She was locked in this room," Ava said slowly, as if explaining to a small child. "Which means she needs our help."

Tiernan eyed the girl for a long moment. "She was locked in this room for a reason. Maybe *we* need protection from *her*."

The girl swallowed nervously, watching him like a skittish colt, her legs twitching with what he suspected was an instinct to run. With a resigned sigh, he lowered the weapon to his side.

Ava moved around Tiernan, ignoring his warning grumble. The girl swiveled her anxious gaze to Ava, watching as she came closer until her knees finally bumped the edge of the cot. The girl was young—maybe fourteen or fifteen—her dark hair chopped at odd angles, the chin-length strands streaked with blue and purple. Cheekbones carved sharp shadows on her face, echoed by the straight lines and corners of her thin limbs and joints. She wore no contact lenses, so her eyes were her most compelling feature—almond-shaped, one almost black, the other pale green. She stared at Ava without blinking, giving the impression she saw much more than most.

"We won't hurt you," Ava said quietly, feeling the tension in the room. "We can help you get out of here. Who are you?"

The girl swallowed nervously. "Emma."

"Emma? That's your name?"

She nodded. "Emma Reiko."

Ava smiled encouragingly and sat down next to her, smoothing her hand over the rough woolen blanket. "I'm Ava. This is Tiernan."

Tiernan peered back out into the tunnel. "We don't have time for this."

Ava tipped her head slightly in acknowledgement. "We're looking for someone," she told Emma, trying to rein in her anxiety with steady breaths and gentling tones. "Was there . . . someone else here? A man with dark hair and blue eyes? He might have been wearing glasses."

Emma licked her lips, swallowed hard again, and darted a glance at Tiernan. Turning back to Ava, she nodded, whispering, "You mean Caleb."

Ava tensed. "You know Caleb? You saw him?"

Emma nodded again, loosening the hold on her knees so she could slide off the cot. She pointed out the door to the other room across the tunnel. "They kept him in there, I think."

Without another word, Ava shot to her feet, racing out into the tunnel and pounding on the metal door as she shouted Caleb's name. Tiernan touched her shoulder, but she shrugged him off and reached down for her gift. Instead of a slow build, it shot forward in a burst of power, the metal door buckling in the center before slamming into the wall, all but folded in half. She rushed into the room, coming to an abrupt stop in the center of the dirt floor. A cot similar to Emma's sat folded against the wall, but other than that, the room was empty.

Tiernan walked in behind her, staying close to the wall as he watched her carefully. Ava sighed, her power settling as quickly as it had surged.

"He's gone," she said, almost mystified by the overwhelming sense of loss. "I didn't feel him, but I hoped . . ."

Tiernan bent over to touch the cot and closed his eyes a moment. "He was here, though. Not too long ago. An hour. Maybe two."

Ava's senses tingled, pushing her anxiety and despair aside with a rush of fear. "They're coming back." She left the room with one last longing glance and found Emma waiting for them in the doorway to her own cell. Tiernan passed them, heading down the tunnel, his gun held at the ready.

"Emma. We can take you away from these people. To someplace safe," she said, tentatively reaching out to touch her shoulder. "But we have to go now. Before they come back."

The girl paled, eyes wide with undisguised terror as she scrambled away from Ava and backed up against the wall. "No. If I run, they'll come after me." She shook her head slowly and took gasping breaths between panicked words. "It'll be worse. It's always worse if I try and run—"

Ava worried the girl was going to hyperventilate. "It's okay," she said, keeping her voice low and soothing.

"You don't understand—"

Tiernan's hissed voice echoed down the tunnel. "Ava! Now!"

She approached Emma with outstretched hands, compassion overriding the urgency of the moment. "I know you're scared," she said. "But I'm telling you, we can keep you safe."

"You can't—"

"We *can*." Ava gripped the girl's shoulders gently and looked into her eyes with reassurance. "I know you don't know us and this is all scary, but time is running out. If we're going to go, we need to go now.

"You need to trust us. Let us help you." Ava squeezed her shoulders. "Please."

Emma stared into Ava's eyes for a long moment, then let out a shaky breath and nodded once. She cast a worried glance toward the door before ducking to grab a coat and a small bag and slipping it over her head and one shoulder. She took Ava's hand and allowed herself to be led through the tunnel after Tiernan.

They found him huddled behind the crate by the tunnel entrance, peering around the corner.

He didn't look back as Ava came up behind him. "How far?" he asked. "Do we have time to get out?"

Ava reached out with her gift, a sinking feeling settling in her stomach. "No. They're too close. Probably already at the cave entrance."

Tiernan's jaw flexed as he looked around the cavern, trying to come up with a plan of action. He signaled for them to follow him as he crossed the room, taking up a spot against the wall next to the opening leading to the tunnel going outside. He flexed his fingers around the gun, and said in a low voice, "You'll have to create a distraction again. With any luck, we can get them headed down that other tunnel before they realize we're here. Maybe with so many Race imprints, it will be hard for them to pinpoint our exact location."

"You think that will really work?" Ava asked.

"Probably not." He shrugged. "So you might have to reenact that trick with the door—maybe with that crate over there." He gestured with the gun across the room, looking at her sideways. "Do you think you can do that?"

Ava knew what he was asking. Could she hurt someone? Could she possibly kill someone? She'd done it before, with Arthur, but that was spur-of-the-moment, unplanned—a them-or-us situation where she didn't have time to think about it beforehand. This was different. She looked at Emma, clutching her hand, innocent and scared, and thought of Caleb.

Caleb.

Somewhere out there. And once the Council learned Caleb was still on the run, they'd most likely take matters into their own hands. In other words, hunt Caleb down. She couldn't let that happen. They had to find him first.

With grim determination, she nodded sharply. "I can do it."

They waited in silence, and Ava could feel each step as the group got closer. She could tell when Tiernan felt them as well. He squared his shoulders, clenched his fists, and braced his feet in a wide stance, preparing for a fight. She turned to the tunnel across the room and readied her own weapons, calling on her gift as the first footsteps echoed through the cavern. She reached out for the metal door she'd knocked down, picking it up and letting it clatter against the stone floor. The sound amplified in the tunnel, and it wasn't long before their pursuers ran into the cavern. They huddled in the shadows as the four Rogues scanned the room, but to Ava's surprise, they didn't even seem to notice them.

Then she realized it wasn't only her own gift she was feeling. Where she held Emma's hand, she felt the tingle of unfamiliar power running along her skin. She gaped at the girl, whose eyes were closed and brow creased in concentration, and watched as the Rogues took off down the far tunnel.

Tiernan tugged on Ava's sleeve, and she stumbled after him.

The three of them ran down the tunnel in the opposite direction, and Ava felt a rush of hope as the light of the entrance finally showed ahead.

They raced out into the sunshine, and Ava stopped and turned around.

"What are you doing?" Tiernan snapped, tucking his gun back into his pants. "Let's go."

"Just buying us some time," Ava said, calling on her gift again.

With a low rumble, the front of the cave shuddered and collapsed in on itself, kicking up a cloud of dust. When it finally cleared, a pile of dirt and rocks lay where the entrance had been.

"Nice," Tiernan said with an appreciative grin. "Remind me never to tick you off."

They turned and headed toward the car at a slightly slower pace, knowing their pursuers would have to do some digging before they could take up the chase. Emma kept eyeing Tiernan with something between awe and fear, and Ava finally nudged her shoulder lightly.

"He's big and scary looking, but he's not so bad," she said, earning an irritated glare from Tiernan. She ignored him and asked, "Was Caleb all right? Did you see . . . did they hurt him?"

Emma shook her head, but she wouldn't meet Ava's eyes.

"Did they hurt you?"

Emma didn't answer; instead she bit her lip and reached up to tuck a lock of purple hair behind her ear. "Are you a friend of Caleb's?" she asked.

"Yes. I think he's in trouble. I need to find him." She glanced at Tiernan. "*We* need to find him."

Emma nodded, her pale skin seeming even more translucent in the bright sunlight. "Can I come with you? To find him?"

"Absolutely not," Tiernan snarled as he topped a hill and stomped heavily down the other side.

"What Tiernan means," Ava said pointedly, "is it's probably going to be pretty dangerous. It's better if we take you somewhere where you'll be safe."

"But I . . . I need to go with you," Emma said, her voice taking on a pleading tone. “I need to fix him.”

Ava’s skin chilled and she stopped in her tracks. “What do you mean, ‘fix him’?”

Emma wrapped her arms around her stomach, her fingers digging into the puffy red coat she wore. “I did something . . . they made me do . . . something to him.”

Ava felt her gift flare in a rush of possessive alarm, remembering the feel of Emma’s power in the cave. “What did you do to him?” she asked, fighting to keep control. Her power pushed against that control, poking at it angrily.

“They made me do it,” Emma said, eyes wide as her voice wavered. “They said it would be worse for both of us if I didn’t.”

Ava took a deep breath, searching for some compassion, some reassurance as she started walking again. “What did you do, Emma? Please tell me.”

They crested another hill and followed the trail leading back to the Jeep.

Emma eyed Ava carefully and said, “I can affect people’s minds. Block memories sometimes, other times change them.”

“Change memories?” Tiernan glanced back, suddenly interested.

“Yeah. Or change the mind itself—how people think, their personalities sometimes. They—the Rogues, did you know they’re Rogues?”

Ava nodded.

“They had me change Caleb. They needed him to work with them—to forget his loyalty to the Council. So I had to instill doubt in him. Make him doubt the Council, the Law, his purpose as a Protector. Open his mind to the possibility of something different.”

Ava felt nauseous as a wave of panic curdled her stomach. “You made him want to work with the Rogues?”

“I didn’t *want* to do it,” Emma said, pleading. “They made me. That’s why you have to let me come with you. I need to fix this. I can put Caleb back to the way he—” With a choked shriek, she flew backward and slammed against a tree.

It took Ava a moment to realize she’d done that. Her power enveloped her, feeding on her fear—her rage—and Emma stared blankly back at her, terror sparking tears in her eyes. The pounding of Ava’s heart echoed in her ears, blood rushing under her skin as her gift held Emma tight against the tree. She could hear Tiernan speaking to her in a low voice, but at first it was just a muddle—white noise under the screaming of her anger.

“Ava, let her go.”

She felt cool fingers against the heated skin of her wrist and blinked down at Tiernan’s hand carefully wrapped around it.

“She’s a victim here. Just like Caleb. Don’t hurt her.”

She looked up at him.

“You need to calm down,” he said. “Let her go.”

Ava took a deep breath . . . and another. Slowly, resentfully, her gift receded, and Emma slid down the tree into a shivering heap, curled up among the gnarled roots.

"I'm sorry," Ava whispered. "I didn't mean—"

"We need to talk about this later." Tiernan reached down, and Emma shrank back. He rolled his eyes and offered her a hand, which she took at last, allowing him to haul her to her feet. "Jeep's just over the rise," he said, releasing Emma as he took off in long strides.

Ava and Emma followed behind at a distance, neither meeting the other's eyes.

Once they'd finally reached the Jeep, Emma slid into the backseat and shrugged out of her coat. She pulled her legs up, wrapping her bony arms around her knees, and wiped at her nose with the back of her hand.

Ava looked through the windshield, ignoring Tiernan's significant glances. It was only when they pulled out onto the main road that she finally sighed heavily and turned around to look at Emma. "I'm sorry," she said. "I shouldn't have done that back there. I know you didn't hurt Caleb on purpose. It's just that . . . Caleb is important to me. I need to make sure he's all right."

Emma unfolded her body and reached over the seat to touch Ava's shoulder tentatively. "I can help you," she said. "I will. I'll undo what I did and he'll be . . . Caleb again. The Caleb you know."

Ava wasn't sure that they had an alternative. If Emma changed Caleb, she'd have to change him back. Who knew if there was anyone else who could undo what she'd done, and it wasn't as if they could spend the time looking.

"How long have you been with the Rogues?" Ava asked.

Emma sat back, resuming her curled up position as she looked out the window. "Since I was a little girl."

"How old are you?"

"Seventeen. Almost eighteen," she said the way seventeen-year-olds did, with a slight lift of her chin.

Ava smiled briefly. "And what you did to Caleb—did they make you do that to other people, too?"

Emma's gaze darted back out the window as she swallowed thickly, her eyes fluttering closed. "They made me do a lot of things."

"How?" Tiernan eyed her through the rearview mirror, ignoring Ava's reproving look. "If you could do to Caleb what you say you did, why didn't you fight back? Make them let you go?"

Despite her protective feelings toward the girl, Ava found herself almost breathless, waiting for the answer.

Emma picked at a loose thread on her sweater, avoiding Tiernan's hostile gaze and Ava's more concerned one. "They have ways," she said, her voice low and almost brittle. "Drugs and . . . pain." She rubbed at her temple, eyes drifting shut as if remembering something unpleasant, and when she opened them again, they were glazed and almost blank. "Let's just say I'm not the only one able to affect someone's mind. Maybe it makes me a coward, but after a while, I . . ." She looked away and swallowed heavily.

Ava felt a rush of empathy for the girl and blinked back a prickling of tears. She swiped at her eyes and turned to Tiernan. "So, what now? Are you going to call Andreas again?"

Tiernan glared at her, with a significant jerk of his head toward the backseat. Obviously, he still didn't trust Emma, regardless of what she said.

"We're kind of in this together now, I think," Ava said, barely resisting the urge to roll her eyes. "A little late for suspicions, don't you think?"

Tiernan apparently got what Ava wasn't saying—that if Emma had the power she said, she could have turned either of them over to the Rogues at any point. Really, if she could do what she said, and they had pretty good evidence that she could, she could have made them turn themselves in. Or even turned them Rogue.

Ava felt a bit nauseous at the thought. Still, it seemed apparent that they were on the same side. And she couldn't get past the fact that they needed Emma if they were going to help Caleb.

Tiernan may not have been a mind reader, but it didn't take him long to catch up with Ava's train of thought. With a disgruntled noise, he picked up his phone and called Andreas.

Chapter 8

North. According to the sensor, they were to head north.

Tiernan clenched his jaw in frustration. He hated depending on Andreas and his super-sensor, but Caleb's trail had disappeared before they'd reached the Jeep and he really had no alternative. Someone was helping Caleb evade them. Someone was covering his trail, and apparently, even masking his shifts, making it more difficult for the sensor to track him.

So . . . north. That was the extent of their instructions.

"So what's north?" Ava mused, half to herself. "Idaho, Wyoming, Montana . . ."

"Canada," Tiernan said when she paused. He might have imagined it, but he could have sworn Ava stiffened a bit at that. "What?" he asked.

Emma leaned forward over the seat. "I think Canada," she said.

"Why do you say that?" Tiernan made a turn onto the highway and floored it. The Jeep shuddered in protest but slowly sped up.

"I overheard some of them talking," she said. "They said something about Ontario."

"Ontario?" Ava seemed nervous for some reason, and she avoided his gaze. "Why would they send Caleb to Ontario?"

Emma shrugged. "I don't know. I didn't hear much. They stayed away from me when they didn't need me."

Tiernan eyed Ava curiously, watching as she stared purposefully out the passenger window. "What is it?" he asked.

"Nothing." She bit at a hangnail, frowned when it started to bleed, and an instant later was healed. "Kind of anxious about everything, you know?" She gave him a weak smile, and he let it go, even though he was far from convinced.

About an hour later, Tiernan pulled into a gas station and set the pump as Emma and Ava went inside for supplies. He pulled out his phone and dialed Andreas again.

"What is it?" The Council member didn't seem happy to hear from him.

"We've picked up a passenger," Tiernan said, keeping his eyes on Emma through the glass walls of the mini-mart. "She claims to be a Rogue prisoner with a particular gift for dealing with memories. She says she's altered Caleb's mind and wants to help us find him so she can undo what she's done.

"I thought you'd want to know," he said. "And maybe check her out."

"I see," Andreas said slowly. "And this girl's name?"

"Emma Reiko." Tiernan waited a beat, but got no response. "You heard of her? She said she's been held by the Rogues since she was a child."

"No. The name doesn't ring a bell," Andreas replied, but Tiernan could hear the tap of computer keys in the background. "I'll look into it. In the meantime, keep the girl with you. It's possible with such a gift she could prove useful to the Council. I don't need to tell you how important it is to keep her away from these Rogues."

"Understood."

"She hasn't influenced you, has she? Or Miss Michaels?"

"No, sir." Of course, how could he be sure? Tiernan didn't like that thought, so he put a bit more conviction in his voice. "My loyalty still lies with the Council, sir."

"Good." After a beat, Andreas asked, "And Ava?"

"Sorry?"

"Is her loyalty with the Council as well?"

Ava and Emma shoved open the mini-mart doors, carrying several bags and chatting quietly. "It's no secret she has no love for the Council, sir." He lowered his voice, hoping she couldn't hear him. "But she's no Rogue."

"Very well," Andreas said. "I'll be in touch."

Tiernan put his phone back in his pocket and grabbed a couple of bags from Ava, peeking inside. "No doughnuts?"

"Other one," Ava replied, taking Emma's bags so the girl could get into the Jeep. "You eat too much sugar, you know."

Tiernan shrugged. "It tastes good."

"But it's bad for you."

"Doesn't matter," he said, thumping his chest lightly. "Race, remember?"

Ava shook her head and got into the car. "You know, just because you *can* eat it, doesn't mean you *should*."

"Why not?" Tiernan took a little too much pleasure in watching her flounder for an answer.

"You just . . . you just shouldn't!" she snapped at last, and Tiernan laughed as they pulled out of the parking lot and headed north.

It was late that night when they crossed the border from Montana into North Dakota. Despite the chilly temperatures, Ava sipped at an iced coffee —lukewarm and watery from sitting in the Jeep—while Tiernan finished off the last of the stale doughnuts. Emma lay curled up on her side in the backseat, sleeping peacefully, as she had been for the past few hours.

Ava yawned and noisily slurped up the last of the coffee, ignoring Tiernan's annoyed huff as she stuffed the empty cup into the bag they'd deemed for trash. She'd picked up a disposable cell phone at their last stop, and her thumb brushed idly at the keys. She'd texted the number to Caleb, knowing Tiernan would be furious, but she couldn't bear the thought that he might try to get in touch with her and not be able to do so. She still, however, didn't know what to do about her mom and dad.

"You know you can't call them," Tiernan said, and she wasn't even surprised he knew what she was thinking.

"They're my parents. They've got to be worried sick."

"By now the police are monitoring their phones," he reminded her. "You're lucky your friend used a pay phone, or they'd probably already be on us."

"I know that," she said, throat catching slightly on unshed tears. "This has got to be so hard on them, though. And my dad . . ." She reached up to swipe at her eyes. "He's been sick. The doctors say stress doesn't help."

"What is it?" he asked, throwing the remnants of a doughnut out the window.

"They're not really sure," she replied. "One doctor says MS. Another, maybe lupus. They can't get a firm diagnosis, which only makes it harder. All I know is he has good days and bad days, and something like this is sure to make it worse."

Tiernan cleared his throat. "I'm . . . uh, sorry."

Ava shrugged. It was all anybody could say. "Thanks." She put her phone away.

"I . . . umm." Tiernan rubbed at his neck, as if he could feel the slight color rising above his collar. "Maybe I could ask Andreas to send someone to them. Ease their minds a bit?" His eyes flicked to hers only briefly, but his flush deepened, and he shifted uncomfortably in his seat under Ava's surprised stare.

"Are you being nice to me?" she asked.

Tiernan's eyes narrowed. "Yeah, well, don't get used to it." He bared his teeth in what should have been a terrifying grimace, but instead somehow seemed to lighten the mood.

Still, he *was* being nice, and Ava couldn't tease him too much about it. She reached out to nudge his shoulder. "Thanks."

He grunted.

She smiled and thought about his offer. "I don't know about sending someone to muddle around in my parents' heads, though. I mean, on top of the obvious—I like their brains as they are, thank you very much—"

Tiernan snorted.

"—I just think if the Rogues, or whoever's set me up for this, aren't thinking about them yet, I'd like to keep it that way. It's probably safer to keep my mom and dad as far away from all of this Race stuff as possible, don't you think?"

"Probably." They rode in silence for a while, and Tiernan glanced at Emma in the rearview mirror, a slight frown on his face.

"You don't trust her," Ava said.

He shrugged. "I don't know her."

"You heard what they did to her." She lowered her voice to a whisper. "She's just a kid."

"Kids can be dangerous, too."

Ava wasn't sure how to respond to that, so she just squirmed around in her seat, trying to stretch muscles cramped from being in the car for so long.

"What's in Ontario?" Tiernan asked suddenly.

Ava jolted, surprised at the question. Then she panicked. Again. All afternoon she'd been trying to come up with a plan of action. A way to deal with the fact that she knew—well, she *suspected*—where Caleb was heading.

The Guardian Colony.

The Colony where Caleb had wanted to take her, to hide her from the Council when they'd been on the run.

Rogues were definitely a threat to the Colony, but so was the Council. She didn't know who to go to for help—how to warn the Colony about what was happening. She didn't have any of Caleb's contact numbers—Audrey, who'd relocated to the Colony after the safe house was attacked by Rogues, Bel, or any of the others. Only Caleb knew how to reach them. And Caleb was currently under the control of the Rogues.

"You going to answer me?" Tiernan snapped in an irritated growl. "If you expect me to trust you or trust her . . ." He flicked his eyes toward the rearview mirror again. "It works both ways, you know."

Ava squeezed her eyes shut, the lights from a passing car flickering red and orange behind her lids. "It's not Ontario. But somewhere near there."

"What is?"

"You have to promise me this stays between us," she said. "If I tell you this—if I *trust* you with this—you can't tell anyone. Not even the Council. *Especially* the Council."

Tiernan's jaw tightened, the dashboard lights casting his face in harsh shadows accented by the jagged length of his scar. "You can't ask me to do that."

"Well, I am. If you want to know where Caleb's heading—where I *think* he's heading, it needs to stay between us. We're going after Caleb, and that's all." She turned in her seat, fixing him with a piercing stare. "This is nonnegotiable. Caleb. No one else."

"What do you mean?"

"I want your word, Tiernan."

"How do you know my word's worth anything?" His lip curled, the question bit off by clenched teeth.

She was quiet for a long moment. "I know," she said at last. When he looked at her in surprise, she shrugged. "Well?"

"Why do I get the feeling I'm making a deal with the devil?" He scrubbed a hand over his shaved head and exhaled heavily. "Fine. All right. You have my word. I won't say anything to the Council. Now, where are we going?"

Ava eyed him nervously, the Jeep suddenly seeming way too small. "To a Guardian Colony."

"What?" Tiernan shouted. Emma stirred in the backseat, and he lowered his voice to a near-hiss. "Are you out of your mind? I can't keep that from the Council!"

"We have to." Ava leaned toward him, panic twisting in her gut. "You know what will happen to all of those people if the Council finds them."

"They're criminals."

"Come on, Tiernan," Ava said with an exasperated snort. "Even you know that's not true." She reached out to touch his arm.

He flinched, but didn't shake her off as he glared out at the road ahead, the headlights making his mismatched eyes glitter.

"They're people trying to do what they think is right. Trying to survive," she said. "And you promised."

"You tricked me," he said a little petulantly.

Ava laughed. "Nice try." But somehow she felt she could trust him, that Tiernan would keep his word.

"Can I ask you something?" she asked, desperate for something to lighten the mood.

He shot her an irritated look. "Haven't you done enough of that already?"

"Not a favor, a question," she clarified. "You and Katherine. Who's older?"

He huffed out a surprised laugh. "That's what you want to know?"

"I'm curious."

He eyed her as though he thought she might be a bit unstable. "We're twins," he said finally. "But she's older. By one and a half minutes."

"Does she lord it over you?"

He smirked, his eyes softening slightly. "Constantly."

"How long have you known Caleb?" she asked, encouraged by his unusual openness.

"Oh, let's see." He rounded a bend in the road, lost in thought for a moment. "Katherine met him first. He was only a kid then. I was in South America at the time."

Ava blinked in surprise. Caleb had finally confessed, after much prodding on Ava's part, that Race had a lifespan about five times that of a normal human. It had been a lot to take in, finding out that—at nineteen—she was dating an eighty-five-year-old, but she thought she'd gotten used to the idea.

Apparently not.

"I didn't realize you were older than him," she said.

Tiernan raised an eyebrow. "Considerably."

"Really?" She turned in her seat, tucking a leg underneath her. "How old are you?" She flushed immediately. "Wow. Is that rude? Sorry . . ."

"It's fine," he said with a short laugh. "I'm a hundred and sixty-two." He smirked, sliding her a sideways glance. "Katherine's a hundred and sixty-two, plus a minute and a half."

Ava burst out laughing. "Oh, she's going to be mad you told me that."

He grinned. "I'm counting on it."

"So, tell me again why we can't use one of the regular border crossings?" Ava slapped away a branch, her feet sinking into the wet mud of the riverbank.

The moon cast a bluish glow on the landscape when it emerged periodically from behind the cloud cover as they slogged through a wildlife refuge in north-central North Dakota, heading for the Canadian border. Emma trudged silently behind them, apparently lost in her own thoughts.

Tiernan held up a hand as they neared a narrow gravel road. He searched in both directions before waving them across.

"And why did we have to ditch the Jeep, if there's a road right here?" She groaned, kicking up gravel as she darted across the road.

"Jeep's probably been reported stolen by now," Tiernan said after a heavy sigh Ava found completely uncalled for. "We couldn't risk trying to cross the border with it. And I'd prefer not to have my bag searched by the border patrol."

"Couldn't you just"—she waved her hand toward his head—"push them? You know, the compulsion thingie?"

He glanced at her sideways. "I'm not very good at that." After a moment, he asked, "Could you?"

Ava shook her head. "I'm not very good at it either. Most I can do is get someone to scratch their nose or something like that. Caleb is much better at it." She fought off a wave of sadness at the thought of Caleb and darted a look over her shoulder. "I bet she could have done it."

"I totally could," Emma said, kicking off a glop of mud on her shoe. "I'm excellent at compulsion."

Ava cocked a brow at Tiernan, but he only ground his teeth in response.

She knew what he wasn't saying. That he still didn't trust Emma. That he didn't really like people in general. That he actually preferred to stomp through brush and mud rather than rely on someone else for his safety.

They hiked in silence for a few minutes until they neared a clearing, and Tiernan held up his hand again.

"The border's right there," he said, tilting his head to scent the air. "When we get across, we'll need to find transportation as soon as possible."

Ava kind of appreciated the fact that he didn't point out she was the only reason they *needed* to get a vehicle. Actually, she wasn't sure about that. Maybe Emma was slow, too.

"Go." Tiernan waved her forward, the planes of his face sharp in the moonlight. "Go now!"

Ava ran across the clearing, only to find Tiernan and Emma both waiting for her in the overgrowth on the other side.

Okay, so wrong about Emma.

They walked quickly along the riverbank as it wound north, passing fields and finally spotting a farmhouse with a beat-up pickup truck parked next to a weathered barn. A low growl drew their attention to the front porch, where a German shepherd watched them, his snout curled in a snarl.

"I got this," Ava whispered. "You get the truck."

Her gaze swept the yard in front of the house, finally landing on a stuffed bear discarded in a pile of toys under a newly budded apple tree.

The dog, still growling in a low rumble, took a slow and tentative step down the porch stairs, hackles raised and ears pinned down.

Tiernan and Emma stepped back quietly, and the dog's attention centered on Ava as she smiled. "That's right. Don't pay attention to them," she said under her breath. She felt for her gift, and it responded quickly, reaching out toward the stuffed bear as if it had been just waiting for a chance to help out.

The bear twisted on the ground, then got to its feet and bounced slowly across the lawn toward the porch.

The dog's attention snapped to the toy, head tilted and ears cocked as his growl turned into a confused whine.

"Doesn't that look like fun?" Ava whispered, cartwheeling the bear toward the dog, and bringing it to a stop at the bottom of the stairs.

The dog took a tentative step down as the bear danced back and forth, taunting him. He eyed the stuffed animal with a predator's eyes, a low growl rumbling through his chest.

Ava swept the bear forward to tap the dog on the nose and quickly back, as though it was running away, the stuffed legs barely touching the ground.

With a playful yap, the dog gave chase.

Ava grinned, sliding the barn door open a crack and leading the dog into its dark interior. She tossed the bear across the barn and slid the door shut with her mind, laughing at the playful growls of what she was sure was a German shepherd tearing a teddy bear to bits.

The crunch of gravel tore her attention away from the mayhem in the barn, and she saw the truck rolling silently toward her, Tiernan pushing it with one hand on the steering wheel as Emma helped him shove on the other side. With a last glance toward the house, Ava rounded the truck and hopped in the passenger side after Emma. Tiernan pushed it—Ava helping a little with her gift—until they rounded a corner in the drive. Tiernan popped the clutch and the engine roared to life.

"Nice job," he said once he'd settled behind the steering wheel. "You ever think of taking that show on the road?"

"Maybe if I can find a beautiful assistant. You up for the job?"

"I look terrible in fishnets."

"Why do I get the feeling you know that from experience?"

Tiernan laughed loudly, and Ava couldn't hold back her own giggles.

Emma looked back and forth between them as though they'd lost their minds. "I don't get it," she said, shoving her hair away from her face. They kept laughing, and she shrugged, curled up on the seat, and closed her eyes. "You guys are weird."

Ava watched the girl for a moment, an idea forming that she was pretty sure Tiernan wasn't going to like. "Emma?"

The girl opened her eyes, but didn't sit up.

"When you said you were excellent at compulsion . . ."

"Yeah?"

"How excellent?"

Emma's lips curved into a smile. "Pretty excellent, if I do say so myself."

"What are you up to?" Tiernan asked with a suspicious glare.

"Can you do it long distance?" Ava asked, ignoring him.

"How long distance?" Emma sat up, intrigued at the challenge.

"Like, over the phone?"

"Humans or Race?"

"Humans."

"Oh no," Tiernan said with a frown. "You can't be serious."

"I've never tried," Emma said. She seemed lost in thought as her words faded off, and she appeared to be working through the logistics in her mind. "But humans are easy, so . . . yeah. I think I could. Why?"

Ava pulled the disposable phone out of her pocket. "I'd like you to talk to my parents."

"Ava, this is a bad idea," Tiernan said. "You don't even know if it will work."

"It's worth a try. I can't let them keep worrying."

"Wait a second." Emma held up a hand. "Your parents are *human*?"

Ava let out a heavy breath. "Yeah. Kind of a long story. I was adopted."

"But . . . how? Why?"

"That's the question of the hour." Ava shrugged. "But here's the bigger issue at the moment. I'm suspected of murder."

"Holy crap."

"That's the understatement of the year," Tiernan said half under his breath.

Ava ignored him and focused on Emma. "I didn't do it. Someone's setting me up. Maybe the Rogues. You hear any of them talk about that?"

Emma thought for a moment, but shook her head with a frown. "Sorry, no. Like I said, they left me alone for the most part."

Ava sighed. She hadn't really expected it to be that easy. "Anyway, we don't know for sure it's them, but until we figure it out, I need to keep my parents safe, and I really don't want them to worry.

"Do you think you can push them? Convince them everything's okay?"

Emma bit her lip, considering. "I think so. I mean, I don't know if I can make them *not* worry. They're your parents, after all, but maybe I can help a little."

"Can you do it to them both at the same time?" Ava was already dialing the familiar number.

"If they were Race, no. I'd have to focus on one at a time," Emma said. "But humans? Since the message is the same. Yeah, I can do it."

"It's the middle of the night," Tiernan said gruffly.

Ava checked her watch. "Early morning for them. I don't want to wait."

"And what if the police are monitoring them?"

"We'll keep it quick," Ava said, already dialing. "I mean, it takes them a few minutes to trace a call, right? And it's the middle of the night. They're probably not even listening."

He was running out of arguments. "Well, call the land line, not a cell. That will at least take a little more time."

Ava nodded, listening to the phone ring. "Keep it simple," she told Emma. "I'm safe. I'm innocent. I'll contact them when I can."

"Okay. I've got it." Emma's eyes were bright with challenge.

Ava held her breath, only releasing it when she heard her mother's sleepy voice. "Hello?"

"Hi, Mom."

"Ava? Oh, thank God. We've been worried sick. Are you all right? The police called us—"

"Mom, listen!" Ava clenched her eyes shut, overwhelmed at hearing her mother's voice, but knowing she couldn't linger. "I'm fine. I swear this is all a misunderstanding."

"Well, that's what I told the police, but they wouldn't listen." Sarah Michaels seemed as incensed at the idea as Lucy had been.

"It's okay, Mom, really." She eyed Emma, who nodded encouragingly. "Is Dad there?"

"He's in the kitchen making coffee." Ava heard rustling as her mother got out of bed.

"Can you get him on the extension? I need to talk to you both."

"Of course." She heard her mother call to her father, and the telltale click as he picked up the other line.

"Ava? You okay, honey?"

Ava let out a shaky breath, feeling tears form in her eyes. "I'm fine, Dad. Really. I need you to talk to someone, okay?"

"Who? What's going on, Ava?" her mother asked.

"Just give me a second, okay? This is my friend Emma. She's going to explain everything." Ava handed the phone to Emma, who reached out with her free hand to squeeze Ava's trembling one.

"Hello?" She smiled at Ava. "Hi. This is Emma. I need you to listen very carefully." Emma's voice was low and soothing, hypnotizing, and there was no sound from the other end of the line. Ava's parents were listening, lulled.

"Ava's fine," Emma said in that same soothing tone. "She's safe. The police have it all wrong, but it will be figured out soon, so you don't need to worry." She arched a questioning brown at Ava, who could only shrug in response. Would it be enough? She had no idea.

"Everything's going to be fine." Emma added another layer, just to be sure. "Don't tell the police she called, though. They wouldn't understand. Just go about your business and don't worry, okay?" Ava heard low mumbles in the background, and Emma smiled. "That's right. That's fine. Here's Ava."

Ava grabbed the phone and nodded when Tiernan pointed at his watch. "You guys okay?" she asked tentatively.

"Sure, honey," her mother replied. "But you still haven't let us know about spring break, and it's only a couple of weeks away. Do you think you'll be coming home?"

Ava felt a rush of relief. "I'll let you know, Mom. I really have to go now, though."

"Oh, okay," she replied distractedly. "I need to get your dad to his doctor's appointment anyway."

"Is everything all right?"

"Oh sure," her father answered. "It's just a checkup. I'm all right. No flare-ups this week. A bit of a drive to that specialist, though, so we're getting an early start."

Ava smiled. "Oh, that's good. Okay, then. You guys have a good day, and I'll talk to you soon."

Her parents bid her good-bye and hung up, and Ava slid her phone into her pocket with a smile at Emma.

"Thanks," she said. "That was amazing."

Emma shrugged as if it was no big deal, flushing a little at Ava's praise. "I'm glad to help."

Tiernan grunted a bit and turned on the radio.

They drove in amiable silence for the rest of the night, finally stopping at a seedy motel in Winnipeg to shower and get something to eat that didn't come in a plastic bag. Of course, Tiernan would rather have kept going, but he succumbed to pressure from the two women in the truck, although not without considerable protest and eye-rolling.

"I suppose we should trade cars again," he said when he conceded. "Get something with a little more room. And four-wheel drive."

Emma and Ava exchanged a victorious smile as he pulled into a motel parking lot in the early morning hours.

While Emma was in the shower, Tiernan flipped on the television—loud—and turned his blue-green gaze on Ava. "So where *exactly* are we going?" he asked.

She squirmed a little. Even after getting to know Tiernan a little better, being the center of his focus could still unnerve her. "I'm not really sure," she said. "All I know is it's about twenty miles from someplace called Red Lake. When we—Caleb and I—were heading there, someone was going to meet us in Red Lake and take us the rest of the way."

"And you don't know how to contact anyone at the Colony?"

Ava shook her head. "Do you think the sensor can help?"

"I asked Andreas, but he says the sensor lost Caleb right around here. He thinks Caleb must have a blank."

"A blank?"

"Someone shielding his Race imprint. A Guardian maybe? You think he's contacted them?"

Ava scrubbed her hands over her face. Her eyes burned; the lack of real sleep over the past few days was catching up with her.

"If he did, they'd take him in. They have no reason not to," she said quietly. "And if he is working with Rogues—"

"They'll know exactly where the Colony is. And how many people are there."

Ava thought for a moment. "But why? Why would a handful of Rogues care? The Guardians are no threat to them. Not like the Council."

"The Half-Breeds maybe?" Tiernan replied. "They're lost and confused when they're brought in. Could make them particularly vulnerable to the Rogue message."

"You make them sound like a cult."

"I never used to think so," Tiernan said with a grim smile. "But lately, things have changed. Maybe they're recruiting. Makes as much sense as anything."

"If that's true, Caleb will lead them right to the Colony."

Tiernan stiffened, his mouth a tight line as Emma came out of the bathroom.

"Next?" she asked, rubbing a towel over her hair.

"You go," Ava told Tiernan. "I'm going to stretch my legs. Maybe hit the gift shop and see if I can find some clean clothes."

"Yes." Emma slid on her coat with a longing sigh. "I'll come with you."

"Money's in the bag," he called out over his shoulder before closing the bathroom door.

They left Tiernan to his shower and walked past the faded doors of a half dozen rooms and into the equally faded gift shop, for lack of a better term.

A few T-shirts and baseball caps hung on a swiveling rack, some books and cassette tapes intermixed with questionable-looking canned goods and automotive supplies. Emma flipped through a six-month old magazine with a floppy-haired teen heartthrob on the cover while Ava collected a toothbrush and some deodorant, as well as a couple of clean T-shirts. She was considering throwing a flashlight onto the pile when her phone vibrated with a text.

Are you all right?

Caleb.

Ava's breath caught, and she cast a nervous glance at Emma. The girl didn't seem to notice, though, just continued to flip through her magazine, chewing thoughtfully on her upper lip.

"I . . . uh . . ." Ava clutched her phone with palms suddenly slick with sweat. "I didn't get enough cash from Tiernan. I'll be back in a sec, okay?"

Emma nodded absently and turned the page.

Ava stepped out into the dappled morning sunshine, glancing nervously toward their motel room before hurrying in the opposite direction, around the far corner of the motel. Unwilling to waste any more time, she dialed Caleb's phone, holding her breath and praying that he wouldn't let it go to voice mail.

"Ava?"

She exhaled on a sob. "Caleb? Where are you? Are you okay?"

"I'm fine." He spoke in a low voice, and she wondered if he was trying to hide his conversation from someone as well. "Are you? Are you safe? I heard you were with Tiernan."

Ava hesitated, unsure if she should confirm that and guilt-ridden that she would wonder. "I'm fine. Caleb, what's happening? Why are you running? The Council says you're helping the Rogues."

"The Council." He almost spat the words, then took a deep breath. "There's more going on here than you know, Ava. You have to trust me on this. The Council has kept us down for too long—"

"What are you talking about?" Ava leaned out to peer around the corner of the building. She didn't have much time. "Caleb, we found a girl—Emma. She says she knows you. She says she did something to your mind."

"My mind is fine."

"Are you going to the Colony? Are you leading the Rogues there?"

"Ava, listen to me." Caleb seemed to be fighting frustration, and not very successfully. "This isn't about the Council and the Guardians, or even the Rogues. It's about the Race. All of us. Look, just . . . get away from Tiernan and go home. Whatever you do, stay away from the Colony. And don't trust the Council."

"I can't—"

"Someone's coming," Caleb whispered urgently. "I have to go. I love you."

"Caleb?" But he was gone. She stared down at the phone. "I love you, too."

It took a while for her to realize it was the first time he'd said it. Sadly, it failed to reassure her.

"Well?"

Caleb knew Bartok was standing there, but his voice made him jump slightly anyway. Caleb was jumping a lot lately.

"I told her to stay away."

"And?"

"She'll come anyway. She's stubborn that way." Caleb couldn't keep a small smile of pride off his face.

"And the girl?"

Caleb shrugged. "Emma's with them. Tiernan, too."

"We'll deal with Tiernan." Sloan crossed the hotel room and poured himself a drink from the minibar. "We make our move once they reach the Colony. You know our orders."

Caleb nodded curtly. "And you swear Ava won't be hurt?"

He chuckled. "Nobody wants to hurt your little girlfriend, Caleb. That's kind of the point, isn't it?"

"How will they know where to go?"

Bartok took a sip of his drink, the ice tinkling as he eyed him over the rim of the glass. "Well, you'll need to leave a trail, of course. But don't make it too obvious. Wouldn't want to make Tiernan suspicious."

Caleb turned away, staring sightlessly out the window. "And then?"

Bartok sighed, obviously bored with the conversation they'd had several times already. "Then we get Emma . . . and Ava. And when this is all over and things are settled, the two of you can go wherever . . . and do whatever." He waved a hand dismissively. "Do your part, Caleb, and everything will be the way it should be. The Council's time is over. It's our time now."

Something teased at Caleb's memory. Something that made him feel as if what the man was saying wasn't exactly right, but he couldn't put his finger on it. When Bartok slapped a hand on his shoulder with an encouraging smile, Caleb smiled back.

He was just nervous . . . worried about what was coming. But it would all be over soon, and he and Ava could be together without Protectors watching their every move. The Council would no longer be looking over their shoulders, and they could live in peace.

Yeah. That was what he was fighting for.

Chapter 9

"Are we there yet?" Emma asked from the backseat, sticking out her tongue when Tiernan glared at her through the rearview mirror. "Just trying to lighten the mood," she said. "You seem so tense."

"I'm not tense," he replied. "I'm concentrating." The window was cracked open next to him, and he scented the air periodically.

They'd slept in shifts through the day and driven through the night, picking up Caleb's trail outside Red Lake and following it east. It felt good to rely on his own abilities for a change, and he felt pride that he no longer needed the sensor. The trail was weak—several times Tiernan feared he'd lost it—but then he'd catch a whiff, or find a sign in the damp ground, and knew he was on the right track.

Ava worried him, though. Since they'd left the motel, she'd been noticeably silent—unusual for her—not even taking the opportunity to mock Tiernan when he'd popped in an eighties boy band CD and tapped his fingers on the steering wheel in time with the beat. He'd risked a car rental company this time, procuring a black SUV with one of his fake IDs.

Ava had eyed him curiously. "Couldn't we have done that before?" she'd asked. "Or does car theft give you a rush?"

"As much as possible, I try to be inconspicuous."

Ava had snorted at that, but her smile didn't reach her eyes. And with each mile they'd driven, she had seemed to withdraw into herself. No curious questions or stubborn bargaining. Her unseeing eyes had stayed fixed on the horizon as she'd chewed on a ragged hangnail.

Yeah. He was worried.

Andreas had been concerned as well. He'd made it clear to Tiernan that he was to bring all of them—Caleb, Emma, and Ava—to him personally.

Do not pass go. Do not collect two hundred dollars. Do not talk to the rest of the Council. At least not until Andreas had had a chance to speak to Caleb personally.

"This matter must be handled delicately," he'd told Tiernan. "Once we've established Foster's motivations, his true loyalties, then we can move forward. We need to find Borré, and if Foster has information on his whereabouts, I need to know."

Andreas hadn't said anything more about the girl they'd rescued from the Rogue lair other than her gifts could prove useful in the future.

Tiernan wasn't an idiot. Andreas Petrov was a politician, so whatever he did was motivated by one thing—protecting himself and his position on the Council. Whatever he wanted with Borré—with Caleb and Ava and Emma—was planned solely with that goal in mind.

He suspected Andreas had his eyes on Madeleine's chair at the Council table.

"What can they do?" Ava's voice broke though the cheesy ballad on the CD player, pulling Tiernan out of his own thoughts.

"Who?"

"You're a million miles away," she said.

Tiernan shrugged. "Concentrating," he said again. "Who are you talking about?"

She twisted on the seat, turning to lean her cheek against the headrest. "The Council. They must be very powerful. I mean, more powerful than your garden-variety member of the Race."

"Not really." Tiernan downshifted and turned onto a gravel road. "They all have gifts, of course. Naomi is able to communicate with animals. Kaeden can shift, like Caleb. But they're politicians, so it's their abilities with people that really come into play."

"What do you mean?"

"We all have an ability to read people to a certain extent." He glanced at her, and she nodded, confirming she knew that already. "But Andreas is particularly gifted at that. He can see motivations behind actions. I swear sometimes it seems like he's almost psychic. Madeleine can do that, too, to a lesser extent, and her compulsion ability is unique. She can actually help someone see someone else's point of view."

"I imagine that comes in handy."

"Yeah." He scratched at the stubble on his cheek. "So in the end, our government is not that different from yours. From the *humans'*," he said, correcting himself before she could say anything. "Based on manipulation and appealing to the masses."

"Kind of a cynic, aren't you?"

"I prefer 'realist.' "

Emma draped herself over the back of the seat, her chin propped on the leather. "So why do you work for them, then? They sound kind of corrupt, if you ask me."

Tiernan shot a glare over his shoulder. "They're what we've got. And they've kept us at peace for centuries . . . millennia."

"Doesn't mean it's right." Emma raised her chin a bit as she met his gaze through the rearview mirror.

"Better be careful talking like that."

Emma scoffed. "Or what? Are they going to come get me?" When Tiernan didn't respond, she leaned a little bit closer, as if waiting and watching for his reaction. "At least the humans have free speech."

"She's right," Ava said and nodded at Emma. "The Council seems like kind of a dictatorship, if you ask me."

"Well, I didn't ask you!" The music on the stereo reached its crescendo, and he slapped at the power button angrily, the resulting silence growing thick and heavy. "The Council is the Law," he said in a calmer voice. "It *is* the Race. They preserve our way of life. And I am sworn to follow their directives." Tiernan glanced at Ava and then at Emma—who had sat back and was avoiding his gaze. "My mission is to find Caleb Foster. You're both here right now because I think you can help in that mission.

"I've already bent the rules by swearing to keep the location of the Colony a secret," he said in a gruff voice. "Don't ask me to betray the Council any further."

No one said a word.

Tiernan turned a corner and came to a stop before a washed-out bridge. He got out of the car and the others followed suit. He crouched down and examined the gravel and the dirt and brush along the side of the road. He stood, dusted off his hands, and pointed toward the bridge. "The trail leads that way."

They walked to the bridge and peered over the edge of the broken wood at the crashing river below.

"Now what?" Ava asked.

Tiernan stepped back and crossed his arms over his chest, staring across the expanse for a long moment. Then he started across the bridge.

"Tiernan?" Ava gaped as he quickened his pace, almost at a run when he hit the wooden bridge. "Tiernan!"

With a shimmer, he was gone.

"What happened?" Emma asked, watching in awe.

Ava laughed when she realized the answer. "It's a cloak," she said. "Might have been nice for him to mention it so we didn't think he was jumping to his death, but that's Tiernan."

The man in question chose that moment to poke his head back through the cloak. His head and shoulders appeared solid and healthy, although the rest of him wavered as if he was underwater.

"You coming?" he asked with a smirk. "I think it's probably best if we continue on foot. The trail is stronger over here. I don't think it's far."

He disappeared again, and Ava and Emma walked toward the bridge, Emma hesitating for a moment before she extended her arm through the cloak. Her hand wavered, and she drew it back with a gasp.

"You've never seen one?" Ava asked.

Emma shrugged. "Not from this side. The Rogues used me sometimes to help strengthen cloaks with hallucinations."

"Really? Like what?"

Emma examined the cloak again, apparently trying to see through it to the other side. "Like this, sometimes. Other things, too—a brick wall, muddy bog, field of thistle bushes—anything to dissuade people from going farther."

They started through the cloak, Ava marveling again at the shimmering landscape around them. "It must have been awful, to be held prisoner all those years. Forced to do things. I'm sorry you had to go through that."

Emma swallowed, blinking rapidly, and Ava realized she was fighting back tears. "I didn't mind usually," she said once she'd regained control. "I just . . . I didn't like it when they made me change people. Like Caleb."

They came through the cloak and Ava reached out to place an arm around the younger girl's shoulders. "It's not your fault. We'll find him, and you'll fix it, right?"

"Right."

She swiped at her nose with the back of her hand, and Ava was struck by how young she seemed. A mark on the inside of Emma's left wrist caught Ava's eye, and before she even realized what she was doing, Ava reached out to grab Emma's hand for a better look. It was a simple tattoo—a thick arc followed the curve along the base of Emma's palm. It was linked to another arc by a vertical line crossing in the center of both. Ava had seen the mark before but couldn't quite place it.

"It's the symbol for Pisces," Emma told her, tugging up her sleeve so Ava could see it better. "Highly intuitive, yin and yang . . . the chameleons of the Zodiac. Sounds mysterious, right?" She wiggled her eyebrows with a grin.

"I don't know much about it. It's the fish, isn't it?"

Emma laughed. "Yeah, the fish." She shrugged. "I just thought the tattoo looked cool." She ran her thumb over the ink before letting her arms fall back to her side.

"How do you get it to stay?" Ava asked. "I'd think it would heal, like other injuries?"

"It takes a special talent. Someone who can manipulate the flesh to heal around the ink," Emma said with a shrug. "I don't get it completely. Healing's a bit of a mystery to me still."

They came around a corner and spotted Tiernan walking ahead of them on a narrow trail through some trees.

Emma glanced at Ava as they hurried a bit to catch up with him. “Can I ask you something?”
“Sure.”
“That thing you did back at the cave. Do you do that a lot?”
“Not a lot. I don’t often have a need to create a landslide.” She smiled, and Emma laughed.
“It’s just . . . you’re pretty powerful, aren’t you?”
“I guess.” Ava shrugged. “I still can’t do a lot of stuff, though.”
“Like the running.”
“Like the running. And the heavy lifting.”
“That is kind of weird,” Emma said, her tone all teenage bluntness. “Do you know why?”
“Not really.” They started up an incline and Ava grabbed a branch to steady herself. “I had some kind of psychic block. Caleb thinks some of it might still be there.”
“A block?” Emma said slowly. “I might be able to help you with that.”
“Absolutely not,” Tiernan snapped, glaring back at them from several steps ahead. “You stay out of our heads.”
Ava bristled. “She was only offering—”
“*I* know what she was offering,” he said, his words precise and intentionally enunciated as the tension rippled through his huge frame. “Have *you* forgotten what she did to Caleb?” He spun on Emma, a thick finger in her face. “You’re here against my better judgment because you said you could help with Caleb. But make no mistake, I don’t entirely trust you.”
“Tiernan!” Ava glared at him. “Don’t be such a jerk.”
“No, it’s okay,” Emma said quietly. “He’s right. You don’t really know me. And I did do something awful to Caleb.” She touched Ava’s arm, a light brush of fingers, before she tugged her sleeves down to cover her hands. “But the offer stands. If you want me to try—after this is over.” She glanced at Tiernan nervously, her voice almost a whisper. “Just say the word.”
Tiernan delivered one more intimidating glare—and yes, Ava was getting a bit tired of *those*—before continuing down the trail.
“He’s kind of cranky,” Emma whispered.
Ava snorted. “Yeah, I don’t think he was hugged enough as a child.”
“I can hear you,” he called back before a hair-raising shriek stopped them all in their tracks.
“What was that?” Ava said, careful to stay as quiet as possible.
There was no need for an answer because a crackle of branches drew their attention to a gap in the trees off to the right.
“Something’s coming,” Emma whispered, grabbing Ava’s arm in a frightened grip.
The noise got louder, the underbrush swaying as something moved beneath it—something growling. They watched, motionless, as a mountain

lion slinked out of the brush. It snarled, its lip curled up over curved canines as its tail swished menacingly back and forth.

"Don't move," Tiernan said, so still it seemed he barely breathed.

Ava had never wished for super speed so hard in her life.

The cat didn't advance any farther, though. It simply watched them with piercing black eyes, its ears twitching as it alternated between low, threatening growls and terrifying screams.

"What's it doing?" Ava's instincts kicked in once the rush of adrenaline had slowed a bit, and she realized something about the lion seemed wrong. Artificial, almost. Ava reached for her gift and used it to pick up a branch a few feet from the mountain lion.

The lion didn't flinch, continuing its growling and snarling.

"What are you doing?" Tiernan asked through his teeth.

Ava ignored him and hefted the branch into the air—then hurled it right at the mountain lion's head.

Nothing happened. The branch clattered into the brush as though the cat wasn't even there. Because it wasn't.

"It's a hallucination," Emma said with a relieved exhale. "Another layer to the cloak." She closed her eyes and took a deep breath.

The image of the lion wavered and disappeared.

"Sorry," she said to Tiernan. "Guess I should have asked first."

He just grunted and continued up the trail. "We must be getting close," he said.

"Thank you," Ava said in a loud and emphatic voice, grinning at Emma when Tiernan ignored her.

They passed through yet another layer of the cloak—a sheer cliff rising out of the ground before them—and pushed their way through without even slowing. The click of weapons stopped them in their tracks when they emerged on the other side, though, and it took a moment for them to realize a dozen people blocked a wide roadway in front of them—with a barrage of weapons aimed in their direction.

Ava hadn't even felt them through the cloak, which she would wonder about once she was no longer afraid for her life. Her power flared, rocks and branches vibrating on the ground and levitating a few inches up in response to the threat.

"Probably not a good idea," Tiernan said, raising his hands slowly in surrender as he kept his voice low and calm. "I doubt you're quicker than a bullet."

"Try me." The rocks swirled about them slowly before, thinking better of it, Ava lowered them to the ground and raised her hands as well, followed by Emma, who'd moved just behind Ava's left shoulder.

"Should I do something?" she whispered, even though everyone could obviously hear her.

"No," Ava replied a little louder, her eyes meeting the gaze of each person in front of them. "We don't want to hurt anyone."

A woman about Ava's size, with close-cropped blond hair, scoffed at that, lifting her rifle a little. "Who are you?" she asked. "What are you doing here?"

Tiernan took a step forward, half blocking Ava and Emma. "We're looking for Caleb Foster."

The woman narrowed her eyes on him. "I know you. You're a Protector." She pointed her gun at Tiernan's head. "It's the Council!" she told the others, eliciting a rumble of outrage . . . or perhaps concern. "Get on your knees." She gestured with the tip of her weapon. "And don't try any of your tricks. We have a dampener."

Tiernan dropped slowly to his knees as a man with shaggy dark hair stepped forward and eyed Ava curiously, his head tipped a little to the left. He continued to stare, and she got a strange, prickling sensation down her back, followed by a kind of constricting feeling, like being wrapped in a blanket. She almost felt like she couldn't move and was surprised to find she could actually wiggle her fingers.

"Strange feeling, isn't it?" The blond woman said with a wry smirk. "Being cut off from your gift like that?"

The dark-haired man continued to stare, his black eyes piercing—as though he could see through her.

It reminded Ava of when Caleb tried to blur her memories back when she first started to suspect he wasn't quite what he seemed, and with a stunned realization, she reached for her gift. It was still there, she noted with relief, flickering around her consciousness, but . . . distant, almost. She called to it, felt it well up a bit, fighting against the dampener.

His black gaze narrowed as he focused and drove Ava's gift back down.

"I think I can stop him," Emma said under her breath, her fingers brushing against Ava's.

Ava stopped fighting him and reached back to squeeze Emma's hand in reassurance. She had a feeling she could stop him as well, but that wasn't their purpose at that moment.

"Look," she said, addressing the blond woman she assumed was in command. "We're not here for the Council. We're here to warn you."

"Warn us about what?"

"It's complicated," Ava said. "But you—the whole Colony—could be in danger. We have to know if Caleb's been here."

"What do you know of Caleb?"

An older man standing at the back of the group stepped forward, and Ava noticed the blonde moved back a little deferentially. The man didn't carry a gun and stood loose-limbed at the front of the group as though he knew they weren't a threat. He was tall, a bit broad in the shoulders, but lean in a way that Ava found vaguely familiar, though she couldn't decide why. His dark hair was cut close to his head on the sides, a little longer on top, his green eyes knowing and intent.

"He's my . . . friend," Ava responded after clearing her throat nervously.

"But something's happened to him."

The man took another step forward, darkness falling over his features as his jaw tensed. "What's happened to him?"

Ava cast a weary glance at Tiernan, who shrugged in response. She turned back to the man and cleared her throat. "He's been manipulated. The Council believes he's working with the Rogues."

"Impossible!" In a flash, he was hovering over her, an angry snarl twisting his lips, and Ava could feel the edge of a blade at her throat, the rough bark of a tree pressed all along her back.

She gasped, disoriented for a moment as he twisted the blade, pricking her skin just shy of drawing blood.

Tiernan started to get up, but he was shoved back to his knees by two men and the woman she'd assumed was the leader, their guns pointed directly at his head.

Emma whimpered, and Ava could feel the girl's power—feel her wanting to fight back.

"No," she whispered, locking eyes with the girl over her captor's shoulder. "Emma, no."

The power receded, tendrils stroking her skin as it departed.

The man pressed the knife more firmly against her skin, his words forced out through clenched teeth. "Now tell me who you really are."

"Maybe pull that thing back a little so I can talk without you slicing my throat?" Ava barely dared to move her lips.

With a quiet grunt, the man slid the knife down a little bit, the tip catching in the cord of her necklace. Her pendant slipped out from beneath her shirt, bouncing lightly against her chest, and his fingers tightened on her arm as he inhaled sharply. In a flash, he spun Ava around and threw her toward another man, who held her arms behind her.

Ava tried to catch her breath, dizzy with the quick movement. "What? What was that for?"

The dark-haired man advanced on her and wrapped his hand around the pendant. "Where did you get this?" he asked stonily.

"That's none of your business!"

He twisted the cord, and it bit into the flesh of her neck. "Answer the question."

Ava lifted her chin stubbornly but relented. "Caleb gave it to me."

"That's a lie." He jerked her closer, Ava's face now inches from his flashing eyes. "You stole it!"

"I didn't! He—"

"He'd never give this away!"

"She's his girlfriend." Emma stepped forward and wormed her way between the angry man and Ava. "They're together."

The man blinked, and his mouth dropped open a bit in surprise. "But he never said . . ." He seemed truly at a loss for words.

Ava seized the moment, thinking quickly. "Look," she said. "I know people here. Bel? Or Audrey . . ." She searched her mind for the last name of the woman from the safe house who'd trained her. "Collins. Audrey lives here now, right? She can tell you who I am."

To his credit, the leader at least seemed to consider her plea. After a moment, he turned to one of the men. "Go find Audrey. Bring her to the conference room."

Ava quietly let out a breath of relief.

"Good Lord." Tiernan didn't often look surprised, but he stared wide-eyed at the man. "You're Gideon Campbell, aren't you." It wasn't a question. "I thought you were dead."

As one, everyone turned toward the Protector.

Ava noted the look of shock on Tiernan's face. "Gideon Campbell?" She looked to Tiernan for an explanation, but he didn't look away from the man —*Gideon*, apparently—he just stared him down, his body vibrating with tension. Ava swore she could hear his teeth grinding. Tiernan was not one for holding back when threatened, and at that moment, he had three guns pointed at his head.

"What's going on?" Ava struggled against the hands holding her, and Gideon turned back to her although he still didn't speak.

He seemed to be taking her measure, his eyes dropping again to the necklace before rising slowly to examine her face.

Ava considered him as well, and then it hit her. Maybe it was the shape of his eyes—narrowed ever so slightly as he studied her features—or the curve of his cheekbones—a bit fuller with the years, but still so familiar—or perhaps the way he stood, loose-limbed, but aware of everything about him. Maybe it was all of it combined, but Ava suddenly knew.

"You're Caleb's father," she whispered, her voice cracking slightly.

He took a deep breath. "Aye," he said, and with that word, Ava detected a hint of a brogue in the depths of his rumbling voice. "I'm his father. And who might you be?"

"Ava. Ava Michaels."

His eyes widened slightly. "I've heard about you. But Caleb never . . ." He stared at her for another long moment, and for some reason, Ava felt her gift flare a bit in response. With a jerk of his head, Gideon ordered the man restraining Ava to release her, and she rubbed at her arm absently.

"All right," he said as the group relaxed and reluctantly lowered their weapons. "I think you and I need to have a talk, Miss Michaels."

Tiernan scowled as he trailed behind the group toward a cluster of large, metal buildings, constantly scanning the area for potential threats. Well, potential threats in addition to the blasted Guardians and Gideon Campbell.

He wasn't exaggerating when he said he'd thought the man was dead.

Neither Caleb nor Madeleine ever spoke of the man—in fact, among the Race, his name was only uttered in hushed tones, if at all. Everyone knew that it was Gideon who broke away from the Council to protest its treatment of Half-Breeds—Gideon who *created* the Guardians along with a handful of other rebels. But as for what happened to him after the fateful day he finally left New Elysia for good, left Madeleine Foster and her young son, no one knew for sure. He'd all but disappeared off the Council's radar, showing up now and then through the years only to evaporate back into the ether. It had been decades since the last sighting, and many—like Tiernan—had assumed he'd been killed, perhaps by a Protector who didn't know who he was or his value to the Council if he were captured rather than eliminated. After all, encounters with Guardians were more of a 'shoot first and ask questions later' kind of thing.

But no, Gideon Campbell was alive and well, and evidently still very much in command of the Guardians. Tiernan couldn't help but wonder if Madeleine Foster was aware of that fact. He half believed she was—and Tiernan wasn't quite sure if the thought made him angry or perhaps sparked a bit of grudging respect for the Council leader who may not be a typical politician after all.

They entered a large building on the far side of the compound, Gideon pressing his thumb to an electronic lock and entering a code before the thick metal door swung open. A few of Gideon's entourage followed them inside, but most took up posts outside the building, casting warning glances toward Tiernan before shouldering their weapons. The blonde, he noticed, stuck close to him, apparently still not sure he could be trusted.

Smart woman.

They walked down a dim hallway lined by crates, filing cabinets, and surprisingly well-organized shelving units, and came to a large room with a conference table in the center and several computer screens, including a large monitor all but covering one of the walls. It was clearly a command center of some kind.

Tiernan noticed all of the screens were blank, and the blonde quickly gathered up a scattering of papers and maps on the table and stashed them in a large drawer.

He made a note of that for later. Just because he promised Ava he wouldn't betray the location of the Colony didn't mean he couldn't do some recon of his own for future use.

Gideon stood at the head of the table, waving his hand in invitation for the rest of them to sit. The blonde took the seat to his right, Ava to his left. Emma sat next to Ava, the dampener on her other side, and Tiernan stood back, his arms crossed over his chest.

"I'll stand, if you don't mind," he said, his tone clear; it didn't matter if Gideon minded or not. Tiernan still didn't trust these people, and he wanted both the exit and his charges in his direct line of sight in case they had to make a run for it.

Gideon shrugged and sat down, turning his attention to Ava.

"Now, before we get started, you should know that Adam"—he glanced at the dampener—"will keep your gifts at bay as long as I feel you may be a threat. And Tyra"—he tilted his head toward the blonde— "is the best shot we have, which says a lot."

She hefted her gun a bit before laying it on the table in front of her, tilting her head with a smirk.

Gideon braced his forearms on the table and leaned toward Ava, gaze intent. "As for me, you should know that I have a talent for seeing the truth. More than the average Race, not to toot my own horn. So I'd advise you not to lie to me."

"I have no intention of lying," Ava said, looking Gideon square in the eye.

"Good." He sat back and folded his hands on his stomach. "Now, why are you here?"

Tiernan fought back an irritated growl and apparently didn't do a good job of it because Gideon cast him an annoyed glance.

"We told you," he said. "We're looking for Foster. We have reason to believe he's coming here. And he could put all of you in danger."

To Tiernan's surprise, Gideon jerked his head in a curt nod. "And why do you think this?"

Emma cleared her throat. "Because of me," she said in a shaky voice.

"It's not her fault." Ava said, shifting a little to draw Gideon's suspicious stare. "She was held prisoner by some Rogues. They forced her to use her gift to alter his mind."

"Alter his mind?" Gideon tensed, his eyes darting to the dampener, who nodded as if to reassure him he had the situation under control.

"Look, we don't have time for all of this," Ava said, slapping the table with an exasperated huff. "To put it simply, the Rogues had Emma mess with Caleb's mind to make him sympathetic to their cause. They needed him to work with them for some reason."

"To help Elias Borré escape Council custody, for one thing," Tiernan said.

"Elias Borré?" Gideon's brows shot up and his body tensed. "That's a name I haven't heard in a while."

Tiernan nodded. "We don't know what else they have planned, but Caleb is headed in this direction, and he's not alone. We can only assume he plans to expose the Colony."

"But why?" Gideon asked. "What purpose would that serve? Rogues have never had a problem with us. If anything, they like that we help divert Council attention away from them."

"We don't know," Ava said with a resigned sigh. "But we need to find Caleb so Emma can undo what she did."

Gideon's eyes narrowed slightly as he took a long look at each of them—Ava, Emma, and finally, Tiernan. He could feel the man probing him but resisted the instinct to try and fight him off. With a distracted grunt, Gideon blinked twice and got to his feet.

"Double the perimeter patrol," he told Tyra. "Take Adam and have Lydia strengthen the cloak. We don't want to keep him out, but I want to know when anyone gets within five miles of us." Tyra nodded and turned for the door, but Gideon grabbed her arm. "No one is to harm Caleb," he said gravely. "Incapacitate him if you must, but I don't want him hurt."

He issued no such warning about the Rogues, and Tiernan knew the Guardians wouldn't hesitate to take them out if necessary. "We need to question the Rogues," Tiernan said. "Find out what they're planning."

Gideon considered that and acquiesced with a grim nod. "But we only need one or two of them for that," he said. "Any extras are fair game."

Tiernan almost smiled. He thought he could very well learn to like Gideon Campbell.

Chapter 10

Ava's instincts were buzzing. She knew Gideon was holding something back. Even with her gift muted by the dampener, she could sense his hesitation—his deception. But the man offered them a hot meal, the first one in quite a while not prepared in a convenience store microwave, so she tabled her suspicions and followed him into another room that apparently served as a kind of common area for the Colony.

Mismatched tables and chairs were arranged around the room—rather industrial with white walls and scuffed gray tile, but a floor-to-ceiling fireplace flanked by large windows looking out onto the wild forest beyond kept it from being too cold and sterile. A handful of colonists were gathered around a big-screen television on the other side of the room, taking turns playing some kind of video game as they lounged on a worn leather sofa and a couple of comfortable recliners. They looked up with suspicion, the room falling silent as Ava, Tiernan, and Emma walked in, but with a nod from Gideon they turned back to their game, although at a much lower volume.

Gideon left them with an older woman named Molly who fed them bowls of soup thick with beef and vegetables and slabs of crusty bread. They ate in silence, all more hungry than they'd realized, not to mention a bit exhausted from their nonstop traveling.

After a while, Ava felt the block of the dampener fade until it vanished altogether. "You feel that?" she asked Emma.

The girl nodded.

Ava could feel her flex her power, testing its limits now that it had been released. "Guess we've been deemed trustworthy, at least somewhat." Ava yawned, breaking apart her last bit of bread into a crumbling pile. "You know Gideon's keeping something from us," she said.

Tiernan snorted. "You're surprised at that?"

"Not really. I mean, he has no reason to trust us. I'm just saying."

He took another bite and peered at her sideways. "What do you think it is?"

"You think he's heard from Caleb?" Emma asked.

Ava shrugged. "I don't think that's it. He seems as concerned about Caleb as I—as *we* are. He just wasn't that surprised when I mentioned Rogues."

Tiernan grunted.

"You think he knows what they're up to?" Emma dipped bread in her soup, watching Ava with wide eyes.

"I don't know. I think he knows *something*."

"You want me to try and get it out of him?" Emma asked, and Ava shivered a little at the anticipation in her tone.

Even Tiernan eyed her with surprise.

"No, I think we can be a bit more subtle," Ava replied. "He's finally called off that dampener. I don't want him to change his mind."

Emma nodded and stirred her soup slowly, looking as if she was working through her own thoughts.

"You should talk to him," Tiernan told Ava.

She barked out a laugh. "Me? It should be you. You two have that whole soldiers-in-arms thing going with the grunting and the looming."

"I don't loom."

"You totally loom. But that's beside the point."

"The point," Tiernan said, pointing at her with his spoon, "is that I'm a Protector. I'm the closest the Council has ever gotten to this place. I'm lucky he didn't throw me in chains on sight."

Ava frowned. She couldn't really argue with that.

They stared at their empty bowls for a while, lulled by the muted sounds of the video game and the quiet rhythm of low voices.

Ava wondered how many of the Guardians playing were listening in on their conversation but found she didn't really care. She was tired of all the secrets. Tired of running. Tired of the lies. And she had a sneaking suspicion that her own doubts about Gideon's candor wouldn't come as a surprise to the man.

"He cares about Caleb," Tiernan said after a while, continuing the conversation as though they'd never paused. "That much is obvious. And I think he believes that you two have at least that in common. He'll be more open with you than me."

Emma cleared her throat. "I think we're about to find out," she said, glancing pointedly toward the door where the Guardian leader in question had entered the room.

He crossed to them, pulling up an empty chair and straddling it backward.

Ava almost smiled at the movement; it was so reminiscent of Caleb. Now that she knew they were related, the resemblance was obvious.

"Everything secure?" Tiernan asked in a gruff voice.

Ava shot him a look that said *grunting and looming, I told you so*, before turning toward Gideon expectantly.

"We're ready," he said. "If they get close, we'll know it."

Ava opened her mouth to speak but was interrupted by the slam of a door and a familiar voice. "Where is she? I can't believe you people. Treating a nice girl like—" And with that, Audrey Collins appeared in the doorway to the common room, all fiery red hair and green eyes, her Irish accent thick with annoyance. She spotted Ava and let out a little squeal.

"There you are!" she said, rushing across the room and pulling Ava up into a tight hug. "Are you all right? Where's Caleb?" She pulled back, gripping Ava's shoulders and barely breathing between words. "What are you doing here?"

Ava felt a weight lift from her shoulders. She hadn't seen Audrey since the attack on the safe house, and although she'd known the woman had survived, seeing her in the flesh helped relieve the ongoing guilt she'd felt at being the cause of the raid.

"I'm so glad to see you," Ava said, her voice cracking with a quick surge of emotion.

"And I, you." Audrey smiled and leaned in with a conspiratorial wink. "Have you been practicing?"

Ava couldn't keep from rolling her eyes. "Constantly."

Audrey laughed. "And?"

"It's helped." For the first time since the whole mess with Caleb started, she felt the stirrings of excitement. "I have better control over my senses, and the telekinesis, too. Caleb says—"

"So I take it you know this girl?" Gideon asked, although his tone suggested he hadn't really doubted it.

"Of course I do, you great lout!" Audrey said with a hint of scorn. "She's a friend of Caleb's. Speaking of . . . where *is* Caleb?" Audrey glanced back toward the door. "What's going on? He didn't come with you?"

Ava sighed heavily. "Caleb's in trouble."

"What kind of trouble?" She turned back to Ava, tucking a strand of the girl's hair behind her ear.

The touch soothed Ava, reminding her of her mother, and she suddenly found herself fighting tears.

"Oh now, none of that," Audrey said quietly, hugging her again and stroking her hair. "It'll all be all right. You'll see." She pulled up another chair and sat down with Ava, never even glancing at the others. "Now, what's got you so upset?"

"She says Caleb's been compromised," Gideon said, sliding a cup of water to Ava, who took a sip, trying to organize her thoughts.

Emma reached out to take her free hand, and Tiernan leaned back, watching the conversation with a detached but critical eye.

Ava explained the situation in terse words. Gideon listened stiffly but added nothing.

Audrey sat back heavily, her fingers pressed to her lips as she looked wide-eyed at Emma. "You did this?"

"It wasn't her fault," Ava said tersely.

"No, no, of course not." Audrey waved a hand dismissively. "It's an impressive gift, is all. I haven't seen such a thing before—not in one so young. Not at any age, actually." She eyed the girl in appraisal. "And you're certain you can reverse the effects?"

"I can." Emma ducked her head. "I *will.*"

"And him?" Audrey jerked her chin toward Tiernan as she spoke to Ava in a low voice. "He can be trusted?"

Tiernan stiffened, but Ava cut him off before he could say anything. "Tiernan gave me his word he won't betray the Colony to the Council," she said. "He won't."

Audrey pursed her lips, nodding slowly as she absorbed that information. She turned to Gideon. "So this is the first time you two have met," she said slowly.

Gideon half glared at the woman, who met his gaze. "Aye," he said.

"Well, then," Audrey said, getting up from the table. "I imagine you have a lot to discuss."

"Audrey," Gideon said in a warning growl.

"She knows Caleb. Better than you," Audrey said sharply. He winced, and she shook her head, her tone almost chiding. "You know she can help."

After a moment, Gideon nodded sharply.

"We can talk more later," she told Ava, patting her arm gently. "I can show your friends to some quarters—"

"We'll stay with Ava," Tiernan said gruffly, his severe gaze brooking no argument.

Audrey's lips quirked. "I assure you she is in no danger." She cast a significant glance toward Gideon, who inhaled heavily, letting the air out in a slow rush as he turned to Ava.

"You can feel that, right? That I mean you no harm?" he asked in a low voice; his eyes seemed to look right through her. "Use your gift. You'll see I'm telling the truth."

Ava reached for her power, letting her instincts sweep away conscious thought for a moment. She nodded. "It's okay," she told Tiernan after a long, searching look at Caleb's father. "I'll be fine."

Gideon nodded and stood up. "I could show you around the Colony, if you like."

Tiernan opened his mouth to protest again, but Ava shook her head at him before following Gideon to the door.

They walked out into the cool evening air, and Ava pulled her coat tightly around her. Gideon led her down the row of buildings—a large, slightly misshapen ring, actually—pointing out a school, a library, and supply shed, before they made their way down a wooded path.

"The living quarters are in the center of the compound," he said, pointing out the specific buildings. "It's best to protect them. The outer buildings pose another layer of protection in addition to the cloaks, which I'm sure you've seen."

To Ava's surprise, the houses were grouped much like a typical neighborhood, but instead of paved streets and sidewalks, the homes lined gravel drives wide enough for a single vehicle. As in New Elysia, she saw no cars; however, there were no garages either, now that she thought of it, only green lawns and covered porches before simple, single-story homes. They appeared to all be roughly the same, but alternating in floor plan—some with the porch to the left of the entry, some to the right. Like the outer buildings, the houses were arranged in a loose ring, and as they rounded a corner, a park appeared in the center of the compound. Ava could see a group of children laughing and climbing on some playground equipment.

"How many people live here?" she asked without thinking, wincing when she realized that Gideon would most likely be wary of sharing too much information with her.

To her surprise, he smiled as he answered, "It varies. We have about fifty families who live here permanently. The rest of the population is transient."

"You mean the Half-Breeds."

Gideon arched a brow. "We prefer not to use that term here, but yes."

Ava nodded. "They don't stay here?"

"Some do. Some choose to help us with the work we do here—help others like themselves. Others want our help to gain control over their abilities so they can go back to live among humans undetected."

"But how do you hide them from the Council?"

Gideon laughed a little and shook his head. "We may live out in the middle of the woods, but we are still Race," he said. "We have technology. We have our own gifts. And we're not the only Guardian Colony around."

Ava wanted to point out that he'd really not answered the question, but decided not to push it. They neared the park and Gideon led her to a bench in the shade of a large pine tree. She stuffed her hands into her coat pockets, but luckily, it wasn't too cold to enjoy the coming dusk. The laughter of children carried to her over the breeze, and for a moment Ava almost forgot that her life had become a gigantic mess over the past few days . . . weeks . . . *months*.

"So," Gideon said after a heavy inhale. "You and Caleb."

"Yeah."

"I heard about what happened before the Council," he said, amusement glinting in his eyes. "I would have liked to have seen Madeleine's face."

She half smiled. "I don't think I'm her favorite person."

Her fingers trailed unconsciously to her necklace, and Gideon's eyes followed the movement, his gaze lingering on the shimmering stones. "No, I imagine not." He chuckled to himself and looked out toward the trees on the opposite side of the park. "She doesn't like to be challenged." His voice sounded like a mixture of amusement and melancholy—almost wistfulness—and Ava couldn't resist the opportunity to find out more.

"You were married," she said.

"We were." He didn't look at her. "We are."

"Still?" Ava couldn't hide her surprise. "I'm sorry. I just assumed. With you here and her . . ." She waved a hand.

"Leader of everything I stand against?" Gideon said wryly, glancing at her sideways. "Yes, that does tend to put a damper on the relationship."

He bent over to pick a blade of grass at his feet and slumped back against the bench, tearing it idly. "Did Caleb ever tell you about how we bond? With our mate?"

Ava flushed. She was so not prepared to have this conversation with her boyfriend's father. "He told me a bit."

Gideon nodded, continuing to split the blade of grass into smaller and smaller strips. "It lasts for life, you know. It doesn't matter if you're together or not."

Ava thought of the void she felt when Caleb wasn't close by—the feeling that something was missing . . . something wrong. And he'd told her the closer they got, the stronger that bond would become.

"So you still feel . . ." She wasn't exactly sure what she was asking, but all of a sudden, she just had to know.

He winced, holding out his palm to let the shredded pieces of grass fall to the ground. "The connection doesn't lessen over time. Every moment is like she was just ripped from me. An emptiness that cannot be filled. And she feels the same."

Ava's heart sank. She could see the pain etched in the older man's features, the loss he couldn't hide when talking about Madeleine, and she could finally understand why Caleb had been so leery to deepen the bond between them. He'd seen what could happen when the bond wasn't enough.

"I'm sorry," she said, the words insufficient but all she could summon up. "Isn't there some way?"

He shrugged. "If there is, we haven't been able to find it. And it's been decades. Since Caleb was a little boy." He stood, shoving his hands in his pockets. "We're both committed to what we believe in. She thinks the Council needs to be the guiding force for the Race, obviously. I think the old ways need to be . . . amended. When I first left New Elysia to establish the Guardians, I'd visit now and then, on neutral territory, but it was really too difficult for both of us. Caleb, too. We agreed it would be best for him if I simply stayed away.

"I tried. But I've watched over him—checked in on him when I could. I was there when he finished school . . . when he was sworn in as a Protector. Watching from the sidelines. I knew Madeleine could tell—that she could feel me nearby—but she let me have those moments. I'll always be grateful for that.

"And after you—" The sadness in his eyes lifted as his lips lifted in a tiny smirk. “After your *encounter* with the Council, Caleb came to me. Well, he came to the Guardians, I should say. He didn’t really speak to me. But I had hoped in time we’d perhaps be able to reclaim some semblance of a relationship. And now . . .”

“Now he’s been brainwashed by Rogues.”

Gideon laughed humorlessly. “Which begs the question—why is he coming here? And why isn’t he here already?”

Ava stood, and the pair started to walk slowly around the perimeter of the park as the sun dipped below the tree line. “That’s a good question,” she said. “*We’ve* been following *him*, and he can shift, so there’s no way we could have passed him. You have any thoughts?”

“Only one thing makes sense,” Gideon replied, picking up a rock and tossing it aimlessly. “He was waiting for you to get here first.”

“But why?”

“That’s the million-dollar question.” Gideon turned to lead her out of the park and back toward the outer buildings. “I don’t have any answers, so I think the only thing we can do is be ready when he shows up.”

“Then Emma can fix him.”

Gideon seemed a bit uncomfortable with that, but he nodded anyway. “Then maybe Caleb can give us some answers,” he said.

The waiting was awful. Now that they had nowhere to go—nothing to do but *wait*—Ava felt like she was going crazy.

The night had been quiet, and fortunately, she’d been able to get a good night’s sleep—the first in a while. Still, she was up with the dawn, only to find Tiernan already outside, scenting the air and examining the ground around the edge of the Colony.

Apparently, he didn’t like waiting any more than Ava did.

“Anything?” she asked, her breath puffing into clouds in the frosty mountain air as she held out a cup of coffee.

“You tell me,” he said shortly.

“What are you talking about?”

He reached into his pocket and pulled out a cell phone. *Her* new cell phone.

“What are you doing with that?” She dropped the coffee and reached for it, but he held the phone away from her. “You had no right—”

“Why didn’t you tell me you’d spoken to Caleb? I thought you were all about sharing information and not keeping secrets. Or does that only extend to other people?”

Ava’s face heated. “I was going to tell you—” It was a lie, and Tiernan knew it.

He barked out a humorless laugh. “Right.” He threw the phone on the ground and smashed it with the heel of his boot. "I thought you trusted me," he said, face carved in a scowl.

Ava saw beyond the anger, though, to the hurt underneath. "I did. I do." When he stalked away, she trailed after him. "I should have told you. It's just that Caleb told me—"

"What?" Tiernan growled, turning on her. "What did your Caleb tell you? Not to tell me? To get *away* from me?" When she didn't meet his eyes, he laughed. "Don't you get it? He's a *Rogue*, Ava. You can try and excuse his actions all you want, but he's not here, is he? He left you to run away."

"Shut up."

"Ignoring the truth won't make it disappear."

"You think I don't know that?" she shouted. "You think I don't know something's wrong with him? I *know* it, Tiernan. I've known it for a while. I've *felt* it, and I ignored it, and maybe if I hadn't . . ." She turned away, wiping tears from her eyes. "I know I should have told you. I guess I hoped . . . I don't know what I hoped.

"But I *am* sorry," she said, glancing at him over her shoulder. "I'm really sorry."

Tiernan didn't say anything for a long moment, and then he exhaled heavily, rubbing a hand over his face. "It's not your fault."

"But maybe if I'd—"

"Ava, it's not your fault," he said more firmly. "This is all so new to you. There's no way you could have known what Emma did to Caleb. You couldn't have seen this coming."

"He said . . ." She cleared her throat, turning back to him. "He said I couldn't trust the Council. He said it's been 'keeping us down' for too long." She used air quotes, earning a smirk from Tiernan. "He denied that Emma did anything to him. Said he's fine. And he . . . he said I should stay away from the Colony."

Tiernan seemed surprised. "Why do you think he'd say that?"

"I don't know. Someone was coming so he had to hang up."

"Strange." Tiernan walked toward the tree line, thinking to himself. "Although anyone who knows you knows that telling you *not* to do something pretty much guarantees you're going to do it."

"Hey!"

"You can't deny it's true," he said with a halfhearted glower. "The fact you're standing here is proof."

Ava sighed. "I really am sorry."

Tiernan shrugged, and his discomfort with the emotion showed in every inch of his tense frame. "I know. It's okay."

Ava cleared her throat. "So . . . have you found anything?"

He shook his head, walking along the edge of the trees as she followed. "Nothing. Any word from Gideon?"

"I checked in with him before coming out. I think he might have been up all night. The cloaks haven't been disturbed, and there's no sign of anyone.

I know I don't feel anything." She reached out again with her gift, just to make sure, but the Caleb-shaped hole remained, untouched and jagged.

"I don't like it," Tiernan muttered, crouching as he examined a blade of grass. "None of this makes any kind of sense."

Ava said nothing, and trailed after the Protector as he continued to scan the perimeter. Her mind wandered to her discussion with Gideon and all that he had told her, and before she could think better of it, she asked, "You ever been in love, Tiernan?"

His frown deepened as he crushed a handful of dirt in his palm. He sniffed it before letting it fall to the ground, standing, and brushing his hand off on his jeans. "That's a weird question."

She shrugged. "It's just . . . Gideon told me last night about Madeleine."

"Ah." He nodded. "You want to know about the bond." He glanced at her briefly before turning back around to stare out through the trees. "Worried about your boy?"

"No," she said, lifting her chin as she crossed her arms almost out of reflex. Ava couldn't deny that she sounded like a two-year-old about to stomp her foot, and tried to cover her embarrassing curiosity best she could. "I was only wondering if it's like that for everyone."

"Well, most bonded pairs stay together. It's rare for them to separate, for obvious reasons."

"So, in all these years, no girl's gotten under your skin?" she asked, keeping her tone light and teasing. "Or are you waiting until you're older to settle down—like maybe when you're in your three hundreds?"

"Ha, ha," he grumbled. "The bond is no laughing matter. It can destroy as much as it strengthens."

Ava was taken aback at his tone. "I'm sorry. I didn't mean—"

"No, it's . . . it's fine." Tiernan took a deep breath and appeared to be considering his words carefully. "You've never asked about my scar."

Ava's step faltered. She was a little stunned by the change in topic. "I didn't think it was any of my business."

"Weren't you curious?" he asked. "Why I would have a scar when we heal so quickly?"

Unconsciously, Ava lifted her hand to her own scar on the back of her head. "Caleb told me . . . if a healer isn't skilled, and the wound is bad enough . . ." She felt sick and wished Tiernan had never brought the subject up. In fact, she wasn't sure how they'd even gotten on the subject.

"Yeah," Tiernan said, coming to a stop and gazing out into the forest. "Or if you won't let a healer near you."

Ava gasped. She'd almost gotten to the point where she didn't even notice Tiernan's scar, but now the jagged line running down his face shone white and angry against his flushed skin. "Why would you do that?" she asked.

"There was a woman," he said, jaw tight as he looked away. "We had a bond. She betrayed me."

"How is that even possible?" Ava couldn't stop herself from asking.

"The bond doesn't *change* you," he said tightly. "It doesn't affect what you *want*, your personality. Greed, corruption . . . a thirst for power. If they are ingrained deeply enough, not even the bond can overcome them."

Ava swallowed hard as a heavy feeling settling in her stomach. "She became a Rogue."

"She thought I could help her—use my connections with the Council somehow. I'm not even sure. When I refused . . ." He touched the scar, tracing his fingertips down the jagged skin and seemed lost in the memories. "She wanted to leave, but she couldn't. Because of the bond." His words were monotone—dull, lifeless. "She wasn't strong enough."

"She tried to kill you."

He blinked, turning away. "She tried. She failed."

"And the bond?"

"Broken."

Gideon's words came back to her. *"It lasts for life, you know. It doesn't matter if you're together or not."*

She could guess how the bond had been broken, and she didn't want to make him say it. "I'm sorry," she said instead.

"It doesn't matter anymore. It was a long time ago." He shook off his melancholy and started back toward the Colony buildings, Ava hurrying to catch up to him. "I only told you so you know what you're dealing with. The bond is a two-sided coin. It's not something to rush into." Tiernan bent to pick up a rock and threw it into the forest, where it lodged in the trunk of a tree.

She raised a brow. "Yeah. I'm beginning to see that." When Tiernan ignored her comment, she opted to change the subject, eyeing the rock still embedded in the tree. She thought about picking up her own rock but knew it would just bounce off. "It's still so frustrating to me, you know. The whole strength and speed thing."

Tiernan, for some unknown reason, seemed to be able to follow her train of thought. "Maybe you need to focus more."

"That's what Caleb says," she replied. "But I've tried, and it doesn't seem to help at all. You don't have to focus, do you?"

Tiernan grunted noncommittally, but when they reached the center building, he led Ava around the side.

"Where are you going?" she asked.

"Found it earlier this morning," he replied when they came to a high fence with a padlock hanging open on the gate. "Think it's just what the doctor ordered." He shot her a half grin as he swung open the gate, and extending a hand along with a slight bow, he gestured for her to precede him through.

She rolled her eyes a bit, but curiosity won out, and she walked into a large fenced area about the size of a football field, with a full track running around the perimeter of the grassy expanse. One side of the field looked to be laid out as some kind of obstacle course, with zigzagging barbed wire, a swinging rope over a big muddy puddle, several wooden platforms, and a high wall at the far end.

He led her to the other end of the field, littered with colored cones, some large black balls, and metal boxes in various sizes. Tiernan approached one about four feet square and slapped a palm on top, the sound echoing around them. "Let's start with something simple," he said.

"This isn't going to work," Ava all but whined. "Caleb's been trying for months—"

"I'm not Caleb," he snapped. "Now, no more excuses. Come over here and put your shoulder to it . . . unless you'd like to start with running," He indicated the track with a flick of his eyes, and Ava winced. She wasn't much of a runner, and keeping up with Tiernan was sure to be an exercise in frustration.

"Okay." She relented, but not altogether graciously, and stalked over to the box, fighting down her negative attitude with every step. The fact that Tiernan actually wanted to help her was incredible, to say the least, and she wasn't going to let the opportunity go to waste.

Or he could have been as antsy as she was waiting for something—*anything*—to happen, and was looking for a distraction. Not that she could blame him.

With a doubtful glance at the box, she took a deep breath and squared her shoulders. "What do you want me to do?"

"Try again." Tiernan ignored a twinge of compassion at Ava's sweat-dampened hair and red face.

Her breath puffed out with exertion, teeth clenched as she shoved her shoulder against the weight block.

Again.

They'd been at it for about an hour, and the girl still showed no sign of accessing her Race strength. If she had any to begin with, and Tiernan was seriously beginning to doubt she did.

Ava grunted, and he could tell she was pushing against the block with all her might. He knew it wouldn't be easy. The block was thick-walled steel, and even though he'd moved to a smaller one when it became obvious Ava couldn't move the larger one, it still weighed close to five hundred pounds.

He'd tried everything—leading her through meditation techniques, hard-core drill-sergeant tactics, even encouraging her, as much as it went against every fiber of his being. He was about out of ideas.

"Maybe you're just . . ." Tiernan winced slightly. "Not very strong."

She scowled at him, turned around, and pushed her back against the block, feet digging into the ground. "You think?" She turned back around, shoving it—or *failing* to shove it—with her hands again. "I don't know why I even worry about it. It's not like I need it. I can just use my gift."

"You can't always rely on that," Tiernan said, reminding her of the reality of the situation. "There are dampeners out there—and people like Emma, who can mess with your mind, despite your gift. You need every weapon at your disposal if it comes to that."

Ava grunted, obviously annoyed, but she kept pushing, so Tiernan took that as a win. It didn't make any sense, though. Ava was Race. She should be able to do it. Perhaps she only needed a good incentive.

"Come on, Ava," he said, forcing a note of cheer into his voice. "If you move it an inch, I'll give you a . . ." He searched his mind, at a loss at what to offer. "Cookie?"

Ava slumped against the metal block, and she seemed unable to hold back a laugh. "A cookie? Seriously?"

Tiernan wasn't sure why he said that, but he wasn't backing down now. "I like cookies," he said, trying not to sound defensive.

Cookies are good. Cookies are tasty. Nothing wrong with a good cookie.

"No offense, big guy," she said, straightening and patting his chest—a little condescendingly, he might add. "But cookies aren't gonna do it."

"Yeah?" Tiernan considered her carefully as another idea came to mind. He rounded the block to the side opposite Ava. "Maybe you just need the right motivation." Without warning, he shoved the block toward her a few inches, and Ava stumbled back in surprise.

"Hey!" She regained her footing and glared at him. "You almost smashed my foot."

"Maybe you should push back, then." He nudged it forward a bit more, trying not to grin.

Ava narrowed her eyes and put her shoulder to the block, her jaw tight with determination.

"Come on!" Tiernan taunted her. "Put your back into it!" He pushed lightly at the block—enough to keep Ava on her toes. "Don't think so much. Let your muscles do the work. They know what to do."

"I really don't think they do," Ava said, punctuating each word with a pained grunt. "I think my muscles are pretty clueless, to be honest."

"Don't be such a wimp."

"Shut up!"

"Shut up?" Tiernan shoved the block a little more. "I think *you* better shut up. Put all that energy somewhere useful." Maybe if he could get her to forget about everything for a moment, her innate nature—the Race blood rushing through her veins—would take over.

Ava had her eyes shut, her brow furrowed, and her muscles strained to move the block. Tension radiated from her body, and he knew she was giving it all she had.

Maybe just a little bit more . . .

"Good thing Caleb will be back soon. Looks like you *need* someone to protect you."

Before he knew what was happening, Tiernan found himself on his back with the weighted block on his chest. He gasped, confused for a moment that he could breathe at all. In fact, the block wasn't exactly lying on his chest. Instead, it hovered about an inch above him, and when he pushed at it, it didn't move.

Ava's smug face appeared over him. "Now who needs protection?" she asked with a smirk.

"That's not fair," he protested.

Laughter drifted to Tiernan in his rather humiliating prison, and he realized they were no longer alone. He shoved at the block again and glared at Ava. "Get it off me."

She hesitated, and he thought for a moment she was going to make him say *please*. With a challenging arch of her brow, she turned her attention back to the block, and it flipped to Tiernan's side, where it landed in the grass with a quiet thunk.

He rolled to his feet and found Audrey and Gideon approaching them, amused grins on their faces.

"Looks like you've met your match," Gideon said to Tiernan.

"She cheated."

"Cheated, schmeated," Ava retorted. "I used what I have at my disposal."

"It's astounding," Audrey said. "You've come so far in such a short amount of time."

"Your telekinetic power is impressive." Gideon nodded at Ava, and her irritation seemed to lighten a bit. "I don't know if I've seen many with that kind of control."

"Have you seen a lot?" Ava asked.

"In my line of work, I've seen it all." He turned to lead them back to the main building, Ava on one side, Audrey on the other.

Tiernan followed behind, listening carefully. Perhaps nursing his ego a bit.

"I'm able to detect gifts in others," Gideon told her.

"Like a sensor?" Ava glanced back at Tiernan.

Gideon shook his head, but it was Audrey who answered.

"A sensor can detect Race," she said, clarifying the difference. "In some cases, track them using their electrical imprint. Gideon's gift is different." She tipped her head to him, inviting him to explain.

"I'm able to sense a particular gift within an individual. Your telekinesis, for example. And your Race intuition, your instincts, they're particularly strong." Gideon stopped, gnawing on his lip as he studied Ava, his eyes narrowed. "There's something more, though. It's strange. I can usually see it so clearly, but it's like there's something . . . *hidden,* something . . ." He shook his head as if to clear it. "Whatever it is, it'll have to wait. I have news."

Tiernan stiffened. "News about what? Has Foster been spotted?"

"Not yet," Gideon replied. "But I may have an idea what the Rogues are up to."

Chapter 11

Ava's heart pounded as they gathered around the conference room table, and Gideon excused everyone else with a nod of his head. Once they were alone, he leaned his elbows on the table and scrubbed his hands over his face. He looked tired. He looked *worried.*

"What is it?" Ava asked.

He exhaled heavily. "We've been hearing rumors for months—nothing concrete, nothing specific—that something is going on with the Rogues."

"Something?" Tiernan sat rigid at Ava's side, his hands curling into fists.

"The word *conspiracy* is being thrown around." Gideon turned to Ava. "I know you're new to all of this, but Rogues don't usually act in groups. They're solitary creatures, living for their own pleasure and usually eliminating anyone who gets in their way."

"Caleb told me," Ava replied, her blood chilling as she remembered her time in the Rogue lair. "Even the Council couldn't figure out why so many of them would join together to take me."

"Not to mention track you since you were a child," Tiernan said, pointing out exactly how long she had been on everyone's radar.

"Really?" Gideon's eyes widened. "I wasn't aware of that."

Ava sighed. She didn't like thinking about Arthur's betrayal for a lot of reasons. Still, she couldn't deny that it could help them figure out what was going on, so she told Gideon all about it—how he'd been her neighbor, her best friend, how he'd apparently been watching her all of her life and was the one who lured her to her own kidnapping.

"And he said you were one of them," Gideon mused, rubbing at his lips, deep in thought.

Ava felt tired all of a sudden. "He kept rambling about having a higher purpose . . . about me having some kind of destiny to help the cause."

"The cause?"

"That's what he said. It was all a lot of crazy talk, to be honest," Ava said with a sigh. "He even called himself a revolutionary."

"Well, that fits with what I've been hearing, actually." Gideon stood and began to pace behind his chair. "Our contacts have been talking about Rogues joining together, although nobody could really figure out why. But what you're telling me, combined with what I just heard . . ." He sat back down, his palms flat on the table.

"I have a source close to the Council," he said, his gaze darting between them. "And from what I've heard, it's possible that the Rogues have plans to make a move on the Council. My contact says they fear a coup." He focused his penetrating stare on Ava. "They're particularly interested in getting you back to New Elysia."

"No way." Ava laughed. "They know that's not going to happen."

"You may not have a choice."

Ava turned on Tiernan, hiding her uneasiness with an icy stare. "Did you know about this?"

"It's no secret the Council wants you," he said, refusing to meet her eyes.

"But do they plan to try and force me?"

His jaw twitched, and he looked down at his hands.

"Tiernan?" Ava felt the familiar twist of betrayal, still so tender after Arthur. "Tell me."

"I don't know the Council's plans!" He shoved away from the table, and the chair screeched as it scraped the floor. "I get my orders. I do my job. At least I did until I crossed paths with you! Now, apparently, I disregard orders and do what I want and hide things from the Council and—"

"Sir!" A man appeared at the doorway and approached Gideon with long strides. "We have a breach of the outer cloak."

Gideon shot to his feet. "Is it him?"

But Ava already knew. She felt the twinge along the edges of the Caleb-shaped hole inside her—her gift reaching out to his, even at a distance. Not quite like slipping a missing puzzle piece into place, but more fumbling with it a bit, trying to line it up just right.

"It's him," she said in a frightened whisper.

Even Caleb had to admit the cloaks were impressive, and he'd seen a lot of cloaks. The animals, so realistic, the bridge—he'd almost fallen for that one the first time he'd visited the Colony, and if he hadn't been told it was a trick, he probably would have tried to find an alternate route.

They're close now. So close.

He could feel himself draw nearer to Ava with every step, the void within him filling slowly, like glittering sand dribbling grain by grain into his soul. It had been difficult—more difficult than he'd imagined, even given his particular knowledge of the bond—to be away from her. He'd thought that keeping his distance, at least initially, would have kept it from forming quite so tightly, wrapping its greedy fingers around his heart, but he'd been wrong. And he could only imagine what it would be like once they were truly joined. In his most honest moments, it was a thought that both exhilarated and terrified him in equal measure.

"Foster! Get your head in the game!" Bartok snapped.

He was a few feet off to Caleb's right, slipping silently through the trees. The guy did everything silently—invisibly—which was what Caleb assumed made him as good at his job as he was. Well, that and a general lack of anything resembling a conscience.

Caleb nodded curtly and shifted farther up the trail, scouting ahead for more cloaks or any other hazards. "All clear," he whispered, knowing they could hear him, before shifting forward again in the leapfrog pattern they'd perfected on their journey north.

Caleb was impatient. He couldn't wait to get to the Colony . . . to get to Ava, and for this whole thing to be over and done with. He'd left a trail as Bartok had ordered and doubled back, where they'd dallied in a seedy motel at the border for far too long, in Caleb's opinion. Bartok wouldn't tell him what they were waiting for, only that they'd get the go-ahead when the time was right. Apparently, now was the time.

He shifted again and could just make out the familiar rooftops of a group of metal buildings through the trees, maybe a hundred feet ahead. He froze at the sound of voices and shuffling feet stumbling through the underbrush and quickly shifted back to his group.

"They've spotted us," he said in a warning whisper. "They're coming."

Bartok nodded. "We knew this would happen. We're ready. Spread out, everyone!"

As they'd practiced, they formed a wide line and proceeded through the trees, Bartok to Caleb's right, Christopher, the pyrokinetic, to his left, and everyone else scattered through the trees. Caleb walked with them instead of shifting, keeping the formation.

"Diversion." Bartok said to the man at his right, and in a few minutes, Caleb heard a loud crash somewhere in the distance.

They stopped, listening intently.

At the sound of shouts and pounding feet, Bartok grinned. "That should give us time to get past the perimeter," he said.

"Then what?" Caleb asked, although he knew.

"Then we fight."

"But not Ava." He'd lost count of how many times he'd said those words since the whole thing started. "Ava's not to be hurt."

"Well, that would kind of defeat the purpose of all this," Bartok said with a roll of his eyes. "Your girlfriend will be fine. We're not here to hurt anyone. We'll grab her and the scrambler and be on our way."

The brain scrambler. Bartok's not-so-flattering nickname for Emma Reiko.

Caleb felt a flash of uneasiness at his words. Emma was so young. But no. There was a reason for all of this. A greater purpose. Their future was at stake. The Council must be stopped.

Caleb switched the gun he was holding into his left hand so he could wipe his sweaty palm on his jeans. Taking a firmer grip, he followed Bartok to the edge of the perimeter. They stopped in the shadow of the trees, peering into the cluster of buildings, and Bartok gave the order to advance with a jerk of his head.

It was all he needed. They'd gone over the plan time and time again.

Find the girls. Get them out. Do what you must to the others.

With a shout, Caleb joined the others as they launched an attack on the Guardians.

It all happened so fast.

Ava followed Gideon as he ran to the control room, where they monitored the cloaks as well as more conventional security cameras and sensors. The room was abuzz with activity, save for a man and woman—siblings or possibly twins, if their matching blond hair, pale skin, and patrician noses were any indication—who sat off to the side, their eyes closed as Gideon demanded information in a quiet, but firm voice. Apparently, they were the organic portion of the cloak or perhaps more sensors.

"How many?" Gideon asked.

"At least a dozen," the man replied. "They have a blank, so it's difficult to tell for certain."

"And Caleb?"

The woman shook her head, a hint of frustration cutting through her calm veneer. "I can't be sure."

"This is a waste of time." Ava grabbed Gideon's sleeve. "I can feel him coming. He'll be here any second."

Gideon faltered for a moment, his eyes flitting to the cameras before nodding abruptly at Ava and following her outside.

Tiernan stopped once they'd hit the open air and tilted his head back to scent his surroundings. "That way," he said, pointing to the southeast.

They started in that direction, but a loud crash—or maybe some kind of explosion—had them stopping in their tracks, and as one, Gideon's men started in the opposite direction.

"No!" Ava shouted. "No, not that way!"

They hesitated, looking to Gideon for guidance.

"It's a diversion," she said, willing him to believe her. "I can feel it."

Gideon's eyes narrowed as he studied her for a quick moment.

She could feel a flicker of . . . something and realized he was somehow reaching out to touch her gift, to see if she *knew*, or was being swayed by wishful thinking.

Abruptly, he turned to Tyra. "Take half the men and see what that was," he told his second-in-command, dismissing her with a nod. "The rest of you, spread out. Take up your assigned positions. The civilians are to be protected at all costs."

He spat orders as they strode to the southeast, and Gideon's soldiers peeled off to take up defensive positions around the Colony.

Emma appeared at Ava's side, wide-eyed and frantic. "What's happening?"

"Caleb's coming," Ava whispered, "and he's not alone."

She'd been waiting for this moment for so long, but now found she almost dreaded it. The fact that Caleb had been manipulated, that he wasn't *him*—not really, not anymore—frightened her, if she were to be honest. "You're really sure you can fix this?" she asked Emma, a touch of panic seeping into her words. "Put him back the way he was?"

The girl reached for her wrist, her fingers locking around it tightly as she looked intently into Ava's eyes. "I can. I promise."

Ava's anxiety quieted, but in the next moment, the snapping sound of gunfire had her moving on instinct. She swept Emma behind her as they ducked around the corner of a storage shed. "Stay down," she said.

"But I can help."

"No," Ava said firmly. "You need to stay safe. We can't risk losing you. Can you mess with the Rogues from here?"

Emma clung to her wrist, nodding against Ava's back. "Yeah. I can help."

Tiernan and Gideon were ahead of them, hiding behind some trees as they waited for the Rogues to appear.

Ava breathed deeply, willing her heart to slow and reaching out to feel Caleb's approach. The puzzle piece adjusted, twisting as it aimed for the empty spot.

A man burst from the tree line, brandishing a rifle, with a second man carrying two handguns close behind him.

Instinctively, Ava swept the guns from their hands and threw them back into the forest.

Tiernan glared at her. "Leave some for the rest of us."

She shrugged, fighting a hysterical giggle. Then all hell broke loose.

A fireball burst from the forest, smashing into the trees over Gideon and Tiernan and forcing them to dive for cover. Tiernan rolled to the side, yanking a gun from beneath his coat and firing into the forest. Ava noticed he shot into the air, more as a warning than anything else, and knew he was waiting until they laid eyes on Caleb before he truly started to fight.

Another fireball flashed through the air, and the Rogues attacked, descending on them in a smattering of gunfire. Ava held her breath, overwhelmed for a moment by the cacophony of shouts and blur of bodies moving at Race speed, unable to focus on where to aim her own gift. Someone, however, didn't have the same problem, for after only a few seconds, a handful of Rogues let out pained shouts, their guns falling to the dirt and sending up wafts of steam where they hit the damp grass.

"What happened?" Emma poked her head around the corner, eyes widening in awe. "Looks like the Guardians have a thermo." At Ava's confused glance, she tried to quickly explain. "Thermal manipulator—someone who can heat or cool things by messing with the atoms."

"Of course," Ava said, stunned. She shouldn't have been, really. This was her life now.

With most of the weapons out of the mix, she'd thought the Guardians could dominate easily, but apparently the Rogues had a few tricks up their sleeves as well. In seconds, Guardian weapons were flying into the forest, and the hand-to-hand combat began.

A Rogue charged at Tiernan, but he stopped suddenly and lay down on the ground as if he was going to take a nap. Emma giggled when Tiernan gaped at him in surprise for a second before knocking him out.

Ava barely noticed. She scanned the tree line as her fingers clung to the corner of the building, feeling Caleb nearby . . . almost there. Her gift flared, excited at his proximity but confused why he was still so far away.

And then he wasn't.

One moment, Ava turned her attention to a Rogue, throwing him off Tiernan's back—without so much as a thank you from the Protector, she begrudgingly noted—and the next she whirled around to see Caleb appearing a dozen feet before her, breathing heavily from repeated shifts, but whole and healthy and looking exactly as he should.

Not as if he was under some strange mind control. Not as if he was a Rogue puppet.

Just Caleb.

Perhaps a little thinner than usual, a little more tired, with dark smudges staining the skin below his eyes—no glasses, she noted absently, and no contacts, his eyes the same mismatched blue and green as Tiernan's. Caleb's shoulders seemed stooped a bit more than normal, breath rasping in and out as his gaze searched the surrounding bodies. He didn't spot her at first, tension radiating from his clutched fists as he shouted her name.

She stepped out from behind the building, wrenching her wrist free of Emma's tight grip. She ignored Tiernan's shouted warning as the sounds of fighting—fists slamming into flesh, bodies hurled into buildings or each other— dulled to a low roar under the blood rushing in her ears.

Caleb whirled around, his blue-green gaze locking on hers as his mouth dropped open on her name. His eyes fluttered closed briefly as relief swept through his tall frame, and he started toward her, heedless of the battle around him.

Ava's gift propelled her forward, impatient, and like the heroine in some old black-and-white movie, she ran into his arms. He held her close, his warmth seeping into her bones as he breathed in her scent. And just like that, the puzzle piece slipped into place—the gaping hole inside her filled to overflowing, and her gift seemed to sigh in satisfaction.

"Are you all right?" Caleb whispered into her hair.

She nodded frantically, clutching at his back.

He pulled away. "We've got to get out of here," he said, taking her hand in his and pulling her into the cover of some trees as the fighting continued around them. "Where's Emma?"

"What?" Ava still felt a bit disoriented, almost drugged, by having him so near. She reached up, sliding her palm over his shoulder and up the back of his neck, her fingers slipping into his hair.

"Emma." He turned back to her, taking her face in his hands. "Focus, Ava. We need to get Emma and get out of here. I can't shift again. Something's blocking me."

"Adam," she said slowly, her mind racing to catch up with what was happening. "He's a dampener."

Caleb cursed under his breath. "We'll have to make a run for it, but we need to get Emma first."

"No." Her voice was weak . . . wavering, but she shook her head, trying to gain her footing again. "No. Caleb, Emma is safe. The Guardians won't hurt her."

"You don't understand," he said distractedly, watching the fighting and searching for the girl. "You and Emma are important. You're part of the plan. We need to get you—"

"Plan?" Ava's stomach churned, her palms sweating as she remembered what Emma had told her.

"They had me change Caleb."

She'd thought she understood, but she'd denied the truth this whole time. "What plan, Caleb?"

He huffed in frustration, fingers clutching his dark hair. "We don't have time for this!"

"What plan, Caleb?" She reached for his arm but hesitated. Her heart ached at that hesitation.

"The plan, Ava," he said, turning wide, urgent eyes on hers. "The Council has had too much power for far too long . . ."

"They needed him to work with them—to forget his loyalty to the Council."

"They think they own us. They think they can keep us down . . . make us all but slaves to the humans . . . keeping down our own kind, for God's sake . . ."

"So I had to instill doubt in him. Make him doubt the Council, the Law—his purpose as a Protector. Open his mind to the possibility of something different."

"But we're the ones with the power, don't you see?" He gripped her shoulders, pleading with her to understand. "The Council has let the humans all but destroy this world. It's our time. It's our turn. We can fix this!"

"Caleb, no . . ." Ava's voice cracked.

He didn't seem to hear her, instead turning away to scan the area again. "But you and Emma are part of it. We need you both."

"We?" She grabbed at his arm, desperation snaking through her. "They're *Rogues,* Caleb. You said it yourself; they destroy whoever gets in their way!"

"Sometimes sacrifice is necessary," he said, brow furrowed as if he was concentrating, pulling the words from deep within him. "None of us likes it, but sometimes it can't be helped."

Ava's skin chilled. In that moment, she truly understood what Emma had done to Caleb. What the Rogues had done to him. With tears sparkling in her eyes, she reached for her gift.

Caleb examined her face and his own softened. "We can talk about this later. You'll understand . . ."

Ava could only shake her head and whisper, "No."

Her gift drifted out to wrap Caleb in tentacles of restraint. It took him a moment to realize, to struggle. "Ava? What are you doing?"

Gideon appeared in her peripheral vision . . . Tiernan . . . there was Emma. Ava absently noted the fighting was over, but couldn't find it in herself to care. They watched, frozen in place, as she bound Caleb tightly, lifting his body so his toes barely scraped the ground. Adam stood off to the side, and she spared a moment to wonder how he blocked Caleb and not her. How he picked and chose where to target his gift. Odd the things you focus on when you're breaking someone's trust.

"Ava?" Caleb's eyes were wide . . . betrayed.

"I'm sorry." Tears streamed down her face, blurring her vision.

A hand on her shoulder startled her, and her gift lashed out, shoving Tiernan back roughly. He staggered, but came toward her again, not touching her this time.

"Ava," he said, his voice soft and soothing as she hadn't heard it before. "You can let him go. We'll take him."

With a choked sob, she nodded, pulling back until Caleb slumped, held upright by his father.

He didn't even seem to notice; his shocked gaze was still focused on Ava. "How could you?"

"I'm sorry!" she cried, reaching for him and then letting her arms fall to her sides, empty. "They're going to help you. They're going to fix you."

"Fix me?" Caleb shouted. "I'm not broken, Ava! What have you done?"

She felt a thick arm encircle her shoulders and allowed herself to be pulled into Tiernan's broad chest.

"Oh, is that how it is?" Caleb's bitter voice cut through her quiet sobs. "Tiernan, Ava? Really?"

"He doesn't mean it," Tiernan said quietly. "It's going to be okay."

"You let him touch you now?" Caleb shouted as Gideon led him away. "Is that what you want?"

And in that moment, she did. She curled into the heat of Tiernan's solid bulk and gave into her tears.

Caleb knew it was of no use to struggle. He couldn't shift, and he was surrounded by Guardians, including his own father, the worthless bastard. He grimaced as he spotted the group of Rogues, including Bartok, on their knees in the middle of a patch of grass, surrounded by armed Guardians, and the man he assumed was Adam, the dampener. He absently wondered about the man's range—if he could continue to block Caleb when he got far enough away from the rest of the group. Such hopes were dashed, however, when Gideon simply stopped, watching as Emma Reiko walked into the midst of the Rogues, closed her eyes, and took a deep breath.

After a while, she smiled with satisfaction, and wound her way back to Gideon. "I've removed the memories of how they got here—everything about the Colony," she said. "Your men can take them back to Ontario. They'll be kind of out of it for a while."

"You're not going to kill them?" Caleb asked in disbelief as he glared at his father and struggled to shake off the Guardian hands holding him captive.

"We're not animals," Gideon said calmly. "And we don't have the facilities to hold them long-term. We only want to be left in peace." The Guardian leader turned back to Emma. "What about Caleb?"

Caleb froze. "What about me?"

"I'll need somewhere quiet," Emma replied, ignoring Caleb's outburst. "He's a bit more complicated." She glanced over to where Ava stood talking quietly to Tiernan. "Is Ava all right?"

"I think she'll be fine once Caleb's back to normal."

Caleb glared at his father. "Stop talking about me like I'm not here."

"You're not," Gideon said gently. "At least not entirely."

"What's that supposed to mean?" A wave of fury swept through him, along with a niggling uneasiness he couldn't quite put a finger on.

"Your mind has been tampered with."

Caleb flashed a glance at Emma.

"Yes," Gideon said, maintaining a calm and even tone. "The Rogues had Emma alter your thoughts."

"That's ridiculous." Caleb knew he was fine. There was no way anyone had messed with his mind. "I've just seen through the lies of the Council."

"Think about it, Caleb." Emma stepped before him, looking deeply in his eyes. "You've never felt that way before."

Caleb felt her reaching into him, invading his mind, and he stepped back abruptly to break the contact. "Stop that."

"I think you'll have to restrain him," Emma told Gideon as they turned to go into a large metal building, one of the Guardians holding tightly to Caleb's elbow. "It looks like he's going to fight me on this."

"Damn right," Caleb said through gritted teeth.

Yet, something was off about all of it. He'd known his mission when they'd arrived at the Colony. Get Ava and the girl and fall back to regroup. Evade the Guardians. Wait for further orders to be relayed through Bartok.

Orders . . . from *who? Why?*

Why did they need Emma and Ava? The question sent a stab of pain through his head, and Caleb fell to his knees, clutching at his scalp.

"What's happening?" he heard Gideon ask. "What's wrong with him?"

"I'm not sure. Get him in here and on the table."

Strong arms lifted him, dragging him along down a dark hallway and into a brightly lit room. The pain in his skull ebbed to a dull throb, and he blinked in surprise to find himself looking up at the ceiling.

"Where's Ava?" he rasped.

"Hold him down," Emma said, her voice gruff and businesslike. "This might hurt, and he's not going to like it."

Something heavy bracketed Caleb's chest and held his limbs immobile. He struggled, unable to move an inch, and squeezed his eyes shut. Slender fingers pried them open, Emma's mismatched eyes appearing inches away from him. They almost matched, actually, the pupils blown so wide that only a thin circle of pale green differentiated one from the other.

"Try and relax," Emma said, her cool palms framing his face.

He felt her prod at his mind, and in a flash of white-hot pain, Caleb screamed.

Chapter 12

Ava could hear Caleb's agonized bellows from where she stood with Tiernan, wringing her hands and overcome with guilt.

Sure, she knew it was useless. She knew it was unwarranted. She'd done what she had to do to help Caleb. Still, she couldn't help how she felt. The look of betrayal in his eyes had cut her deeply, and she knew it was something that would haunt her for a long time to come. She could feel Caleb fighting against whatever Emma was doing to him, and her gift longed to reach out and help—to fight off whatever was hurting him.

"He'll be fine," Tiernan told her, trying to assure her again.

Ava wasn't convinced, but she nodded just the same. She wanted to believe it—*needed* to believe it.

Finally, the screams stopped, the last of them echoing through the treetops before fading away into silence. Ava could feel Caleb calm, and with a choked gasp, she ran toward the building, Tiernan on her heels.

She sped through the hallway and jerked to a stop when Emma and Gideon emerged from a room and closed the door behind them. Gideon looked up at her approach and held up a hand.

"He's asleep," he told her. "We gave him some R-cubes, but he really needs the rest, I think. It took a lot out of him."

"But he's . . . is he . . ."

Is he fixed? Is he him? Is he Caleb?

"He's fine."

Emma was trying to assure her, but Ava turned to Gideon for confirmation. She still couldn't shake the lingering tendrils of anger that Emma had done this to Caleb in the first place, no matter how undeserved that anger was.

"He's back to normal," Gideon said. "As far as I can tell, all the effects have been removed. He also remembers everything about his time with the Rogues, which should prove useful. He wanted to tell us everything, but he's so exhausted." He glanced back at the door, pride on his face. "Brave kid."

It took a moment for his words to register with Ava, and when they did, the rush of adrenaline drained out of her, and she slumped against the wall in relief. "So he's all right."

"He's all right." Gideon reached out to lay a hand on her shoulder. "He kept asking for you."

Ava blinked back tears.

Perhaps he'd forgive her. Perhaps he'd understand.

"Can I see him? Can I . . . I'd like to stay with him." Now that he was back, she couldn't bear the thought of being away from him. Even if he was sleeping.

Gideon seemed to understand. "I'll check on you later," he said before heading down the hall to the control room.

Tiernan eyed her carefully. "You okay?"

"Yeah. Yeah, sure." She nodded briskly, brushing away her tears. "I'm fine now."

He cleared his throat, jerking a thumb over his shoulder. "Then I guess I'll . . . go . . . debrief or something."

Ava fought a smile. "Yeah. Go and loom and grunt with Gideon."

To his credit, Tiernan just rolled his eyes and walked away.

Emma, however, reached out to take her hand. "Come on," she said gently, reaching for the doorknob. "See for yourself. He's going to be fine."

She let Emma lead her into the room, only letting out a breath when she saw Caleb lying peacefully on a small bed against the wall.

Caleb slept deeply, his chest rising and falling under a thin blanket. Unable to resist touching him any longer, Ava left Emma standing at the door and rushed to his side. She brushed the hair away from his forehead, and he shifted into the touch, a pleased sigh slipping from his lips. Her gift settled within her, finally calm and quiet.

"I can do the same for you," Emma said, startling Ava slightly. She hadn't realized the girl had moved to stand next to her.

"What do you mean?" Ava whispered.

Caleb let out a quiet sound, his head rolling on the pillow, and Emma pressed a finger to her lips and indicated the door with a tilt of her head.

Ava nodded, touching Caleb's cheek lightly before following the girl to the other side of the room.

"I know you're having trouble with your gifts," Emma said. "And I'd like to help you." She glanced at Caleb. "Now's not the time, of course, but when you're ready, let me know."

"You really think you can lift the rest of the block?" Ava asked. "How would that even work?"

"I'll explain it all later. But for now, Caleb needs you." She smiled. "And I can see that you need him, too." With that, she stepped out of the room and closed the door behind her.

Ava blinked in confusion, a little scared about Emma's proposal but intrigued, nonetheless. Caleb let out a quiet whimper and she hurried to his side as his eyes fluttered open.

"Ava?"

"I'm here."

"I'm . . . what happened?" he mumbled, his voice thick with sleep.

"Shhh . . ." she whispered, her fingers smoothing lightly over his forehead. "Just rest for now."

He settled, and she moved toward the padded chair next to the bed, but Caleb reached for her, his hand flailing until it rested on hers. "Don't go."

He tugged on her hand, and she smiled, kicking off her shoes. She slid into the bed next to him, fully clothed, and rested her head on his chest, his strong heartbeat reassuring her that he really was going to be all right.

"I'm not going anywhere," she whispered as she curled up against him and joined him in sleep.

The sun had shifted low in the sky when Ava opened her eyes again. She had no idea how long they'd been asleep, but daylight had melted into dusk, so it had been at least a few hours. Caleb was a warm, firm presence half under her, one arm wrapped around her waist, the other thrown over his head on the pillow. She fought the urge to stretch luxuriantly and instead attempted to slip out of the bed without disturbing Caleb. His arm tightened around her, though, halting the movement.

"Where are you going?" he rasped, although his eyes remained shut.

She felt suddenly self-conscious, nervous after all that had happened. "You're awake."

"Sort of," he said, his lips quirking. "My head feels like somebody took a jackhammer to it."

Ava reached for the jar of R-cubes on a side table and touched one to his lips. "Well, that'll happen when someone goes picking around in your brain."

He opened his mouth for the cube and chewed and swallowed quickly before he took a deep breath and finally opened his eyes. "Remind me never to do that again."

Silence thickened in the air as Ava searched for the right words. "About before—"

"Listen—" Caleb said at the same time.

"I didn't mean—"

"No, it was my fault." Caleb rolled to his side, leaning on his elbow over her. "I hate what I did. What I said to you—"

"That wasn't you." Ava reached out tentatively to touch his face. "I'm sorry for hurting you. Using my gift against you."

"Hey." He ran his fingers lightly over her lips and leaned in to kiss her softly. "You have nothing to apologize for. You did what you had to do."

Despite it all, Ava couldn't hold back a snicker. "So, essentially, we're both sorry, but neither one of us should be."

Caleb smirked. "Sounds about right."

Ava sobered, laying her hand against his cheek.

He sighed, leaning into her touch, and her gift flared, mingling with his in quiet contentment.

"I'm so glad you're back," she said.

"Me, too."

They lay there for a moment, indulging in the peace and quiet, and Caleb let out a heavy breath.

"As much as I'd like to hole up in this room with you for about a month, I think I should go talk to Gideon." His jaw tensed under her hand at the mention of his father.

"Are you sure you're ready for that?" she asked. "You've been through a lot."

He sat up, flipping back the covers. "I think he needs to know what the Rogues are up to. And there are things you should know as well."

"Me?"

"This is bigger than we thought, Ava."

"Gideon said the Council suspects a conspiracy."

"He knows?" Caleb's eyes widened in surprise.

"Not for sure," she replied. "But I take it he's not far off?" A knock at the door kept Ava from pursuing the issue, and Caleb waited for her to get out of bed before answering it.

"Good, you're awake," Tiernan filled the doorframe with his massive bulk, glancing at Ava before turning his attention back to Caleb. "Gideon wants a debriefing, if you feel up to it."

"Yeah . . . yeah, okay." Caleb rubbed the back of his neck idly, walked over to grab his shoes, and settled in the chair next to the bed to put them on.

Ava slipped into her own, ran her fingers through her hair, and secured it into a ponytail before taking Caleb's offered hand.

"Ready?" he asked.

"As I'll ever be."

They walked down the hall behind Tiernan, and Caleb spoke to her in a low voice. "I learned things about you—about your background. I'm not sure if you want Gideon to know."

She watched Tiernan's broad back. He kept up his steady pace, showing no sign he was listening, though Ava knew he could hear them. "Is it bad?" she asked.

"No. I just . . ." He glanced at Tiernan and stopped, letting the man get a few feet ahead of him. "I don't know that I trust Gideon."

"He's your father." Ava couldn't keep the surprise out of her voice.

"Not in any of the ways that matter," Caleb replied through gritted teeth.

Ava scrubbed a hand over her face, tired and a little frustrated that they were having this conversation in front of Tiernan, of all people.

To his credit, he had stopped to wait for them but was leaning against the wall pretending not to pay attention.

"We don't have time to go into this now." Ava strove to be patient and hoped she was getting somewhere close. "Your issues with Gideon aside, I think we can trust him. We *need* to trust him," she said quickly when he opened his mouth to interrupt. "I don't think we can handle the Rogues on our own, do you?"

Caleb clenched his jaw. "No."

"And personally, I'm not ready to go to the Council with this, are you?"

"No. Not yet, at least."

"All right, then," Ava took his hand firmly in hers. "Let's go talk to him and try to figure out exactly what's going on and maybe what our next move should be." She started to walk, and Caleb reluctantly let her drag him along.

"When did you get so bossy?" he asked.

"I've always been bossy."

"Not this bossy."

Tiernan snorted.

"Shut up," Ava snapped as she passed him.

Caleb gaped, looking from Ava to Tiernan in shock.

"Don't ask," she said with a grumble of annoyance. "He's kind of a pain, but he's all right."

Tiernan barked out a gruff laugh. "*I'm* not the pain."

Ava wanted to argue the point, but they'd reached the conference room. Her smile fell as she followed Tiernan inside, nerves sweeping through her stomach at the sight of the Guardians waiting for them.

Emma sat huddled in a chair in the corner, her knees drawn up under her chin. She jumped to her feet when she saw them, hurrying over to Ava and grabbing her arm. "Is he okay?" she whispered, looking nervously at Caleb.

"I'm fine. And before you say you're sorry, don't. I know you didn't want to do what you did—and you did set it right . . ."

Emma's mouth twisted awkwardly before curving into a small, relieved smile. "Well, I *am* sorry."

Caleb smiled back. "I know."

"Where's Audrey?" Ava asked as Gideon approached. "Is she all right?"

"She's fine." Gideon gave a small, reassuring smile. "She was called on to help with the wounded—not many, thanks to you—and I ordered her to get some rest. She'll see you in the morning." He eyed Caleb carefully. "I know you're tired, but I thought we should talk."

Caleb cast a significant glance around the crowded room. "I'd prefer we speak more privately."

With a jerk of his head, Gideon cleared everyone from the room except for Tyra, who sat with her feet propped up on the conference table, fiddling with her nails. Ava, Caleb, and Emma sat down across from her, with Tiernan leaning on the wall in a shadowed corner, as usual. Gideon took a seat next to Tyra at the head of the table and nodded at Caleb to proceed.

"Ava said the Council suspects a Rogue conspiracy, and in this case, they're right."

Tyra sat up, her booted feet thudding hard on the floor. "What kind of conspiracy?"

Caleb took a deep breath, squeezing Ava's hand under the table. "They plan to overthrow the Council—have been planning it for years, actually. Decades." He turned to Ava, gaze focused and intent. "It's why they want you, Ava."

"What does Ava have to do with it?" Gideon asked.

Caleb faced Gideon. "What do you know of Elias Borré?"

"Borré? I know that name's coming up a lot lately." Gideon pursed his lips, thinking for a moment. "Powerful man. Brilliant scientist. Very influential until he went Rogue."

Ava tried to follow the conversation. "Borré. The Rogue the Council had in custody—the one they said you helped escape?"

"I *did* help him escape."

Gideon stood abruptly, shoving his chair back as he rubbed the back of his neck in frustration. "Maybe you should start at the beginning," he said. "How did the Rogues get to you, and what did they want?"

Caleb leaned back and lifted his eyes to the ceiling as he took a deep breath to gather his thoughts. "I was transporting a Half-Breed here. A sensor named Evan."

Gideon stiffened. "You said he ran away."

"To be honest, I have no idea what actually happened to him." Caleb rubbed at his eyes and groaned in frustration. "I *thought* I'd delivered him. That I'd spent a few days here—talked to Bel—"

"Bel Castro?" Gideon shook his head in confusion. "Bel hasn't been here in months."

"I know that now." Caleb scrubbed his hands over his face. "Emma planted the memories."

"Your mind did, actually," Emma said, offering a bit more clarification and clearing her throat as she looked nervously around the group. "I had to make you think Evan had been delivered and that you'd been here instead of with the Rogues. Your mind filled in the logical details on its own."

"No wonder they call you a scrambler," Caleb muttered before glancing up at the girl. "Sorry."

She shrugged and turned her attention to her shoelaces.

"What was his gift?" Tiernan asked after a moment. When Caleb looked at him blankly, he clarified the question. "The Half-Breed, Evan?"

"I have no idea. Bel never mentioned it." He turned to Gideon. "Do you know?"

"We think he was a sensor," he replied.

Tiernan stiffened, and Ava turned to him with wide eyes.

"Do you think?" she asked.

Tiernan shrugged. "He said the sensor was newly acquired. It makes sense."

Both Gideon and Caleb spoke at the same time. "Who?"

"Andreas Petrov," Tiernan said. "It's how we were able to track you," he told Caleb. "I don't know for sure that the sensor he used was your boy, but it could be that the Council ended up with him after all."

Ava wasn't sure if she should feel relieved that Evan escaped the Rogues, or worried about what the Council would do to him.

Caleb reached out and took her hand, obviously feeling her ambivalence. "Anyway, a group of Rogues intercepted me," Caleb said. "They drugged me, took me to the caves in Utah. Then Emma . . ." He glanced at the girl, who wouldn't meet his eyes. "Well, you know what Emma did. When I came to, I had this deep-seated distrust of the Council, bordering on downright disgust." He rubbed at his eyes in frustration. "It seems so ridiculous now, but at the time, it made sense. It was all so . . . logical."

"I'm sorry," Emma said quietly. When Gideon turned his attention to her, she added the reasoning. "They wanted him loyal to the cause. I didn't know anything other than that."

"They sent me back to Missouri. Told me to keep an eye on Ava and I'd be called on when I was needed."

Ava fought a chill at his words, realizing that Caleb hadn't really been *Caleb* for longer than she'd thought—before she'd even noticed the changes.

"They sent me on a few missions, I suppose to see if I really was trustworthy, if the tampering had stuck. Then I went with them to free Borré."

"Why?" Ava said the word, but everyone was wondering.

"Somehow, Borré brought Rogues together—dozens of them—making promises of taking over the Council. Taking over the world, basically," he said wryly. "Big words about how we're superior to the humans. How they've screwed up the world on their own and it's time for us to take control. This was years ago, before you were born," he told Ava.

Ava shuddered, remembering Caleb saying those very same words and believing them.

"As you said, Borré is a scientist, and he began experimenting with genetic engineering on our own people. Like so many megalomaniacs before him, he wanted to create the perfect specimen. Race superior to Race. And use them to overthrow the Council.

"Among the Rogues, they're called The Twelve," he said, not meeting

Ava's eyes at first. "Borré's followers hid them among humans, using psychic blocks and genetic manipulation to keep their identity secret from the Council . . . from the Protectors. It's why they have no Veil," he said, and Ava's blood froze. "He made them look human. He needed them to *be* human, as far as the Council was concerned. Until the time was right for them to emerge."

"I know of The Twelve," Emma said quietly. "I heard the Rogues talking about them once when they didn't know I was listening. They said Borré chose the most gifted Race women to serve as mothers of The Twelve. He himself was the father."

Ava swallowed and tried to get her mouth to form the words. "And you—and you think . . ." She couldn't bring herself to say it.

"Yes." Caleb's hand was firm and reassuring around hers, grounding her as he said the words she dreaded hearing. "Elias Borré is your biological father. And I'm afraid, he wants you back."

Hours later, when they were once again curled up together in bed, Caleb whispered, "Are you all right?"

Ava wasn't sure. She'd sat, numb, through the rest of the debriefing, trying to comprehend the awful truth that she was the product of some maniac's plan to take over the world, and that maniac was, in fact, her biological father.

"No," she said finally. "I really don't think I am."

He rubbed her back gently, his warm palm comforting, and she tucked her head under his chin. "It's only where you came from, Ava," he said. "It's not who you are."

"It's still a lot to take in," she said. "I mean, what do they want from me? And why take you?"

He sighed. "They thought I could get you to join Borré," he said. "If not, at least get you away from Tiernan so they could . . . compel you."

"Using Emma?"

He nodded. "But then you helped Emma escape, so the mission changed. We—*they* needed both of you."

"But why me?" she said again still unable to take it all in. "Sure, I have the whole telekinetic thing, but that's about it. I'm not even as strong as you."

Caleb huffed a little in indignation.

"You know what I mean."

He pulled her close, pressing a kiss to the top of her head. "I don't know the details," he said. "But you definitely have something they want. It only confirms to me that there's still more to you than meets the eye." He kissed her again. "Not that I ever had any doubt."

Ava snorted. "Sweet talker."

Caleb yawned, unable to hold it back.

"Go to sleep," she told him. "We can talk more tomorrow."

"You sure?" His voice was already heavy with exhaustion.

She stroked his hair. "I'm fine. Go to sleep." After a moment, she leaned in and whispered against his cheek, "I love you."

"Mmm . . . you, too." And he was out like a light.

Ava, however, wasn't so lucky. She lay there for what felt like hours, unable to slow her racing mind. When a quiet knock sounded at the door, she slipped out of bed, surprised to find Emma on the other side.

"Got a minute?" she asked. "I thought we could go outside. Take a walk and talk?"

They made their way out of the building, and followed the same path to the park that Ava had walked with Gideon the day before. Ava felt peaceful for the first time in weeks, and simply allowed herself a moment to enjoy the feeling. Emma seemed to be content to walk in silence, breathing deeply in the cool night air.

When they got to the park, Emma took a seat on one of the swings and motioned for Ava to take the other one. With a smile, she said, "I'd like to help you."

Ava dragged her feet in the gravel under the swing. "That's what you said. Help me how?"

"Lift the rest of your psychic block. Put things right, like I did for Caleb."

Ava froze, her fingers gripping the cold metal chain. "You agree with Caleb. You think it's still there." She'd thought she'd destroyed it months ago at the Rogue lair; she'd felt it crumble down. It was how she had saved Caleb. How she'd killed Arthur. She shivered at the memory.

"Yeah, at least bits and pieces of one," Emma said. "I can't believe I didn't feel it before—of course, you kind of warned me against swimming around in your head." She grinned. "But it's there. It's weak, broken in places, but it's there."

Ava let the swing move again, Emma's words sinking in as she pushed slowly back and forth. "And you can . . . you can remove it? All the way?"

Emma was silent for a moment, and Ava glanced at her. She had her eyes closed, breathing deeply, and Ava could feel her prodding—a flicker of a touch in her mind before she pulled away.

"I can," Emma said.

"Will it—" Ava swallowed, remembering Caleb's screams of pain. "Will it hurt?"

"Not if you help me," Emma replied, reaching out to touch her hand. "Caleb fought me. That's why . . ." She looked away, swallowing thickly. "I didn't want to hurt him."

Ava felt uneasy; the idea of anyone messing with her mind didn't sit well with her—especially not someone who'd until recently been working with the Rogues. Still . . .

"What will happen when it's gone?" she asked.

Emma shrugged. "I'm not sure. I can't tell exactly what it's designed to block."

"Maybe my strength . . . my speed?" Ava couldn't ignore a rush of excitement at the idea.

"Could be. Or maybe more psychic gifts?" Emma bit her lip. "Or, it's possible nothing will happen. No way to know for sure until it's gone."

A nervous thrill ran through Ava—half eager, half terrified.

"It's up to you," Emma said.

"I think . . ." Ava twisted the swing until she faced Emma head on. "I think I'd like you to try."

Emma's face lit up with a sunny smile. "Great! Okay, close your eyes—"

"Wait a second. You want to do it right now?"

Emma's smile fell a little. "Well, yeah. Don't you?"

"I figured you'd need to prepare or something." Nerves fluttered in Ava's stomach.

"I don't. Do you?" Emma cocked a brow, a smile teasing at her lips.

"No," Ava replied defensively. "I can do it. I'm . . . I'm ready." Tiernan was going to kill her for doing this on her own. Not to mention Caleb. Still, she squared her shoulders and closed her eyes. "Now what?"

Emma turned to face her, reaching out to lay her hands gently on Ava's head, fingers spread wide. "Try to relax," she said, breathing deeply to demonstrate. "And when you feel me, don't fight me. It'll go against your instincts, but let me in. I'll try to show you the block, and you can help me remove it."

"But how—"

"Just breathe," Emma said, her voice barely a whisper. "Stay calm. You'll feel it."

Ava concentrated on breathing deep and slow, willing her muscles to relax and her pulse to slow. After a moment, she felt Emma's gift and gasped at the intrusion, her gift flaring up in defense.

"Shhhh . . ." Emma murmured. "Don't fight it."

Ava exhaled slowly, corralling her gift, almost reassuring it. She felt Emma prodding in her mind, a quiet pressure—not unpleasant, but a little unsettling.

"There," Emma said. "Do you feel it?"

"No, I—I don't know . . ."

"I'm going to try and lift it now. Help me if you can."

Ava felt what she could only describe as a pull . . . then a push . . . deep within her mind. "I can feel it."

"Use your gift," Emma whispered, tension evident in her voice. "See if you can help me."

Ava called on her power, feeling it well within her, almost eager to follow her directions. She focused on the point in her consciousness where she could feel the block and urged her gift to work with Emma's.

"That's it," Emma said. "Keep going."

Ava's jaw clenched as she concentrated, the harsh breaths from both girls cutting through the air around them.

"Almost there," Emma whispered.

With a rush, Ava felt it lift and disappear. Her gift swelled, consuming her wholly for the first time, and she fell forward off the swing and landed on her hands and knees in the gravel.

Emma dropped to her side, wrapping an arm around her shoulder. "Are you all right?"

Ava nodded, breathing heavily, her gift sparking along her skin—along every nerve ending. She'd thought it remarkable before, but now . . . now it rushed through her, thickening her blood, filling her with sizzling energy.

"It's just . . . so *much*." She tried to catch her breath, overwhelmed.

Emma helped her up, got her situated back in the swing, and knelt before her. "Try and breathe through it," she said. "It's part of you, but it's been held back for so long. You have to get used to it."

Ava nodded again, closing her eyes and trying to get hold of her heaving breaths.

"Don't hold it back," Emma said. "Let it be. Just . . . let it be."

"You're quoting the Beatles now?" Ava gasped out.

"Who?"

"You've got to be kidding me." She opened her eyes and stopped fighting. Instead of pushing back, she let her gift swell and felt it reaching out, beyond her skin—beyond her body. She watched in awe as the gravel all around the swing set began to float, higher and higher. Her necklace warmed against her skin and started to hum with vibrations.

"That's it." Emma smiled encouragingly. "That's it."

Ava let it go . . . the gravel floating and swirling around them, forming intricate patterns—spirals and stars—smaller pebbles orbiting larger ones. She laughed, her gift reaching further, larger rocks lifting into the air, the swing set itself shaking, tugging against its moorings.

"Now, try and bring it down," Emma said quietly. "You're not fighting *against* it. It's you. It's like putting down a pencil when you're done writing."

Ava nodded, letting the gift wrap around her, withdrawing to within the boundaries of her skin once again. The swing set settled, and slowly the rocks . . . then the pebbles lowered to the earth, the last settling into place with a quiet plink as the necklace stilled, its warmth lingering comfortingly.

"Wow," Ava said, voice cracking. She cleared her throat with a choked giggle. "Wow, that was amazing!"

Emma's smile fell, her brow creasing in concern.

"What?" Ava asked. "What's wrong?"

"Your nose."

Ava reached up with a trembling hand to touch it, surprised when her fingers came away red and wet. "I'm bleeding."

Emma fumbled in her coat pocket, pulled out a crumpled tissue, and pressed it to Ava's nose. "Just an aftereffect of lifting the block," she said in an attempt to reassure Ava. "You've been through a lot. It's only natural."

That made sense. Ava took the tissue and pressed it more firmly against her nose. She had a feeling Emma had released more than her gift. Her body felt stronger, vibrant with energy, although her mind felt tired, her head aching.

"You should rest," Emma said, helping her to her feet.

Ava let herself be led back to the main building. She was more than ready to curl up next to Caleb and sleep. She sniffed slightly. Tomorrow, she'd see just what Emma had freed up.

Yeah, What's a little nosebleed, anyway?

Chapter 13

"I don't understand why we need to wait for Tiernan," Caleb said grumpily, sipping coffee from a paper cup as Ava led him to the training area behind the Guardians' common building. His head no longer hurt, but he was a bit irritated at being dragged out of bed shortly after dawn. He'd liked the feeling of Ava pressed along his side, her head pillowed on his chest as their gifts mingled, wrapping them in soothing warmth, and had hoped to indulge that feeling until at least noon.

Ava, however, had other ideas. She'd bounced out of bed, a bundle of nervous energy, words tumbling out as she told him Emma had lifted the rest of her psychic block and she felt strong and fast and powerful and . . .

"Come on, Caleb, I want to go try it out!"

Which was why he was huddled in his coat in the frosty morning air when there were other things he'd much rather be doing, thank you very much. He eyed Ava a little hungrily and let out a heavy sigh. It had been so long that they'd been apart. He craved some time alone with her now that the immediate danger had passed.

Is that so wrong?

"I have a bit of a score to settle with Tiernan," she said, bending over to stretch her leg muscles and then straightening up to reach over her head. "That guy is more of a slave driver than you!" She grinned, leaning up to kiss the corner of Caleb's mouth. "No offense."

"None taken," he said wryly, chasing her mouth when she pulled away.

She smiled, letting him pull her close into a deeper kiss, a victorious rush of endorphins kicking in when he felt her tremble, her fingers tightening on his jacket as her knees buckled a little. She didn't move away when he released her, instead leaning her forehead against his shoulder with a shaky sigh.

"What are we going to do?"

There was something in the question, the whispered words accompanying her sigh, that made him realize the toll everything had taken on her. Not only the running and the fighting, but the understanding that she wasn't who she thought she was—and all that that entailed.

"We'll figure it out," he said and pressed a kiss to the top of her head. "I'm not leaving you again. We're in this together." She leaned closer, wrapping her arms tightly around his waist, as he did the same, one hand stroking up her back to tangle in her hair.

A throat cleared and they pulled apart in time to see Tiernan approaching with Adam in tow.

Ava propped her fists on her hips, arching a brow at the presence of the dampener. "What? You don't trust me?"

Tiernan smirked. "Not as far as I can throw you." He considered that. "Although, now that I think of it, I could probably throw you pretty far, so I should say, not as far as *you* could throw you."

"That doesn't even make sense."

Tiernan shrugged, making his way over to the largest weight block on the grass and looking at her expectantly. "Well? You dragged me out of bed at this ungodly hour, are you ready or not?"

Ava started toward him, but Caleb stopped her with a hand on her wrist.

"You sure about this?" he asked quietly. Tiernan was the strongest of the Protectors, and with Adam present to dampen her telekinesis, Ava would have no weapon against him if her strength failed her yet again. "Maybe you should try it with me first."

"Yeah. If you don't think you can handle it," Tiernan called out, goading her.

She cast him an irritated glance before turning back to Caleb. "I'm sure. It'll be fine. I promise."

Caleb wasn't convinced, but he watched her approach the block, reaching out to strengthen her power with his own. She smiled back at him, obviously feeling it, and he nodded in encouragement.

Adam didn't interfere and seemed to be focused on dampening Ava's telekinesis, nothing else. He stood off to the side with his hands in his pockets, watching the proceedings with mild interest.

"Ready?" Tiernan asked.

Ava pressed her hands flat against the block. It was almost as tall as her, and she took a deep breath to center herself before answering. "Ready."

Tiernan seemed unworried, simply leaning forward against the block, but not putting any real strength behind it. Ava, however, closed her eyes, her muscles tightening as she shoved against it and her feet slipping on the damp grass. She dug in and gasped when the block moved. Only an inch or so, but it definitely moved. She straightened, gaping at the block—then at Caleb.

"Did you see that?" she asked, breathless. "Did you see that?" She jumped up and down, a laugh bursting from her lips.

"Try again." Caleb moved closer with an encouraging smile.

Ava nodded excitedly, putting her shoulder to the block.

Tiernan braced himself on the other side. "Go ahead," he said.

Ava gritted her teeth as she pushed, the toes of her shoes digging into the dirt. The block moved, and Tiernan tensed, pushing back just a little. Caleb watched in awe as the shoving battle continued for the next several minutes, amazed at the tight set of Tiernan's shoulders, the bulging of his biceps and faint sheen on his skin.

Ava's making Tiernan sweat.

He couldn't keep down a rush of pride at the thought.

Tiernan grunted with exertion, casting a glance at Adam. "Is she?"

Caleb realized he suspected Ava was cheating and grinned when the dampener shrugged and shook his head, disproving that suspicion.

Emma had managed to unblock whatever had been keeping Ava from her Race strength. And when it came to that strength, apparently Ava had a lot of it. To Caleb's surprise, the block started to move, and Tiernan's feet slid backward as he tried to keep it from happening.

With a shout, Tiernan stumbled backward as Ava pushed the block toward him for several feet before he dodged out of the way.

She gave it one more mighty shove before raising two fists victoriously over her head. "Yes!"

"I can't believe it." Tiernan braced his hands on his knees as he breathed heavily. "I just can't believe it. What happened?"

Caleb watched in amusement as Ava did a little victory lap around Tiernan before shoving at his shoulder.

"Emma lifted my block. I'm a hundred percent Race now. Want to wrestle?" she challenged.

"Shut up." He glared at her. "I can't believe you let her tamper with your brain. Not that there's much to tamper with."

"Oh, now, don't be a poor sport," she said.

"Then don't gloat," he snapped. "It's not pretty."

She fluttered her eyelashes at him. "Caleb thinks I'm pretty." Ava ran over to Caleb and jumped into his arms with a whoop.

He swept her around in a circle, laughing against her mouth as she kissed him soundly.

"I'm strong," she said breathlessly when he finally set her down. "Like, *really* strong."

"I noticed." Her excitement was infectious, and soon, even Tiernan was shaking his head and smiling.

"Come on," Ava said, grabbing Caleb's hand and dragging him to the edge of the grass.

"What are we doing?"

She stopped when they got to the track circling the field, taking his coffee cup and tossing it into the trash. "We're going to race." She stood, elbows bent and legs braced in a starting position. "I have a sneaking suspicion that I'm fast, too."

"Oh, yeah?" Caleb shrugged off his coat and moved next to her on the track. "That sounds like a challenge."

"Oh, it is," she said with a grin. She tilted her head, studying him for a moment, then shouted across the grass. "Hey, Adam. Don't let him shift, okay?"

Adam waved a hand in acknowledgment, never looking up from whatever had his attention on his cell phone.

"After all we've been through, you don't trust me?" Caleb asked in mock outrage.

"Just taking precautions," she said with a laugh. "Ready?"

"Ready."

With a shouted *Go!* they took off around the track.

As it turned out, Ava was right. She was fast.

She was *very* fast.

Ava felt like she was flying. Running around the track with Caleb at her heels—falling farther and farther behind her, she might add—the wind whipping through her hair as her shoes slapped on the hard ground felt wonderful. She couldn't hold in a thrilled giggle. It was exhilarating. Even more than shifting with Caleb because it was all her. *Her* muscles flexing. *Her* arms pumping. *Her* body moving at impossible speeds.

Not so impossible anymore, thanks to Emma.

As if summoned by her thoughts, Emma appeared at the gate, along with Audrey.

Ava slowed to a trot then stopped before the two of them, barely breathing heavily. "Did you see?" she asked Emma. "It worked. You freed up everything!"

Emma's grin matched her own. "Well, *we* did," she said.

With a joyous laugh, Ava pulled the girl into a tight hug, the two of them bouncing in excitement.

"Thank you," Ava said.

"It was the least I could do, after . . . everything," she said, glancing at Caleb as he joined them.

"I was going to offer to help," Audrey said with a grin, "but it looks like you hardly need it."

"You think there's more?" Ava asked, tingling with excitement. "I feel like there's more."

"You won't know until you try."

There *was* more. Much more. She still couldn't shift. Her compulsion skills, although slightly improved, were nowhere near as strong as Caleb's, let alone Emma's. But as they sat cross-legged in a circle on the grass, Ava uncovered yet another pleasant surprise. They were taking a break, and Tiernan and Adam were talking near the gate before the dampener left the area, no longer needed.

Ava was hungry and tired, and she rubbed her temples as the beginnings of a headache throbbed through her skull. Her stomach rumbled, and she flopped back on the grass, closing her eyes to the warmth of the sunlight on her skin.

"My mom makes the best fried chicken," she mumbled distractedly. "It's so crispy and juicy and incredible. I'd smell it cooking and my mouth would just water. What I wouldn't give for a piece of it right now." She inhaled deeply. "I can almost smell it."

"Umm, Ava?" Caleb's voice cracked a bit.

"Hmmm?" She was still a little lost in the sense-memory of her favorite food—the scent of the chicken, the warmth of the kitchen—steamy-humid from the crackling-hot oil. The weight of . . . *something* . . . on her stomach.

Her eyes fluttered open. She stared up at the sky, the smell of chicken even stronger somehow. "What's on my stomach?"

"You did it," Emma whispered in awe.

"What did I do?" Ava still didn't dare look at her stomach. She was beginning to think she knew what she'd find and wasn't quite certain she could handle it.

"Ava, look," Caleb said quietly.

She curled up on her elbows and peeked down, her eyes widening in surprise. A plate of fried chicken sat on her belly, steam wafting in the cool air. She steadied the plate—almost surprised to find it solid in her hand—before sitting up, still gaping at it as she held it gingerly before her.

"It's . . . chicken."

Emma giggled.

"But how?" She looked around the circle from Emma to Caleb to Audrey. "Where did it come from?"

"Did she shift it?" Emma asked Audrey.

"From Oregon?" Audrey laughed. "I don't think so."

"Then . . . you think?" Emma sat up a little bit, turning wide eyes on Ava.

"Yeah," Audrey said.

"Yeah, what?" Ava was getting a little irritated that the three of them seemed to know something that she didn't, not to mention were talking about her like she wasn't sitting right there. Holding a plate of chicken. That she really wanted to eat, actually.

"I've never seen anyone manifest something so complex," Caleb said, reaching out for a drumstick.

Ava fought the urge to snatch it away, instead watching as he took a bite.

"S'good," he said and licked his lips. "Try it."

Ava took a piece, offering some to Emma and Audrey before taking a bite. The skin crackled, and juice slipped out the corner of her mouth before she caught it on her thumb.

"Does it taste like your mom's?" Audrey asked, her green eyes appraising.

Ava took another bite, swallowing before she answered. "It does. It . . . *is,* isn't it?" She couldn't believe what she was asking.

"I think so." Audrey took a bite, nodding in approval.

"But . . . how?"

Emma finished her chicken and tossed the bone over the fence before wiping her fingers on her jeans. "You manifested it."

"Manifested? Like . . ." She waved a hand in the air. "Abracadabra? Watch me pull a rabbit out of my hat?"

Caleb laughed. "No. Like, you realigned the atoms around you to create your mother's fried chicken."

Ava's mouth dropped open. "But—but that's impossible!"

"Rare," Audrey said, holding up a finger and eyeing the chicken. "But not impossible."

Ava's mind raced with the possibilities as she gnawed on a chicken wing. She stopped mid-gnaw and asked, "How does it work?"

"I don't really know," Caleb said, reaching for another piece. "I've only met one guy years ago who could do it, but all he could manifest were ice cubes."

"Ice cubes?"

"Yeah. He could pick water atoms out of the air and condense them." Caleb took the plate from Ava and set it down before her. "Nothing this complicated, though. This is . . . well, it's extraordinary is what it is."

"You think you can do it again?" Emma asked, rolling over until she was lying on her stomach, her chin propped on her fists.

"I have no idea." Ava couldn't take her eyes off the half-empty plate. "I don't know how I did it in the first place."

"Well, if it's like shifting, it's a matter of visualization," Caleb said as he switched into teaching mode once again. "You were thinking about your mom's chicken. Your memories must be particularly vivid—maybe that helped."

"It's like using your Race sight." Audrey leaned forward to emphasize her words. "Try to see all the details. Look within as you imagine it."

"You also seemed pretty relaxed," Emma said. "Don't think too hard about it."

Ava took a deep breath and let it out slowly. "Remember. Focus. Look within. Relax. Got it." She lay back down in the grass, laced her fingers together over her stomach, and closed her eyes. After a moment, she popped one back open. "What should I try?" she asked Caleb.

He shrugged. "Maybe try to make the chicken disappear?"

"Disappear?" Ava frowned. "Isn't that the opposite of manifesting?"

"Not really." Emma shifted her weight to one hand, waving the other dramatically. "You're just putting the atoms back where they were."

Ava wrinkled her nose. "Just like that."

"Just like that." Emma frowned. "Well, except for the pieces we ate."

She looked to Audrey as if wondering if the pieces in their stomachs would disappear, too, but the other woman shrugged. Apparently, this was new to all of them.

Caleb crawled over to sit by Ava's shoulder. "Don't overthink it," he said, laying a hand on her shoulder.

She could feel his gift mingling with hers, boosting it, and she sighed into his touch.

"Imagine the spot where the plate is," Audrey said. "Then imagine it . . . gone."

"Gone?"

"Gone."

"Okay." Ava sighed, closing her eyes again and ignoring her persistent headache. "I'll try."

In the end, it wasn't as difficult as Ava thought it would be. It only took about half an hour before she was able to make the chicken disappear . . . and reappear . . . and finally transform it into a football, of all things.

She found she could only manifest things she had personal experience with—things she could imagine in precise detail. She tried, for example, to manifest a copy of *Moby Dick*, but although the cover looked realistic, the pages were covered with gibberish.

It excited her, though, to explore her new abilities. In addition to the manifesting, her telekinesis had strengthened as much as her body, and Ava's control had grown exponentially. By midafternoon, she found herself standing in the middle of the training field, weight blocks and pieces of the obstacle course whirling in the air around her. She laughed, her arms spread wide, manifesting balls and chairs and whatever popped into her mind. Her gift surged forth, and it felt like it swept out to encompass everything around her.

"Ava!" Caleb shouted.

She was vaguely aware of a pulsing in her head—the headache wouldn't go away, but she couldn't be bothered with it. She spotted a bench across the field and picked it up into the air, stacking it on top of a pyramid of weight blocks. She heard a rattling sound and realized the fence surrounding the training field was vibrating—the roof of the common building, no, the building *itself* shaking as well.

"Ava, stop!" Caleb ducked under a flying rock and ran toward her, but she barely noticed.

The ground quaked beneath her feet, and she looked down in surprise as a narrow fissure opened up beneath her. Power rushed through her, lifting her off the ground, her toes barely brushing the grass as the earth cracked beneath them.

Caleb slammed into her, grabbing her around the hips and tackling her to the ground.

With her concentration broken, the blocks and boulders fell to the ground and the tremors stopped abruptly. Ava's breath grew harsh in her ears—now that everything else was silent—her chest heaving with every inhale, her skin tingling with the aftershocks of her power.

"Holy—" She sat up, untangling herself from Caleb. "Did you see that? It was incredible!"

"Ava—"

"I felt so amazing . . . so alive—"

"Ava!"

She blinked at Caleb, confused at his look of concern, a similar expression on Audrey's face. "What's wrong?"

"Are you all right?" Audrey asked.

"Of course I am. I'm great! I don't understand—"

Caleb cut her off with a look. "Ava, look around."

She did, then, getting to her feet and turning in a slow circle. The training field was . . . well, a mess, actually—rocks, balls, and various other things were scattered haphazardly around, the bench overturned and lying on a broken section of fence. She spotted Emma watching from a distance, half hiding behind a storage shed; the shed itself was slightly crooked, one wall crumpled by a wayward rock. Her eyes dropped to the cracks in the ground, for the first time realizing the extent of the damage she'd wrought.

"I'm sorry," she whispered. "I—I didn't realize."

"You're bleeding," Caleb said quietly, handing her a handkerchief.

She pressed it to her nose, a headache suddenly pounding behind her temples. "I don't feel so good," she mumbled, dropping down to sit on the grass while she put her head between her knees.

Gideon and Tyra burst through the gate, followed by a half dozen armed Guardians.

"What in the world happened?" Gideon shouted as he stepped around an upended weight block with its corner stuck into the ground. "We thought it was an earthquake at first."

"No, no earthquake," Audrey said. "Believe it or not, that was Ava."

"I'm sorry." Ava started to get up but sat down heavily again, overcome by dizziness. "I'll fix it. I can fix it."

"What's wrong with her?" Gideon asked, crouching down next to Caleb.

"I'm not sure."

"It's nothing," Ava said, rubbing at her temples. "It's normal. Emma said it's probably an aftereffect of the block. It'll be fine."

Emma had finally left her hiding place and stood on the edge of the circle, and they all looked to her for confirmation. "It should go away as she gains more control," she said.

"See?" Ava tried to get up again, leaning heavily on Caleb. "I'm fine. I'll be fine. I just need more practice."

"I think that's enough practice for the day," Caleb said, wrapping an arm around her waist.

"But I should clean up—"

"It can wait," he said.

Gideon reached out to touch her shoulder. "Caleb's right. You should get something to eat and rest. We can deal with all of this tomorrow."

At the mention of food, Ava's stomach growled. The few bites of chicken had long since worn off and she was tired and hungry, so she didn't put up a fuss. She let Caleb take her into the kitchen, fix her a sandwich with a side of R-cubes, and tuck her into bed.

She fell asleep almost immediately, too exhausted to notice when he left the room.

"Got a minute?"

When Gideon looked up from his computer, Caleb entered his office, taking in the sparse furnishings and simple metal table and chairs with a disinterested glance.

"How's Ava?" Gideon asked, pushing the laptop aside and folding his hands over a pile of maps and papers on the tabletop.

Caleb rubbed at his eyes and drew a heavy breath. "I don't know."

"Did the R-cubes help?"

"She said they did."

"But?"

"I think she was lying. Or she didn't want me to worry."

Gideon waved toward an empty chair, and Caleb hesitated only a moment before sitting down.

He was tired, he had to admit. The past few days—weeks, really—had taken a toll that was catching up to him. He never thought he'd be sitting with his father, of all people, about to pour out his thoughts and worries. But really, there were very few options. Tiernan. No, not going to happen. Tiernan wasn't really a talk-out-your-feelings kind of guy. Emma thought he was overreacting and said Ava would be fine. She just needed time. It made sense, but he couldn't help worrying. Still, he wasn't exactly sure how to start the conversation.

"She's very powerful."

Gideon huffed out a laugh. "That's putting it mildly. From the state of the training field, I'd say she's one of the most powerful people I've ever met. And that's saying a lot."

Caleb cleared his throat and scooted closer to the desk. "That's what I wanted to talk to you about. You've seen it all, pretty much. But have you ever . . . it seems like there's something . . . *wrong*, doesn't it?"

"You mean the nosebleed."

"It's more than that," Caleb replied, unsure exactly what he meant. "There's just something wrong. Her gift—it feels . . . too much, maybe? I don't even know."

Gideon eyed Caleb. "You've bonded with her."

Caleb flushed, not meeting his eyes. "To an extent, yes." This was not a conversation he wanted to have with his estranged father. Still, he couldn't see an alternative.

"And her gift feels wrong?"

"I don't know." Caleb stood up quickly, the chair scooting back along the floor in his haste. "It feels . . . different."

"Well, that's understandable. The block—"

"It's not just the block," he said. "If it was only that, I wouldn't be so concerned." He paced a few steps and back again. "She got a headache."

Gideon sat back, crossing his arms. "Really."

"I think it was worse than she let on. And there are the nosebleeds."

"Nose*bleeds*? As in more than one?"

Caleb nodded. "One when Emma initially lifted the block. Another today."

Gideon seemed to consider that as he ran a finger idly over a map on the table. "What does Emma say? She's young, but she really has more experience with this than any of us."

"She's lifted other blocks and says it's normal."

"You disagree."

Caleb sat back down and adjusted his chair so he could lean forward on the table. "What do you think? Like you said, you've met a lot of people—Race, Half-Breeds—have any of them had headaches after using their gifts? Nosebleeds?"

Gideon puffed out a breath. "Well, no. But Ava's kind of a unique situation." He propped his elbows on the table, his fingers laced against his lips. "If she's part of this Rogue conspiracy, basically bred to be some kind of super Race, it could account for the problems she's having."

Caleb's heart sank. It was what he'd been thinking as well but was too afraid to put it into words. "You think she's in danger?"

"It's too soon to say that, I think. Maybe Emma's right. It could pass."

"So what do we do?"

He turned back to his laptop and clicked a few keys. "I've put out some feelers. There are some out there who might know what's going on—or at least more than I do. We can run some tests."

"She'll love that."

"Well, she'll love this even more," Gideon said with a wry twist of his mouth. "Like I said, we can run some tests, but we're not set up to do much more than the basics here. If she doesn't improve, you'll have to go to someone with more resources."

It was irritating how Gideon kept putting Caleb's fears in front of him—stating what he already knew but didn't want to face. "You mean the

Council. Ava will never agree to that."

"She might not have a choice." Gideon stood up, rounded the table, and leaned on the edge next to Caleb. "Look, you don't have to do anything right now. We can help her train, keep an eye on her, like I said—run a few tests and see if we can figure out the headaches. Hopefully, in time, she'll be fine."

"And then there are the Rogues."

Gideon laughed humorlessly. "And then there are the Rogues. Yes. But, given Ava's little demonstration, it seems we have a pretty good weapon in our corner if it comes to that."

"She's not a weapon," Caleb said with an irritated glance.

"I know she's important to you, son—*Caleb*," he said when Caleb stiffened. "But given what you've told me about the Rogue plan—and seeing with my own eyes what she can do?" He exhaled heavily, a concerned frown on his face.

"I'm beginning to think a weapon is *exactly* what she is."

Chapter 14

Ava wasn't certain what woke her. She jerked a little, disoriented for a moment until the feeling of warmth along her back and the arm wrapped around her waist reminded her of where she was. Something was off, though, and she couldn't put her finger on what it was. Slipping quietly from the cozy bed, she tucked the blankets back around Caleb and went to the window to peer through the metal blinds.

Night had fallen, the full moon high in the sky and casting the area in a cool, blue glow. Ava's eyes swept the grounds, searching for—she didn't really know, but something. She felt unsettled, waiting . . .

There.

Movement off to the left caught her attention, and she had to move over to the edge of the window and press her cheek flat against the wall to see what it was.

"Emma?" she whispered.

What is Emma doing outside at this time of night?

Ava watched the girl walk purposefully into the forest until she lost sight of her in the trees. Biting her lip, Ava felt for her gift, her instincts on high alert and urging her to act. To do something. In a quiet rush, she slipped on her shoes, grabbed her coat, and left the room, with Caleb sleeping peacefully behind her.

She hurried out of the building, no one awake to intercept her now that the immediate Rogue threat had passed, and jogged in Emma's direction, entering the forest where she'd seen the girl disappear. She kept to a narrow path, unsure what else to do—unsure what she was doing at all, if she were to be perfectly honest—simply following the flutter of Emma's gift, which felt familiar now that Ava had become so intimately acquainted with it.

Ava walked deeper into the forest, the branches overhead cutting off the light from the moon, but she had no problem seeing, her vision sharp and clear, even in the darkness. A flash of red—Emma's coat—caught her eye, and Ava quickened her steps, feeling an urgency she couldn't quite explain. The brush grew thick and tangled, the path barely visible, and she fought her way through, ducking under branches and stepping over fallen logs. Her instincts led her to a twisted mass of branches—almost a wall of greenery—and with a determined breath she shoved her way through, stumbling as she came out the other side.

Brushing off her clothes, she straightened to find Emma standing in the middle of a small clearing, her hands tucked into her red parka. The girl smiled as if she'd been expecting her.

"Emma? What are you doing out here?" Her breath drifted through the clearing on the breeze, carrying her words.

"Waiting for you."

"Waiting for—" Ava took a few steps closer, a strange tingling sensation starting at her toes and slowly drifting up. "Why?"

"To help you, of course." Emma's mismatched eyes grew dark, her pupils growing to consume all but a sliver of green in one eye, and the other, completely black.

Ava could feel a prodding at her gift, a gentle tug. The tingle grew stronger, and warmth suffused her body.

"Help me . . . what?" Her whisper floated through the clearing as her power responded to Emma's call, filling her, up and out . . . reaching into her surroundings.

"That's it," the girl said, encouraging her. "That's it. Let it go."

Ava's gift swelled, flashing through her like a wildfire, and instead of trying to contain it, she let it flow—out from her fingertips and down into the ground beneath her. It burst forth from her skin, invisible but hot and electrifying, filling the clearing and not stopping.

How far can it go?

In response, the rocks and branches around her flew into the air and began to circle above the clearing. Emma walked toward her slowly, her eyes still focused on Ava, who could feel the girl boosting her gift, prompting her . . . urging her to keep going . . . to push it as much as she could. To test her limits.

Ava wanted it.

She wanted it all.

It was giddy, the feeling of vast and unrestrained possibility, and she laughed at the thrill of it, the trees around her swaying and creaking in response. She was vaguely aware of the heat and vibration of her necklace against her chest and the low throb of her headache returning, but she couldn't be bothered with it. Emma stood before her, toe-to-toe, as the rising wind whipped around them.

"Keep going," Emma shouted over the gusts, her palms held out slightly from her body as she fortified Ava's power. "It feels fantastic, doesn't it? Not to fight it anymore. To be all that you're meant to be."

It really did.

Ava tilted her head back to watch the swirling wind—a hurricane of debris with the two of them at the eye. She closed her eyes, her power bursting forth to manifest a boulder . . . a huge snowball about three feet across . . . a crystal chandelier. Emma laughed, and Ava opened her eyes to see her watching the whirling cyclone, a chair and potted plant appearing overhead, then melding together into a blob of red clay . . . a ceramic vase.

"Can you do something bigger?" Emma shouted, bracing herself as the ground trembled beneath her, branches snapping off nearby trees and joining the melee.

Bigger. Something bigger.

Ava manifested a chest of drawers . . . a refrigerator . . . then with a frown of concentration and an exultant shout, the crumpled body of a Volkswagen bug.

Ava's head pounded, but the pain faded into the background. It was nothing compared to the exhilaration of using her power—of letting *it* use *her*. She felt moisture on her top lip, wiped at it with the back of her hand, and smeared the blood on her jeans with an irritated sniff. She turned her gaze to a large pine tree at the edge of the clearing, and it groaned, its roots cutting up through the ground.

Emma's thrilled "Yes!" made her smile.

The tree pulled free with an explosion of dirt and rock and joined the spinning vortex of everything Ava controlled, everything she *created*. The tree spun around, smashing the snowball and sending down a shower of ice crystals.

Ava laughed, twirling in the floating white flakes.

"More," Emma demanded.

Ava wiped at her nose again distractedly, caught up in the moment. She could do more. She could do *anything*.

With a deep breath and a harsh exhale, her gift slammed out in a powerful burst. Emma grabbed Ava's arms, steadying herself, and Ava felt her power erupt outward. Shockwaves rippled out through the forest, taking everything with them. Ava watched as boulders ripped through the underbrush and the tree she'd uprooted slammed into another until they both fell to the shuddering ground. The metal of the VW folded in on itself before wrapping around yet another tree. Then the wind died down abruptly, leaving them both gasping, and the forest fell silent around them as it absorbed Ava's destruction.

She should have felt tired, but she didn't. Instead, her gift danced along her skin, energy pulsing through every inch of her body.

"You should try something else," Emma said, her dark eyes still focused on Ava's. "Something alive."

"Alive?" Ava stared into Emma's blown pupils, bewildered. "Is that even possible?"

"You can do it. I know you can."

"But, what?" Ava's voice was small, unsteady, and confused. "I don't know—"

"You can do it." Emma's fingers tightened on Ava's arms. "Don't you feel it? The power coursing through you? It wants you to push it. It *wants* to do it."

Ava nodded slowly, mouth parted and lips dry. She licked them, leaning into Emma for support. She knew so much more about this. It was as if she knew Ava's gift better than Ava did. "What should I . . . a rabbit? A dog?" she whispered.

"Don't sell yourself short, Ava," Emma snapped.

Is she mad?

"Bigger?" Ava asked.

"Bigger." Emma smiled in satisfaction. "Now, concentrate."

Ava closed her eyes, feeling the reassuring pressure of Emma's hands on her arms. She cast about for something bigger. Something that would impress Emma, make her proud. She'd done so much to help her. It was the least Ava could do.

And with a soft smile, she decided. She pictured it in her mind—muscular shoulders covered in thick, silver-tipped black fur, paws the size of dinner plates, curved claws digging into the dirt. She called on every memory she had to perfect the size—three hundred pounds? More? Ava shrugged, opting to let her memories guide her. She visualized it at the edge of the clearing and knew by Emma's gasp that she had succeeded before she even opened her eyes.

"Yes," Emma whispered, her eyes wide with awe.

Ava followed her gaze to the shadow of a large pine tree, tilted at an odd angle, half its roots out of the ground. Before it, immense and powerful, stood a grizzly bear on its hind legs, its eyes black and ferocious. It roared, the sound echoing through the dark forest, and Ava faltered for a moment, stepping back.

"It's . . . magnificent." Emma cast an admiring glance her way, and Ava couldn't keep down a rush of pride at her accomplishment.

The bear fell to all fours, letting out another bellow, and Ava smiled. A smile that slowly fell when the bear collapsed onto the ground, its roars morphing into something else. It bayed, writhing in the dirt and debris, and Ava realized it was in pain.

"What's wrong with it?" she asked, taking a few steps toward the bear.

It growled in warning, black eyes turned on her as its lip curled in a snarl.

She could see the twitches of agony rippling the animal's thick fur and turned to Emma for guidance.

The girl sighed. "It's not right," she said.

"What do you mean?" Ava asked a little frantically.

Emma took her hand, squeezing gently. "It looks right on the outside—

it's what you know. But something's wrong on the inside. It's not your fault. How could you know?"

Ava watched in horror as the bear twisted on the ground, whimpering and frothing at the mouth. With sick realization, she absorbed Emma's words. She'd tried to manifest something—a *living* thing—with no real knowledge of the intricate biology that made it up.

She was a spoiled child playing God.

Ava fell to her knees, retching onto the dirt, blood and bile seeping into the ground.

"You have to help it," Emma said, her voice steely as she dropped to Ava's side.

"But . . ." Ava swiped a hand over her mouth, fighting back another rush of nausea. "How? I don't know how."

Emma's mismatched gaze locked on hers again. "It's suffering, Ava. You have to put it out of its misery."

Ava's eyes blurred with tears as she turned back to the bear. It whined pitifully, and she choked on her own sobs. "I'm sorry," she whispered.

"You have to fix this, Ava," Emma said, her voice low and soothing, but with a biting edge. "You know what to do."

"What?" Her voice was rough, ruined. "Make it go away?" She turned toward the suffering bear.

"No," Emma said firmly. "You must face the consequences of your actions."

"How?" But as Emma stroked a hand over her head, Ava knew. She knew how she had to pay for her mistake. It was so clear.

Ava nodded, tears running down her cheeks as her eyes fluttered closed. She pictured the bear—its image imprinted so clearly on her mind—looked closer . . . closer . . . until she could see inside. Pictured the beating heart, so inadequate and imperfect, and squeezed it tightly with her mind—her gift a fist closing about it. Teeth gritted, she bore down, tightening the grip until the low whimpers became staggered breathing, harsh in her ears, then nothing. Silence, broken only by her own soft keens. She fell forward into the dirt and curled up in a ball, sobbing uncontrollably, unable to look at the helpless animal she'd created and destroyed. She felt Emma rubbing her back, her voice soothing as she tried to comfort her.

"It wasn't your fault."

Ava gasped. "How can you say that? You saw what happened."

"Ava, sit up."

She hesitated only a moment before complying, wiping the still-streaming tears from her cheeks. For a moment, Emma looked far older than her seventeen years, her eyes dark with remembered pain and something else Ava couldn't quite put a finger on.

"It's not your fault," Emma said again, shaking Ava's shoulders slightly to emphasize the point. "You're new to all of this, and I shouldn't have pushed you so hard. Next time—"

"Next time?" Ava said harshly, outraged. "Are you kidding? There's not going to be a next time!" Ava felt sick at the very thought of it, another wave of roiling nausea twisting in her stomach.

Emma rubbed her shoulders gently, her gaze penetrating. "Relax, Ava. Calm down. Take deep breaths."

Ava nodded, breathing in sync with Emma.

"It's okay," Emma said, soothing her with her words, her touch. "You didn't mean to do it, did you?"

"No." Ava hiccupped. "No, of course not."

"Then you're not responsible for it," she said firmly.

Ava found herself nodding again, her thoughts calming. "I'm not," she said, swiping at her tears. "It wasn't my fault."

"Of course it wasn't. You'd never hurt anything on purpose, would you?"

"No."

"No, you wouldn't. Not unless it was trying to hurt you . . . or someone important to you, right?"

Ava nodded again. Her head felt muzzy, full of cotton, Emma's words the only thing cutting through. The only thing making sense.

"You're so strong, Ava," Emma said, smoothing a hand over Ava's hair. "And you're only going to get stronger with time. You'll see."

A crackling of branches had them both jumping to their feet, one of Ava's boulders doing a half-hearted defensive jump.

Caleb appeared at the edge of the forest, climbing over a downed log as he took in the destruction around him with a mixture of shock and confusion. His gaze landed on the bear and he choked slightly, taking few hurried but cautious steps toward Ava.

"What happened, Ava?" he asked. "What did you do?"

For a moment, Ava was overcome by guilt and shame—confusion as she saw what she'd done through his eyes. Emma ran a hand down her arm gently.

"It's all right," she said in her calming, hypnotic voice. "He just doesn't understand."

Yes. That's right.

Caleb didn't understand. Maybe Ava could explain it to him.

He stood a few feet away, watching her carefully. "Ava, are you all right?" he asked. "Your nose is bleeding again."

Ava raised a shaking hand. Her chin and lips were wet. She stared blankly at the red smudges on her trembling fingertips.

What? Why?

"It doesn't matter," Emma said, pulling a napkin from her coat pocket. "It will be fine."

"It's fine." Ava nodded slowly, Emma's dark gaze calming her fears.

Emma cast a glance over her shoulder at the bear. "You can make it go away now."

Ava didn't look at the bear, only into Emma's hypnotic eyes, visualizing the empty space where the dead bear used to lie.

Emma looked over again. "Good," she said. "You're doing so well, Ava." She rubbed a palm over Ava's head again, smoothing her hair. "It's going to be okay."

"Ava, what's going on?" Caleb asked, stepping forward slowly. He seemed worried. In fact, he looked almost . . . *afraid* of her.

"I was practicing," she said. Her throat felt raw and she swallowed thickly.

"In the middle of the night?"

Ava shrugged. "I couldn't sleep."

"You don't have to explain yourself to him." Emma patted her arm. "He doesn't understand."

"Understand what, exactly?" Caleb asked, turning his attention on Emma. "And why are you here?"

"I'm helping."

"Yeah. I can see that." He looked around at their ravaged surroundings and focused, wide-eyed, on the twisted pile of fallen trees.

"She's very powerful," Emma said. "You can't hold her back."

"I don't want to hold her back!"

Ava felt a wave of irritation at how he was talking about her as if she wasn't standing right there.

"I also don't want to see her hurt," he said.

"I'm not hurt," Ava said quickly. "I'm fine. Emma's helping me." Her head throbbed and she rubbed absently at her temple.

Caleb came toward her, his face softening. "You're not fine, Ava. You're pale as a ghost, and you're covered with blood. Something's wrong. You're pushing yourself too hard."

"Don't listen to him," Emma snapped. "He doesn't know what he's talking about."

She turned to Emma, confused. "I don't understand."

"I know." She squeezed Ava's shoulder gently. "It's all right. I'm going to help you. But you have to see, Caleb is only keeping you down."

Ava glanced at Caleb, a tingle of worry twisting in her gut. "He wouldn't do that."

Would he?

"Not on purpose, but people fear what they don't understand."

"Ava, don't listen to her." Caleb stepped forward, taking her hand and holding it firmly. "She's doing something to you. You can't trust her."

"Of course you can trust me," Emma said in her low, reassuring voice.

Ava couldn't keep herself from looking into the girl's eyes. They pulled at her . . . comforted her. They told her that Emma understood her. She wanted to help her.

"He doesn't want you to reach your full potential," Emma said sharply. "He's afraid of your power."

"Caleb?"

"Come with me, Ava," he begged, tugging on her arm. She didn't move, and Caleb glared at Emma. "Let go of her."

Emma laughed. "I don't know what you're talking about."

"I don't understand . . . what's happening?" Ava swayed a bit on her feet. Emma turned back to her, giving her power a boost, and Ava steadied.

"He wants to take you away from me," Emma said. "He wants to keep you for himself. Keep you weak."

"That's not true. Don't listen to her, Ava."

Emma continued as if he hadn't spoken, and Ava couldn't look away. "He's afraid of you, Ava. He knows you're going to become one of the most powerful people on earth. Much more powerful than him. He's jealous."

"Ava, she's twisting your mind." Caleb's voice came to her as if from a great distance and then faded away.

"You have to show him," Emma said, her eyes piercing and black, that little sliver of pale green the only lightness in her gaze. "Show him he can't keep you from what's rightfully yours."

"Mine?"

"He'll put you at the mercy of the Council. Or worse, the humans. You're better than that, Ava. You deserve more than that."

Ava blinked. She didn't like the sound of being at anyone's mercy. She turned to Caleb. "Why?"

"Ava, no." His face crumpled. "You can't believe that. You need to come with me. I can help you."

"Help me how?"

"We can run some tests. Find out what's happening to you."

"I heard him talking with Gideon." Emma brought a hand up to cup her cheek, her fingers pressing in hard. "They want to take you to New Elysia."

"Is that true?" Ava asked, feeling sick with betrayal at the expression on Caleb's face.

"Only as a last resort," he said. "And not against your will, Ava."

She shook off his hand. "How could you?"

He reached out to grab her again, and her gift flared up, throwing him backward.

"You can't trust him, Ava," Emma said, standing next to her.

"She's the one you can't trust!" Caleb shouted, getting to his feet.

"You know that's not true." Emma took her hand, and Ava relished the feeling of Emma's power surging through her, making her stronger. "There is something I didn't tell you Ava, because I wasn't sure you were ready. I think you are now."

"What? What is it?"

Emma raised their joined hands, and Ava caught sight of her tattoo—the curved lines, parentheses facing opposite directions, a line crossing both in the center.

Like a sideways H.

Ava turned Emma's arm slightly.

Like the H on the corner of the baby blanket back home.

"Yes," Emma breathed. "You know it. Don't you?"

"It's . . . on my blanket."

Emma nodded. "You remember what I told you?"

Ava stared at the symbol, now so obviously the same. How had she not noticed it before? "It's the symbol for Pisces," she said, her words slurring a little. Her head throbbed as she tried to understand what was happening. "Your sign."

Caleb started toward her, but Ava held him back without conscious thought, her gift protecting her.

"Not really my sign, no," Emma told her, tilting her head with a slight smile. "In the Zodiac, it's the twelfth sign."

"Twelfth?" Ava's mind whirled.

The blanket. The symbol. Destiny.

"The Twelve."

"Yes." Emma smiled. "I'm one of The Twelve, as well. My father is Elias Borré." When Ava continued to gape at her, she added with gentle touch to Ava's cheek. "We're sisters, Ava."

Sisters?

Caleb pressed his palms against the invisible barrier keeping him from Ava, feeling his way along it in hopes of finding a hole—an opening of some kind. But no. Ava didn't even seem to be paying attention to him, but she was somehow keeping him at bay. Her gift, it appeared, had developed the ability to work without her direct control.

And Emma, it appeared, had control of Ava.

He could feel her presence inside Ava, a foreign presence mingling with her gift. A thick black stain tainting what had once been pure. What had once been *his.*

"Ava!" he shouted. She paid him no heed, though, absorbed in Emma's words.

"I wasn't hidden, not like you," she told Ava. "I was the last to be born. The one who put the blocks in place was killed by Protectors, so Father needed me, you see? You all needed me. And Father kept me close so I'd be ready when it was time to bring you all home."

"Home?" Ava swayed on her feet a bit, blood trickling from her nose. She wiped at it absently, and Emma caught her wrist, brandishing Ava's red-stained palm.

"Once we get home, back to Father, it won't hurt anymore," she said, wiping Ava's hand with the bloodied napkin. "He helped the others. He'll help you too. You'll see."

Ava said something incomprehensible, and Caleb shouted, pounding against the invisible barrier impotently.

"He won't stop," Emma said with a warning glance his way. "He'll take you to the Council, and they'll keep you imprisoned, drug you, dampen your gifts—anything to keep you under their control. You know they're afraid of you already. If they knew what you could really do, they'd never stop trying to get their hands on you."

"He wouldn't . . ." Ava shook her head slowly, but her eyes, wide and almost glazed, remained focused on Emma. "Caleb wouldn't do that. He loves me."

The wall wavered, and Caleb took one cautious step forward and then another.

"No," Emma said firmly. "He'll never let you use your power. He's afraid of it."

Caleb took another step toward Ava silently, afraid to shift and startle her.

"I'll never betray you, Ava," Emma said, her palms on Ava's cheeks. "We're sisters. We're family. I only want what's best for you."

Caleb reached out and took Ava's wrist.

She turned on him, her eyes flashing as she ripped her hand from his grip, threw it up, and threw him away. He flew through the air, slamming into a half-uprooted tree.

"Ava, no," he pleaded, panting as he tried to center himself. "Please. Come back to the Colony with me. Let me help you." He started toward her once more, but she threw him again, and he landed in a heap on the ground.

"No!" she shouted. Then in a quieter, uncertain voice, she said, "No. You can't . . ."

"That's right," Emma said with an icy smile in Caleb's direction. "No one can stop us."

Caleb got to his feet, staggering a little as he held his hands up in what he hoped was a placating gesture. "Ava, you know me. I *love* you. I would never hurt you."

She slammed him against another tree and held him there, the bark cutting into his back, his feet dangling above the ground.

"Stop, Ava. Please." His voice cracked as Ava's hold tightened. "Remember what Emma can do. She changes memories, twists your free will. She's manipulating you. She's using you like she used me."

Ava took a step toward him, her head tilted as she watched him fight against her invisible bonds.

"She's a Rogue, Ava. You can't trust her."

"No," Ava whispered, tightening her grip even further.

Caleb couldn't breathe; his ribs cracked under the pressure.

"It's a lie," Emma snapped. "Finish this. He can't be trusted."

"Ava, no." He gasped for breath, his head swimming at the lack of oxygen. "I love you." Darkness crowded in at the edges of his vision, shadows taunting him with images of his death.

"Please . . . Ava. I love you." And Caleb couldn't tell if the words actually made it out of his mouth or simply echoed in his head.

Ava looked deeper . . . inside.

Just like the bear.

She rooted under and around, through skin, muscle, and sinew, searching for Caleb's most vulnerable places. The tender spots that would get him to *stop*. To *listen*. To *understand*.

"No . . ." He was quieter. No longer shouting.

That's good.

"Ava. End this! "

Ava faltered when she felt his power. It seemed so familiar, somehow.

Peaceful.

It sparked memories of soft touches and warm smiles. It reached out to her, curling tendrils tingling with warmth tracing over her skin. She could see . . .

"Kill him!"

His heart. Beating so slowly now. His power pulled away from her . . . reluctant, almost pleading.

"No . . ."

His heart.

"No . . . I can't."

Her heart.

"Kill him!"

"No!" Ava whirled on Emma, and the girl flew across the clearing and landed in the dirt with a grunt. Without waiting another second, Ava ran to Caleb and threw herself into his arms.

"Ava, no!" Emma shrieked as she staggered to her feet, shaking off her surprise and reaching out to Ava with her gift. "You can't!"

"Caleb." Ava sobbed, her head tucked into his neck as she clung to him. "Please . . ."

Without wasting another second, Caleb wrapped her in his arms and shifted them away.

Chapter 15

Ava's knees buckled when they hit solid ground, and Caleb was no better, both of them slumping to the damp grass in a pile of limbs. He drew a deep breath, and she felt him shudder before pulling her gift back enough to release him.

"I'm sorry . . ." Ava's mind swam with confusion—thoughts of Emma, her *sister*, Caleb . . . blurry images of what she'd done, and the world tilted on its axis as Emma's compulsion weakened.

Hands turned her over, examining her for injuries, and Ava realized for the first time that they were back at the Colony, and they weren't alone. Gideon hovered over her with Tiernan, the sky lightening slowly behind them and casting their faces in shadow.

"What happened?" Gideon asked. "Whatever you were doing set off warning bells with Simeon—our sensor," he told Ava when she looked at him blankly. "Good lord, Ava, you're covered in blood."

"I'm fine," she said, her voice wrecked and raspy as she wiped at her nose. The flow had lessened considerably.

"It's Emma." Caleb coughed, sitting up and holding his ribs. "She's a Rogue. About a quarter mile due east." He gasped out the words, gingerly lifting an arm to point in the direction of the trail.

"On it," Tyra said, already gathering men and weapons and heading off through the woods.

Tiernan shot another worried glance Ava's way before joining the group.

Gideon helped Caleb to his feet, wincing at his pained whimper. "Are you all right?"

"Fine. Few cracked ribs, I think, but they're already healing." He didn't look in Ava's direction.

She felt sick. Things were beginning to fall into place now that the cloud of Emma's influence was lifting. She'd believed what Emma told her, felt it true to the very core of her being.

She'd hurt Caleb.

Gideon turned to help Ava, and Caleb snapped, "Be careful."

"I'm not going to hurt her."

Ava's heart sank when Caleb flushed and looked away. "He's not worried about you hurting me. It's the other way around," she said flatly, getting to her feet and swaying at a rush of dizziness. "Emma influenced me, but I'm all right now."

Kind of.

Ava wondered if she'd ever truly be all right again. The thought of someone tampering with her so intimately, so powerfully—she felt violated and ashamed.

"Better get Adam, just in case." Caleb still wouldn't look at her.

"I said I'm fine!"

"How are we supposed to know that for sure?" Caleb asked, nodding at Gideon as he called Adam back over the radio. "I've been under Emma's control. It's not an easy thing to escape."

"Well, I'm not trying to kill you, am I?" Ava shouted, and her face crumpled as she broke out in sobs and collapsed back down into the grass. She was so tired. Her head ached, throbbing pain with every heartbeat. Breathing was a chore.

It was only a moment before Caleb's warm arms encircled her, his gift reaching for hers just as his body did.

She slumped into his chest, whimpering, "I'm sorry . . . I'm so sorry . . ." over and over again.

He murmured reassuring things as he rubbed her back with big, warm strokes. She couldn't decipher the words, but they soothed her nonetheless. Eventually, she calmed, sniffling quietly into Caleb's strength as he told his father an abbreviated version of what had happened.

"Sisters," Gideon muttered—again—as he helped Caleb get Ava to her feet, the two of them practically carrying her limp body inside.

She shivered, the warmth of the common building a welcome relief. "Half sisters," she said coldly, and Caleb chuckled.

"Good to see you're back," he said.

Ava still couldn't laugh about it, but she forced a small smile, leaning into him and inhaling his comforting scent. "Are you sure you're all right?" she asked.

He leaned down to kiss the top of her head. "I'm fine. Barely feel it anymore." He twisted a little as proof once they entered Gideon's office.

Ava spotted a futon along one wall and claimed it for her own. Caleb sat next to her and drew her close as Gideon paced.

"So you're a part of this grand plan of Borré's." He fumbled in a cabinet for a jar of R-cubes and tossed it to Caleb, who took a couple for himself and handed two to Ava. "And there are ten more of you," Gideon said.

"I'm not part of any plan," Ava said stubbornly and popped the cubes into her mouth as if that ended all conversation on that topic. "There's no way I'll help the Rogues."

"Sorry, wrong choice of words," Gideon said distractedly, obviously still lost in his own thoughts. "But somehow you broke free of her control."

"I could feel her," Ava said finally, the memories clarifying the more she thought about them. "I could feel her doing it, but somehow . . . I didn't care. But when Caleb—" She brushed at her eyes, swallowing thickly. "I could tell something was wrong, but I couldn't break free, not entirely."

"Ava's mind has always been exceptionally strong," Caleb said, his low voice lulling her. "I couldn't blur her memories for any length of time, and my compulsion never stuck. And that was before the block was lifted. Once I shifted her far enough away, it seemed like Emma couldn't maintain the link." His voice held a hint of pride.

Pride Ava felt was unwarranted. "Or maybe she gave up when she realized we'd go after her."

Gideon's radio beeped as if on cue, and he answered gruffly. Ava wasn't surprised to hear the report that Emma had vanished.

She sighed, Caleb's fingers stroking her arm and relaxing her. She yawned, and he pulled her down so her head rested in his lap. The cubes dulled the headache—barely—but she was still so tired.

She fell asleep with Gideon ordering a search of the forest and Caleb's fingers in her hair.

Ava's stomach rumbled, but she couldn't bring herself to eat. She sat between Tiernan and Caleb in the common room, huddled over sandwiches and lukewarm coffee, and she toyed with the bread, breaking off pieces and crumbling them between her fingers. She'd slept for a couple of hours curled up with Caleb on the futon, and she almost felt back to normal.

Almost.

Her head still throbbed a little, a reminder of the huge output of power she'd displayed. Caleb assured her they'd figure it out, but Emma's words haunted her.

"Once we get home, back to Father, It won't hurt anymore."

Her father. A Rogue bent on taking over the world.

Perfect.

Tiernan waved a hand in front of her face, and she looked up to see him watching her carefully. "You sure you're all right?" he asked.

"I wish people would stop asking me that," she grumbled but then sighed heavily. "I'm fine. Just a bit overwhelmed by it all, you know? Not every day you find out you were created for world domination."

Tiernan snorted. "Think pretty highly of yourself for someone who couldn't even move a training block until a few days ago."

"Yeah, well, I can sure do it now." She eyed him, the challenge clear in her gaze. "You want to try me?"

Tiernan laughed, but it was Caleb who spoke. "Probably best not to push yourself until we figure out the headaches and nosebleeds," he said. She knew what he wasn't saying. They had no idea if there was any lasting damage, or if there would be.

"Not to mention the little fact that I'm still wanted for murder," she said with a grimace, shoving her plate away.

"I think it's safe to assume the Rogues are behind that as well."

"But why? What could they possibly hope to gain?"

He shrugged. "Pretty simple, actually. To limit your options. You can't go home. You *won't* go to the Council. Reveal the Colony to the Protector"—he eyed Tiernan— "or to the *Council,* and you have no place here as well. You have nowhere to go but to them."

"But I'm not going to reveal the Colony's location," Tiernan said, leaning back in his chair. "I suppose they didn't account for that."

"Which means the plan isn't foolproof," Caleb said. "They are ahead of us, though. From what Emma said, I think they may already hold the key to what's happening to Ava, physically."

"Well, we better figure it out soon," Tiernan said before swallowing the last of his sandwich and washing it down with coffee. "We're going to need Ava to go up against the Rogues. Especially if there are more of her out there."

"Not more *of* her," Gideon said, taking the seat across from Ava. "Others *like* her."

Caleb nodded and shared knowledge from his time with the Rogues. "Borré is the father of all of them, but they all have different mothers. Each woman was carefully screened and chosen for her unique gifts in an effort to pass those gifts on to the offspring."

"So he created an army of superior Race, each with different abilities?" Tiernan asked.

Gideon nodded. "It makes sense. They'd work together, each having a role in his plan."

Ava groaned, her head falling forward to clunk on the table and narrowly missing her plate. "It's so ridiculous. Like a comic book. He made a Justice League, only with villains."

"You're not a villain," Caleb said.

"So not the point." She stood up, throwing her hands in the air. "Don't you get it? This was all part of his insane plan. Every single bit of it—us finding the Rogue lair . . ." She shot a glance at Tiernan. "Getting Emma . . . that's why it was so easy, you know? The whole mess with Caleb and Borré's escape—probably even Borré getting captured in the first place! He's played us like pawns in his little game, and I'm sick of it!" She collapsed back into the chair at the thought of Officer Simmons. "People have died—*are* dying—and all because of some twisted plan to manipulate me."

"It didn't work." Caleb reached for her hand.

"Regardless," Gideon said, "it looks like the time has come for them to collect these . . . Twelve . . . and put their plan in motion. The good part is —"

"There's a good part?" Ava knew she sounded like a child. She didn't care.

Gideon shook his head slightly. "The good part is that Ava's shown us The Twelve aren't puppets. They have to either be lured to the cause or compelled—which would be difficult to do if they're all as strong as Ava. Perhaps that's something Borré hadn't counted on."

"Which means," Tiernan said, sitting back in his chair and tugging at his lip briefly, "that if we can get to some of them first, we might have a weapon against Borré's plan."

"But how are we supposed to find them, let alone convince them to join us?" Ava asked.

They were all silent for a long moment, exchanging significant glances.

Ava's stomach sank. "Oh no," she said slowly. "You can't really think —"

"It's the only way, Ava. They have far more tools at their disposal," Caleb said, reaching for her hand under the table.

She turned wide eyes on Gideon. "And you agree? After everything, you want to go to the Council with this? They'll lock you up and throw away the key!"

"Not if we do things right," Tiernan interjected. "I can help ease the way. And I'll get Katherine in on it, too. She can be very convincing."

Caleb tried to reassure her. "Rafe will help."

"And Andreas," Tiernan said.

Caleb looked a bit surprised at that but didn't comment.

"But what about . . ." Ava's eyes trailed to Gideon, who was watching her, his expression unreadable.

"Madeleine will do what's best for the Race," he said quietly. "She always does. We'll just have to convince her that working with us is the best option. The only option."

Ava's heart ached for the Guardian leader. After what he'd revealed about his relationship with Madeleine, Ava could only imagine what it would be like for him to face her again.

But if he could do it . . .

"All right," she said, nodding firmly. "Okay. I'm in."

Emma Reiko made her way to a nondescript house in the suburbs of Seattle, ignoring the driver she'd compelled to give her a lift once she'd made it out of the Canadian wilderness. He hummed along with the radio, tapping his fingers on the steering wheel, and the girl huffed in irritation, tempted to push him to drive across the country once he dropped her off, just for the fun of it.

Humans really were so annoying. But his car was comfortable and fast. And with her gift, speeding tickets weren't a concern, so all in all, it was worth putting up with him.

"Turn right at the next corner." She checked her reflection in the visor mirror before snapping it back into place. "Third house on the left."

He pulled to a stop in the driveway and got out of the car, running around to the other side to open Emma's door.

She got out, nodding at him and earning a dreamy smile for her efforts.

So. Annoying.

"On your way, now," she told him, touching his forehead as she toyed with his mind. "You never saw me or this place, all right?"

The man nodded, dazed, and got back into the sports car. The engine roared loudly and the tiles squealed as he drove away.

Emma looked up at the house, knowing what was waiting for her and that it wouldn't be pleasant.

Things had not gone as planned with Ava, not at all. And her father was not going to be happy about what Emma had done. He'd ordered her to get close to Ava—earn her trust and in time, convince her to return home. Not to try and compel her unless as a last resort. And she was supposed to run it by him first.

But what was Emma supposed to have done? The Rogues had failed miserably in their attempt to take Ava, and once Emma had spilled the beans about how she'd tampered with Caleb—which she'd had to do or they would have left her at some safe house, thank you very much—she had no choice but to reverse the effects. Not that he was important anyway. Ava was the important one, and gaining her trust was Emma's primary mission.

A mission she'd undeniably failed.

Emma took a deep breath and started up the walk. There was no putting it off any longer. It was time to face the music. The thought brought a wry smile to her lips as she heard the familiar strains of classical piano through the door.

Emma raised a hand to knock, but the door flew open before she could touch it. Father did enjoy theatrics, on occasion. She walked in, following the quiet music down a hallway to the back of the house.

Father sat at the piano, his eyes closed as he played one of his favorite pieces.

Rachmaninov, Emma thought, although she couldn't be sure. Her tastes trended toward more current artists.

She stood in the doorway, waiting, as he finished the piece, the notes hanging in the air for a moment before he lowered his hands and turned on the stool to face her.

"Well, you've certainly made a mess of things, haven't you?" he asked, eyes glittering in the lamplight. His right was black, like Emma's; the other, gold, like Ava's. His hair was brown and wavy, not like either of them, and Emma often wondered which of her siblings had inherited that trait.

"I'm sorry, Father," she said quietly. "I only did what I thought was necessary."

"Yes, but that's not really your job, is it?" His voice was calm.

Emma knew better than to be reassured by the fact he didn't seem angry. "No, Father."

"You were to get close to your sister. Form a friendship. Earn her trust."

"Yes, Father."

"And you tried to move too fast, in the end, pushing her away." He stood, crossing to Emma, his tall frame looming over hers. "Did any of your work hold?"

Emma swallowed thickly, her eyes on the toes of her shoes. "I don't know."

"No. It. Didn't."

She looked up in surprise before thinking better of it.

"Yes, I *know*," he said shortly as her gaze dropped again. "Of course I *know*. I have eyes and ears everywhere, dear daughter. Nothing escapes my attention. Your sister shook off your compulsion like it was *nothing*." He reached out, his finger sweeping slowly down a lock of hair before tucking it behind her ear. The finger continued down her cheek and hooked under her chin, lifting her face until she met his gaze.

"This is why you must follow my instructions," he said kindly, his thumb stroking her cheek. "Everything we're doing is according to a very detailed plan. Each step must be followed in order as part of a carefully controlled timeline. If you go off on your own . . ." His grip tightened on her chin painfully, and tears formed in Emma's eyes. "You run the risk of ruining everything we've worked for. Do you understand?"

She tried to nod, but he held her tight. "Yes, Father," she whispered, tears of shame trickling down her cheeks. "I'm sorry, Father."

"I know you are, dear girl." He pressed a kiss to her forehead and released her. "This is a setback, but not one we cannot overcome." A wayward curl had fallen forward over his brow, and he swept it back to lie smoothly with the rest. Her father always liked things in order.

"I still have faith your sister will join us, but we need to move forward to bring home the others." He looked deep into her eyes. "Are you up for the task?"

She nodded, desperate to get back in his good graces. "Of course, Father. You know I am."

"Good." He touched her cheek again, a soft smile on his face. "That's good." His smile fell. "Unfortunately, I cannot allow such disobedience to go unpunished."

Emma swallowed nervously, her stomach twisting in fear, but she held his gaze. Father did not tolerate cowardice. "I understand."

"It's for you own good. So you remember next time and don't repeat the same mistake."

"I know, Father." She closed her eyes as his palms pressed against her hair. The dull throb of a headache began behind her eyes, radiating outward and growing in intensity.

"I love you, Emma."

"I love you, too, Father," she whispered before the pain stabbed through her and forced a scream from her lips.

Eventually, she blacked out, awakening some time later curled up on the carpet with dried blood on her mouth and the last remnants of the headache fading away.

Her father sat at the piano playing Beethoven—or maybe it was Bach—and humming along with the melody.

Caleb tracked Ava down at the park in the center of the Guardian living quarters. She sat on a bench, watching a group of children on the swings, a soft smile on her face as she toyed with her necklace. He sat down next her, pulling her hand into his lap and interlacing their fingers before placing a soft kiss to the tip of her thumb. His gift settled with her near, and he wondered how he'd survived such a long separation.

"How'd it go?" she asked.

Caleb had been talking strategy with Gideon, Tiernan, and Tyra. He'd been surprised when Ava had opted out, saying she needed some time to herself. She'd never been one to sit back and let others make decisions, but she'd been through a lot.

"Fine," he said. "I think we actually have a plan. Which is saying something, considering the personalities involved."

She smirked. "Meaning you're all stubborn as mules."

"Hey!" He laughed. "Takes one to know one."

She shrugged but didn't deny it. "Are they going to relocate the Colony?"

Caleb frowned. He and his father hadn't seen eye to eye on that one. "Gideon doesn't think it's necessary, at least not yet. He'll leave Tyra and a contingent here to guard the civilians when we go to New Elysia. He seems to think once we form an alliance the Colony will be welcome there."

"You don't agree?"

"I think he's putting a lot of faith in the Council. I'm just not certain it's warranted." He waved a hand toward the children. "I also don't like leaving innocent people here when the Rogues know where they are."

"I don't think the Colony is in danger," Ava said quietly. "The Council is their target. If anything, they'd want the Guardians on their side."

"So you think they'll be back, just not to attack?"

"Eventually," she said. "But I'm thinking they'll need some time to regroup. I don't think Emma expected to be going back empty-handed." They sat in comfortable silence for a while, and Ava drew in a heavy breath. "I've been thinking . . ."

"Always a dangerous proposition." She elbowed him, but her smile grew, which was his intention in the first place, so he took it as a little victory.

"I was thinking," she said with a mock glare. "About this testing Gideon wants to do."

"Yeah," Caleb said slowly.

"I'll do whatever he thinks is necessary. I trust him, you know." She glanced at Caleb as if expecting him to argue the point, but he didn't. "But if they don't figure it out—"

"They'll figure it out," he said quickly. "If not Gideon, then the Council doctors—"

She held up a hand. "If they don't. If they *can't*. And if it comes down to it, and the Rogues attack . . ."

Caleb didn't like the way this conversation was heading. "Ava—"

"I want to fight," she said firmly. "Especially after what Emma did—" She shook her head as if to eliminate the memory. "If they take control, they'll do it to others. It's not right, Caleb."

"I know, but—"

"There's no 'but,' " she said. "If it comes down to it, I'll use what I have to stop them. And I'm asking you not to try and stop *me*."

"As if I could." He played it off like a joke, but he hadn't answered, and Ava knew it.

"You could," she said softly. "Between you and Tiernan and Gideon and, God forbid, Adam, you could stop me. You would if you thought it was dangerous for me. You know you would."

Caleb couldn't disagree. The thought had crossed his mind.

"I know it's a lot to ask," she said, turning back to watch the children, her thumb rubbing little circles on the back of his hand. "I know what it will do to you if . . . if something happens to me."

"Nothing's going to happen to you." The thought filled Caleb with sick dread. His gift spiked, instinctively wanting to protect, and by Ava's quiet sigh, he knew she felt it.

"Please," she said, turning to look into his eyes and take his face in her hands. "I need you to promise me. I'll do anything—whatever you and Gideon think is necessary. All the tests. Answer all the questions. I don't care. But in return, I need you to promise that you won't stop me if I'm needed."

Caleb fought the rush of anxiety at her words, tears pricking at his eyes as he looked into hers. But in that moment, he couldn't deny her.

"I'll try," he said, choking on the words as he covered her hands with his. "That's all I can promise right now. I'll *try*. I swear."

Ava studied him for a long moment and then nodded, realizing that was the best she was going to get. She scooted closer to him and rested her head on his shoulder.

"It's strange," she said. "To think I have all these . . . siblings out there. And I don't even know them."

Caleb knew what she didn't say: *and I might have to kill them*. He tightened his arm around her shoulders, drawing her close.

"And my parents," she said quietly. "I have to explain all this to them somehow. I have to make sure they're safe."

"We'll keep them safe," he told her, the words quiet, reverent—a vow. "You have a lot of people on your side here, Ava. No one's going to let anything happen to them."

She nodded, leaning into his warmth, and he hoped he could keep that promise.

Eventually, the children went home and the sun slid below the horizon. Caleb pulled Ava to her feet and linked their fingers as they walked back toward the common room for dinner. They stopped on the path before the building came in sight, and Caleb surrendered to an urgent need to pull her close and wrap his arms around her waist. She sighed into the touch, tangling her fingers in his hair as he squeezed her a little tighter.

After a long moment, he pulled back. "No matter what," he said firmly. "No matter what happens, we'll get through this. I'm not leaving you again. We'll face this together, and we're going to make it. I know it."

Ava nodded, her eyes shimmering with unshed tears. "I know."

"And I want . . ." He swallowed thickly, sure but nervous all the same. "I want us . . . together. Forever, Ava."

She froze. "What are you saying? Do you mean . . ."

He nodded, as certain about this as he was about anything. "I've been afraid, Ava. For a lot of reasons. And I want to explain them all so you know just what you're getting into here. But I want you to know that I'm in this for the long haul. And for us, that's a *really* long haul . . ." He laughed, running a hand through his hair. He was rambling, and he couldn't stop. "And I know it's a lot to ask—"

Nothing else came out of his mouth, because Ava chose that moment to pop up on her tiptoes—and a little bit higher, thanks to her gift—to plant a soft kiss on his mouth.

He gasped into the touch of her lips, pulling her close and reveling in the feeling of their power mingling. It was like coming home. And it was only going to get better.

"Yes," she whispered against his mouth when they drew apart to catch a breath.

He grinned. "I'm not sure I actually asked anything yet."

"It doesn't matter," she said, her grin matching his. "Yes. To everything.

Anything. All of it."

Caleb couldn't find it in himself to push the matter, so instead he just kissed her again. And they stood, wrapped in each other's arms long after darkness fell, forgetting all the challenges that stood before them and simply remembering what it was like to be together.

To be meant to be.

About the Author

T.M. Franklin started her career writing non-fiction in a television newsroom. Graduating with a BA in Communications and specializing in broadcast journalism and production, she worked for nine years as a major market television news producer, garnering two regional Emmy Awards, before resigning to be a full-time mom and part-time freelance writer. After writing and unsuccessfully querying a novel that she now admits, "is not that great," she decided to follow the advice of one of the agents who turned her down—*write some more and get better at it*. Her first published novel, *MORE*, was born during National Novel Writing month, a challenge to write a novel in thirty days.

She lives in the Pacific Northwest with her husband, Mike, is mom to two boys, Justin and Ryan, and an enormous black dog named Rocky who's always lying nearby while she's writing. Whether he's soothed by the clicking of the computer keys or just waiting for someone to rub his belly is up for debate.

In addition to *MORE* and *The Guardians*, Franklin penned the Amazon best-selling short story, *Window*, as well as another short story, *A Piece of Cake*, which appears in the *Romantic Interludes* anthology.

Connect with T.M. Franklin

Website: www.TMFranklin.com

Twitter: https://twitter.com/TM_Franklin

Facebook: https://www.facebook.com/TMFranklinAuthor

Goodreads: http://www.goodreadsocom/author/show/
584430.T_M_Franklin

Acknowledgments

To my wonderful editing team, D.J. Gann, Jennifer Matera, and Andrea McKay. Thank you for your expertise and patience—and your dedication to make this book the best it can be. It means the world to me.

To the *MORE* Street Team: Fern, Mich, Leslie, Chao, Nikki, Martha, Alyssa, Ashley, Lauren, Kristin, and Jacqueline. Thank you all so much for your support and for spreading the word about *MORE*!

To Olivia Mandell, Sherry Bellaire, Stephanie Pires, and Ryan Kegley for offering up fresh eyes and honest criticism. Thanks for helping to make this book better.

To Jenny Pedroza, who puts up with all of my crazy ideas with a smile, and is always there to help implement those ideas in any way she can. Thank you so much!

To all the folks at TWCS Publishing House. It's such a blessing to me to work with such a talented, dedicated, and FUN group of people—thank you!

And finally to my family—thank you for supporting this crazy dream of mine. I love you!

Excerpt from *Twelve*: Book 3 in the *MORE* Trilogy Coming in 2014

A block of ice smashed against the wall above Ava, raining down a shower of freezing crystals. She cursed under her breath and made a dash for the adjoining building—a detached garage—and pressed her back against the wall next to Caleb.

"I thought you said she'd be reasonable," she said, sneaking a glance around the corner and ducking back just as quickly when another bowling-ball-sized block of ice shot their way and landed at their feet.

"That's what the intel said," Caleb replied, his eyes darting around as he tried to figure out their next move. There had been a plan, of course. There was always a plan. But as Ava was quickly coming to realize, when it came to the Race, such plans often fell apart.

"We should have brought Adam," she muttered.

"He was needed back at the Colony."

The dampener could mute gifts, sometimes block them altogether, but Gideon was leery to let him go too far from the Guardian Colony ever since the Rogue attack. Caleb had assured his father that he and Ava could handle it. It was supposed to be a routine mission, after all.

"Well, he sure would have come in handy with Miss Ice Ice Baby over there," she said with a disgruntled frown. She spotted a couple of garbage cans propped against the house and an idea began to form. "You think you can shift us behind that tree on the other side of the yard without her noticing?"

Caleb snuck a quick peek. "Yeah. What are you thinking?"

"I need to get where I can see her so I can try and bind her."

Caleb stiffened. "No way."

"Come on, Caleb, it's no big deal." Ava felt a familiar rush of frustration. He'd been like a mother hen lately, and she was *fine*.

"You can't use your gifts. You *promised.* Not until we figure out—"

Another ball of ice ricocheted off the corner of the building and they fell to the ground, covering their heads.

"We need to do *something!*" Ava snapped. "I'm open to other ideas."

They'd received word of a possible Half-Breed named Sophie near the border in Minnesota, and Caleb was supposed to get to her before the Council did. Ava had begged to go along, after nearly going crazy with boredom while holed up at the Colony for almost a month. He'd agreed only because there'd been no time to argue, and no one else to go with him. Since his kidnapping and manipulation, the Guardians had instigated a strict buddy system. Even Caleb was subject to it.

They'd driven to Minnesota, but had left the car at the gate so they could shift into the neighborhood where Sophie lived. Caleb had been careful to materialize out of sight of the house, only to find the girl standing at her mailbox, staring at them wide-eyed and scared out of her mind. When Caleb had stepped toward her, she'd taken off running toward the house, and the ice bombardment had commenced.

A cryokinetic. That's what they called her. Someone who could use cold and ice, like a pyrokinetic used fire.

Ava still couldn't believe this was her life now.

Protectors would be coming soon—within a day or two if their intel was correct, not that Ava wanted to rely on that—but Caleb and Ava had yet to get to the front walk, let alone the front door. Ava knew their only chance was to bind Sophie long enough to convince her they weren't there to hurt her. Convincing Caleb of that, however, was easier said than done.

"We can wait her out," he said as a burst of smaller ice pellets hit them. He pulled Ava into his arms and rolled closer to the wall to shield them from the worst of the blast. "She's panicking . . . afraid . . . and her gift is lashing out. She can't keep it up for long. When she calms down, or gets tired, we'll be able to get to her."

"And how long will that take?" At his silence, she pushed away from him. "You have no idea, right?"

Caleb rolled over to sit braced against the wall and glared at her with a mulish expression, but said nothing.

Ava took a deep breath and crawled over to sit on her knees between his sprawled legs. She reached out to touch his face, the mingling of their power settling them both. "I'll be okay," she said softly. "I won't use much. You know it's only bad when I try to do too much—"

"We don't *know* that."

"I'm *fine*," she said, willing him to believe it and ignoring the ache behind her eyes. "We have to do *something*. It's only a matter of time before a neighbor calls the cops."

As if emphasizing her words, another ice ball crashed into the garage door.

Caleb glared in the direction of the noise, and she knew he was desperately trying to think of an alternative plan of action.

"Come on." She got to her feet and held out her hands. "We need to do this. Now."

Caleb tried to stare her down, but when she didn't look away, he took a deep breath and let her pull him to his feet. "You sure you're okay?" he asked, obviously unconvinced.

"I'm sure." She stepped close and wrapped her arms around his waist as another ice ball flew past them. "Let's go."

Ava closed her eyes as Caleb shifted them across the yard and took only a second to steady herself before peering around the trunk of the tree. She spotted the girl peeking out from the living room blinds. Ava used her gift to rattle the garbage cans by the garage and smiled when another ice ball flew in that direction. She reached out for Caleb's hand, using his gift to boost her own and to ground her.

"Okay, I'm going to bind her so she can't run, then you shift us inside," she said.

"I really don't like this." He squeezed her hand, though, so Ava knew he was with her.

"I can deal with anything she throws at us." She glanced back at him with a wry smile. "You do the talking."

"Great."

"Hey, you're the one with all the experience." Another ice ball crashed into the garage. It was smaller, though, and Ava hoped that was a good sign.

Caleb yanked on her hand a little. "First sign of trouble and I'm shifting us out. She'll just have to take her chances with the Council."

"I'll be fine," she said with a reassuring smile. "Ready?"

He gave a curt nod, and Ava turned back to the window. She let her gift flow up and out—willed it to wrap around the cryokinetic, visualized ropes lacing around her in a tight web. When they heard a muffled shriek from inside, Caleb pulled Ava close and they shifted inside.

Ava swayed on her feet when Caleb released her, and tried to stay focused on keeping Sophie bound. The girl screamed, and a small ice ball shot toward them that Ava deflected easily.

Caleb maintained a safe distance, holding up his hands in a placating gesture. "Please, calm down," he said. "We're not here to hurt you. We want to help you."

The girl struggled against Ava's grip, tears streaming down her cheeks. She was young—maybe Ava's age, possibly a little older—with warm brown skin and curly black hair. She wore jeans and a red sweatshirt tattered at the sleeves. The room was cold, ice crystals forming around the windows, and Ava shivered as she watched the girl's panicked eyes search for an escape.

Eyes like Ava's—one brown, one hazel-gold.

"Caleb," Ava murmured.

"I see it."

There wasn't time to contemplate the discovery, however, as another spray of ice shards flew toward them. Ava stopped them in midair, and they fell to the ground like they'd hit an invisible shield.

The girl choked out a sob.

"Don't be afraid," Ava said in a quiet voice, stepping around Caleb.

Sophie whimpered, and the temperature dropped a little, but there were no more ice balls, thank goodness.

"I'm going to let you go, but don't run, okay? We just want to talk. We're not going to hurt you."

After a moment, the girl nodded jerkily. Ava pulled her gift back, and Sophie slumped to the sofa. "What do you want?" she asked, wiping away tears with the back of her hand. "Who are you?"

Ava smiled and eased down to sit on the other end of the sofa. "I'm afraid that's kind of a long story."

Ava closed the bathroom door quietly and leaned back against it, closing her eyes against the pain in her head. Once Sophie had calmed down, Caleb began to explain about the Race and Half-Breeds, and Ava had been able to excuse herself without much notice.

She left the light off and fumbled in her jacket pocket for the little container of painkillers she'd taken to keeping close at all times. She popped a couple of the pills in her mouth and swallowed them dry, followed by a couple of R-cubes. With a heavy sigh Ava turned to the mirror and winced at her washed-out appearance. She prodded at her nose carefully, glad that she'd at least managed to avoid a nosebleed. There was no way she would have been able to hide that from Caleb.

She'd been hiding a lot lately.

But with the ongoing threat of the Rogues, and the upcoming trip to New Elysia, she knew she was needed. Her gifts were needed. If they were to come under attack, Ava had to be able to fight. If Caleb or the others found out that her headaches were getting worse—that she'd started having them even when she wasn't using her gifts—they'd leave her behind, and she couldn't let that happen. She couldn't let them face the Council, not to mention the Rogues, without her. She couldn't let *Caleb* face that kind of threat alone. Not after she'd come so close to losing him.

Ava bent over the sink and splashed some cool water on her face, swiping it over the back of her neck as she sagged against the counter. She'd see the healer again once she got back to the Colony. Hopefully, he'd be able to help, and since he was bound by the same confidentiality as a human doctor—she'd made sure of that before she had ever approached him in the first place—he'd keep her secret.

It was only for a short time, anyway. Once they got to New Elysia, the doctors there would figure out what was causing her problems and she—and everyone else—would be able to focus on figuring out how to stop the Rogues.

"Ava?" Caleb's muffled voice at the door made her jump. She'd been so lost in thought she hadn't even felt his approach. "Are you all right?"

She turned off the water and wiped her face quickly with a towel. "Yeah. One sec." She checked her appearance once more and brushed her fingers through her hair. The headache had eased, thankfully, and her face had regained its color. Ava reached for the door and forced a relaxed smile before opening it.

Caleb searched her face. "You sure you're okay?"

"Of course," she said, widening the smile a bit. "Everything okay with Sophie?"

"Yeah. We really should get out of here, though."

"Well, let's go then," she replied, patting his chest as she squeezed past him in the narrow hallway. She felt him trail behind her as she made her way into the living room, which had warmed to a normal temperature, the ice on the windows melted and dripping onto the carpet.

Sophie emerged from a bedroom on the other side of the living room, carrying a small duffle bag and a backpack.

"You ready to go?" Ava asked.

Sophie took a deep breath. "I think so." Her lip trembled slightly and Ava crossed to her.

"It's going to be okay," she said, reaching out to gently squeeze the girl's shoulders. "We'll keep you safe. I promise."

Sophie nodded and swiped away a few tears.

Ava led her to the front door as Caleb opened it and poked his head out to scan the yard before waving them through. He grabbed Ava's arm to hold her back.

"Are you *sure* you're all right?" he whispered, glancing at Sophie a few steps ahead on the walkway. "No headaches?"

Ava ignored the curl of guilt in her stomach. She hated lying to Caleb, but she didn't see an alternative. Not if she was going to keep *him* safe.

"I told you, I'm fine," she said, popping up to kiss him lightly.

He caught her around the waist and studied her for a moment, focused and intent as he looked into her eyes.

She forced herself to meet his gaze—not to flinch, even as her heart thumped heavily in her chest.

"Okay," he said finally, sliding his hand down to squeeze her hand. "Let's go."

Ava let out a slow breath as they took off at a jog toward the road. It was probably nothing anyway. Her powers were new and her body was still getting used to them. Even the Colony healer couldn't deny that that was a possibility. Her body—her brain—simply needed to adapt to her new abilities, then the headaches would stop. She'd be fine.

Ava picked up the pace and turned right toward the gate.

She'd be *fine.*

CPSIA information can be obtained at www.ICGtesting.com
Printed in the USA
LVOW12s0139121113

360814LV00026B/492/P

9 781612 131719